About the author

Catherine Yardley has been writing since she was in single figures. She is happiest when she is either reading or writing. She writes women's fiction because she believes women have the right to have their stories told in all of their messy, complex glory. *Ember* is her first novel. She lives in London with her husband and children.

EMBER

CATHERINE YARDLEY

EMBER

Pegasus

PEGASUS PAPERBACK

A CIP catalogue record for this title is
available from the British Library

ISBN-978 1 91090 397 1

*Pegasus is an imprint of
Pegasus Elliot MacKenzie Publishers Ltd.*
www.pegasuspublishers.com

First Published in 2022

**Pegasus
Sheraton House Castle Park
Cambridge CB3 0AX England**

Printed & Bound in Great Britain

D e d i c a t i o n

To my wonderful family

Acknowledgements

A huge thank you to Margaret Graham who read an entire draft and gave me great feedback. Thank you to Claire Dyer for her feedback too. A huge thanks to Jane Cable for all of her support and inspiration over the years. Thank you to my husband for all of his support and to our lovely children. Thank you to Suzanne Mulvey, Vicky Gorry and all of the team for their hard work and for taking a shot on my book. I remain humbled. To my 2022 Debut Author group: thank you for your support and for keeping me sane.

This book was written before the Covid 19 pandemic and that is why it doesn't mention it.

During the process of writing this book I experienced an ectopic pregnancy. This book is dedicated to our baby who did not make it.

'Family quarrels are bitter things. They don't go by any rules. They're not like aches or wounds; they're more like splits in the skin that won't heal because there is not enough material.' F Scott Fitzgerald.

Introduction

'I need you to get out of the car.'

'What?' Rob asks.

'I need you to get out of the car,' I say again trying to be as calm as possible.

Rob stares at me and blinks. Then he looks around. It is getting dark and we are in the middle of nowhere. He was startled awake by the car lurching forward. He looks at me and blinks again. He was sleeping when I put my foot on the brake and he is still half- asleep. I look back at him. Trying to keep all of my emotions down.

'I need you to open the door and get out of the car.'

I can tell he is trying to figure out what the hell is happening.

'What?'

'I need you to get out of the car,' I say again. The irritation in my voice makes me hate myself.

Finally, he opens the door and swings his legs out. He hesitates before the rest of his body follows. Then he spins back around and looks at me again, his hand on the door. He is nonplussed, I can tell. Almost shell-shocked.

'Please take a step back and close the door.'

He does as I ask and I drive off. As I do I hear him coming out of his fuzz to yell, 'That is actually my fucking car!'

Driving is usually how I relax but not tonight. Tonight, something had broken in me. Trying to behave normally was exhausting. I just wanted to scream at the top of my voice. It would be dark in a couple of hours and dusk was already starting to make its mark. The only thing that is bright is the headlights of the car.

I think back to what just happened. How gorgeous Rob looked as he slept. His profile was beautiful. I always loved his strong, straight nose, his high cheekbones and that perfect jaw. His face took my breath away. I felt lucky every moment he was in my life, which is why I tried to ignore the seed that had been planted inside of me. A seed that was growing at an exponential rate. It felt like a cancer that would take away everything that I have, and yet I had not managed to stop the growth, I put my foot on the brake fast and heavy. Then it was done. Leaving only self-hatred and hollowness. I close my eyes and the tears come.

I slow the car down for a moment. No, I am fine. I am fine; if I just say it enough it might even become true. I turn the radio on. I can see the motorway signs for London. I head to my brother's house. It will all be okay then.

Chapter One
Two weeks earlier: 2018

Natalie

When I planned the hen night it was with nothing other than pure escapist fun in mind. I had some reservations about what I had planned for tonight but decided to go for it. Now we were in a tacky, trendy club in Central London. Eighties music was pumping through the speakers and here we all were: inebriated and dancing our hearts out.

Amanda was not usually someone who drank a lot or partied hard; she was more of a homebody, but not tonight. She was giving it all she had, dancing like no one was watching, her huge engagement ring blinding everyone when the light caught it. "Look What You Made Me Do" by Taylor Swift came on and the ladies give it all they have. I take a moment to watch my sister. She is not her usual fashion-forward self. She is wearing angel wings and devil horns. All of the other hens did the cliché slutty fancy costume thing. Alexa was dressed like a slutty nurse, Diane was dressed as a cat and Michelle was dressed like a schoolgirl. An actual schoolgirl. Seriously, I thought Why did they always have to dress for men? There was more to life than the male gaze. Regardless, they all smiled and sang along to the song as another round of drinks came.

'Cheers! To happily ever after,' I said, turning to Amanda.

'Happily ever after, and you are next!' Amanda smiled.

'Maybe,' I muttered under my breath.

From then on, the night descended into debauchery. Stockings were flashed and I spent five minutes trying to get Amanda down from a table she was dancing on. A group of men stared and talked amongst themselves. I hoped they would not come over. One of the men caught my eye and I smiled, understanding passed between us and he turned and started talking to his friends. No trouble came from them. I always loved it when you got a good guy instead of a twat.

'I'm so happy!' Amanda screamed and danced some more. She really was making the most of her last night of freedom.

'Everyone smile!' Alexa said as she snapped away. She had been taking pictures all night. Mostly of herself. I do not know why my sister is friends with such a narcissist.

'Everyone together!' Alexa said.

We all smiled and a picture was taken. One of the waiters offered to take a picture of all of us.

'Thank you so much,' I said and handed him my phone. We all huddled up and smiled at the camera. The waiter handed the phone back. I showed everyone the picture.

'We look great,' Alexa said. She was right. We did. It was one of those rare pictures where everyone looked good. I looked at it, a snapshot in time. It was a perfect moment.

One by one the other women fade away until it is just Amanda and I. I put my arm around her waist to steady her and head outside where our taxi is waiting. She sings songs all of the way home. Her lack of pitch, tone, anything, making the taxi driver wince. When I drop her off at her house Neil looks amused. I kiss her on the cheek before I hand her over. I can't believe my little sister is getting married. She does not seem so little any more.

I straighten out my feet as my last patient of the day leaves the room. It is Friday and I am looking forward to a rare weekend off. Today I am only doing a half-day because Amanda's last wedding dress fitting is later this afternoon. This morning has been as insane as it always is. A blizzard of nervous pregnant women thinking that there is such a thing as a birth plan. I can feel the heat of the sun coming in from the window. Its glow feels nice on my back. It is a beautifully sunny day in Tooting even though it is March. I circle my ankles and then I put my shoes back on. It is time to go, but I have time to grab a quick lunch first. I log out of my computer and gather my things. I say goodbye to the receptionist and head to the main exit of the hospital towards the car park. I almost bump into an elegant blonde woman who is impeccably dressed on my way out.

'Excuse me,' I say to her. She says nothing but gives me a look like she knows me.

I head to the car and drive off in the direction of Central London. The mothers are out in abundance, pushing their prams in pairs as they gossip. Such is this part of South West London.

When I get to Central London, I head to one of those trendy places that serve smashed avocado and almond milk drinks. I go in and order a latte and sit down near the window with it. Ah, this feels good. A moment before more wedding admin. It is all so full on. I take out my phone and I am surprised to see a number of missed calls from a number I do not recognise, along with two voicemails. Strange, I call my voicemail. The moment I hear his voice I regret it.

'Hi, Nat, Natalie. Um. Well, hello it's your father. I hate answer machines. Anyway, get back to me. I was just saying hi.'

I feel a headache coming on and a pain in my stomach. It feels unbelievable that he would think it is okay to call me. Sure, he sounds uncertain, faltering. I delete the message and I do not listen to the other one. I feel anger rising in me. I was having such a lovely moment but it is all ruined now. How did he get my number? I put my phone down and stare at it. I look around the cafe. The place is full of families. Mums and dads with their small children, grandparents delighted by the tiny people carrying on their genes. I wish I could get to the point in my life where seeing a happy family didn't give me a tiny stab of pain. I guess it is always painful when you see other people with something that you have always yearned for, but never had.

I block them out and try to not think about how much of a nightmare the wedding day is going to be. Mostly because he will be there. My father.

Those words sound strange, foreign. I have no father. How can he have done such a terrible job and yet keep the title? That was the problem with people falling in love and getting married; it meant a strange mix of people were continuously thrown together just because they were related by blood or were about to be related by marriage. It was exhausting and full of resentment. I could not wait until it was all over. The wedding administration was endless and tedious.

Not that I told Amanda that of course. Even though Amanda left pretty much all of it to me. I was more of a wedding planner than a maid of honour. At least it was temporary and if it made Amanda happy, it would all be worth it. I look at my phone again. Rob was not there when I woke up this morning which meant he had gone for a run. I miss him and I want to tell him about that bastard calling me. He always put me in a spin. I decide against it.

I put the phone away and head to the wedding boutique. I get there just in time and Amanda is nowhere to be seen. Which is no surprise. She is always late. She thinks it is cute but of course she is wrong. Especially since she is in her thirties and so officially a grown-up. She should know better. I sit down and start to flip through the pile of fashion magazines on the table.

'Can I get you anything? Tea, coffee, water?'

I look up at Serena, the receptionist and smile. We are on first name terms now after the many dress fittings and design meetings.

'I am okay thanks. I just had a latte. I am sure Amanda will be here soon.'

Serena smiles back and returns to her work.

For the second time today I start to relax, just for a moment. It feels blissful.

'Hey, big sis. You are here. Thank you for coming. I am so excited!'

I look up and there she is. All five foot ten inches of my sister. She looks how she always looks: impossibly groomed and glamorous. I worry about her financial future. All of her money seems to go on clothes and beauty treatments. She is fake-tanned, of course. She has gorgeous, thick, curly blonde hair, partly fake, she is wearing full on red lipstick. I wonder if her lashes are fake too. They look voluptuous. I try to not feel intimidated but I do not have it in me. I am not the kind of woman who goes all in for the beauty stuff. Why should women spend time and money looking like a Barbie? But I am not immune. Sometimes I think I should make more of an effort. Especially when I am standing next to the glamazon that is my sister. She is four years younger than me and four inches taller.

I get up to hug her.

'You look great,' I tell her.

'You look,' she starts to talk but then looks me up and down. A tiny frown tries to furrow between her brows. I am surprised it almost succeeds. Amanda gets Botox every few months.

'Great.'

The last word does not have the conviction it needs to be true. I smile, finding it funny. I guess my black trousers and blue blouse are not to her taste. She also does not get why I hardly ever wear make-up. She always tells me I would look 'so much prettier'.

I kiss her on the cheek and she offers me the other one too and then gives me a tight squeeze.

'I am so excited. The wedding is almost here!'

'I know. Two weeks from now and you are a married woman.'

Amanda goes up to Serena, who looks up and smiles at her.

'Hello, Mrs Holmes. I will let Anna know you are here.'

I notice that Amanda does not apologise for being late. She never does. I look at my phone. Our appointment time was thirty minutes ago.

'I hope I did not keep you waiting. Central London is always a nightmare.' I jump. It is almost like she read my mind.

'No, not at all. I was reading some magazines.' I feel bad for being so judgmental now.

'We are ready for you now.'

We turn. The seamstress, a lovely Polish woman with long, thick brown hair, greets us with a smile.

'Follow me,' she says while gesturing with her hands.

Amanda squeals. I am not girly, and I am not a squealer, but even I get caught up in the moment.

'Let's go fit that dress,' I say as I stroke Amanda's cheek.

The dress is hanging up. It is the first thing we see as soon as we walk into the room. It really is stunning.

It is an off-the-shoulder princess dress with a train. It is white with lace detail. It is a girly-girl's dream and Amanda is the girliest girl I know. Anna, the seamstress, brings in two glasses of champagne. Now I am happy. Every day should have a little fizz.

'Oh, thank you.'

I take the glass and have a sip. It is good stuff too. Maybe this wedding planning is fun after all. I nearly spit out the next sip as Amanda turns down her glass. I have never seen Amanda turn down any drink, never mind champagne. Amanda strips down to her underwear and puts the dress on with some help from Anna. I have always respected how Amanda has so few inhibitions. I could never stand in only my underwear in front of a stranger.

I watch my sister admire herself in the mirror. She looks stunning. Like a modern Grace Kelly, except Amanda's beauty is more obvious. She is blonde and busty with hips to match. I feel proud to be related to her. She is a showstopper.

'I love it! It looks great. Can you take some pictures?' Amanda hands her phone to Anna, who takes it politely. Amanda smiles and puts her hands on her hips.

'Natalie, come here. Let's get a few together.'

My sister beckons me and I get up. I stand next to her and smile. God, I hate having my picture taken. Is there anything worse? Finally, it is over and Anna hands Amanda back her phone.

'I took a few. I hope they are good,' Anna says.

Amanda flips through them and seems happy enough.

'I will crop them and put them on Instagram later. Give people a taster before the wedding,' Amanda says to no one in particular.

'I will let you both get on with it. Take some time and let me know if you want any more changes. It looks like it fits to me,' Anna says and then leaves. Amanda watches after her as she goes.

'So, I have some news.'

'Ooh. I love news. Come on, what is it?'

My sister smiles an ecstatic smile.

'I'm pregnant!'

I try to put a smile on my face. I had not expected this so soon and it feels like being hit with a car. I wish I did not feel like this. Through the happiness I feel for my sister is a dull ache. There is another feeling. At first, I think it is jealousy but, no, it is something else. To be jealous would require an energy that I do not have. I just feel sad.

'I am so happy. We just started trying. I mean, we weren't even trying. We just stopped using a condom and the first time: boom. Pregnant.'

'Wow. That is amazing,' I say, incredulous. Just like that. Pregnant with no effort.

'Of course, I was worried about getting pregnant before it happened. I read so many articles in magazines and I kept thinking about how I was in my early thirties. I am thirty-three after all.' Amanda lets out a little scream. 'Scary! Anyway, I am so happy we are pregnant. I never wanted to be one of those sad women who never have children. I mean, can you imagine? If I had never been able to give Neil a child? I can't even think about it. It would not be fair on him.'

Amanda swirls around in her dress feeling very satisfied indeed, but I feel like I have been punched in the gut. My entire world is falling in on me. A wave of nausea hits me and I think I might actually throw up.

'Are you okay?'

I did not notice that Amanda had stopped talking. I had zoned out.

'I'm good. I just think the champagne has gone to my head.'

I look at my sister and give her my biggest smile. I am acting like my life depends on it. I don't want her to know how I am feeling. Or why I am feeling what I am feeling. Especially not now, at such an important time for her.

'Do you mind if I get some air? This alcohol has made me feel funny.'

'Of course! Go right out. In fact, I'll get changed and join you.' Amanda takes the dress off and hands it to me along with the hanger.

'It fits perfectly. Get them to put it back on the hanger and in a cover. Thank you, sis. I love you.'

Amanda starts putting her clothes back on. I head for the door, holding my arms up so the dress does not drag on the floor.

'Oh, Natalie.'

'Yes, Amanda.'

'Do you think all the alcohol we drank on the hen night will affect the baby?'

'No. Not at all. Don't worry. The baby is just a bunch of cells at the moment. The cells will just be replaced by other ones. Once will not hurt.'

Amanda looks relieved and lets out a sigh.

'Phew. I was really worried. I didn't know then, of course. I have felt guilty. Poor little bub. It is so handy having an obstetrician for a sister.'

I smile. My sister is already a mother worrying about her baby. It suits her.

'Well don't. Everything will be fine. Just no more alcohol.'

'Okay. Thanks, sis.'

'You are welcome.'

With that I head back towards the door to find Anna. I see her near the reception.

'It fits perfectly. Can you put it in a cover please? We will take it today.'

'That is wonderful news. I will hang it up for you.'

I stand while she puts the dress back on the hanger and then wraps the dress in a plastic cover.

'There you go.' Anna hands me the dress.

Finally, I am almost near the door and about to get a hit of fresh air when I hear Serena talk to me.

'Can you sign this please? It just confirms you have the dress and have had the final fitting.'

'Of course.' I pick up the pen and read the paper thoroughly. Making sure nothing is amiss. I flip over to the other page and as I do I notice another signature and for the third time this afternoon I feel like I have been punched in the gut.

It is my father's signature. He paid for the dress. He has been here. He will have seen Amanda in her dress. Amanda did not even have the guts to tell me. I sign the piece of paper and I feel the anger rise in me. I plaster yet another fake smile on my face as I see my sister walk around the corner. Another mask to hide my devastation and disappointment and I am sick of it.

When I finally get home, I am furious. I slam the door. Hard.

'Everything okay?' I hear Rob call. I try to respond but I do not have the energy to answer. I crumple against the wall in the hall.

Finally, I can cry. I hear Rob coming down the stairs. He kneels down and kisses me on the top of the head. He puts his arms around me. I need him. I need this.

'What is it? What is wrong?'

I am still finding it hard to answer. I want to curl up in bed.

'I am being silly. Just ignore me.'

'We both know I'm not going to do that. Now, if something has upset you it is not silly. Let's talk.'

I look at Rob. He knows I am terrible when it comes to talking about my feelings. Or my family for that matter. He has developed a skill to get me talking but I do not think it will work this time. I just want to be alone.

'Come on. You are crying in the hall. You have never been much of a crier. I want to do my job: love and protect the woman I love. It is you and me against the world.' He says the last part in a cheesy, jokey way. Giving me a gentle elbow as he does. I laugh.

'God, you are so naff.'

'Naff?'

'Yeah,' I reply, shrugging.

'You can't say the word "naff" to call me naff. That word is…" I see him searching for the correct word.

'Naff?'

We both laugh.

'So come on. What is wrong?'

'My father called me. And Amanda is being a dick.'

Rob looks shocked.

'Your father called you? How did he even get your number?'

'I don't know. Amanda probably gave it to him.'

'No wonder you are calling her a dick.'

'That is not why I am calling her a dick.'

'Jeez, what else has she done?'

'He paid for her dress. I can't believe I am such an idiot. This entire time she has been talking about how I was the only person she wanted there and it was a special thing between the two of us and he's been there. Seeing her in her wedding dress. Paying for the wedding dress. Sipping the goddam champagne.'

Rob kisses me on the top of the head. I love it when he does that.

'She has always been biased towards him. Don't let it affect you. I know it is hard, but she has always had issues. Maybe one day she will see the truth.'

I think about what Rob is saying. Amanda always had our father in her life. She loved him despite everything. And I know that this is not what is upsetting me most. I weigh up whether I should tell him the truth, but it is just too painful.

He has come to me when I need him and loved me. Just like he always does. He is the best man that I have ever known. He is caring and loving. Kind and decent. He is everything I have ever wanted and I can never live up to that. I can never give him everything and yet he gives me everything. It is not fair and it does not line up.

'You are right. I should not let it get to me. It is nothing to do with me. Their relationship is their own business.'

I smile at him and then I hug him. My perfect man. He hugs me back and I breathe him in.

'That's my girl.'

He holds me tight and I want him to stay there forever.

Then: 1993

I guess you could say my father never had great timing. Like when he broke our family apart on Christmas Day.

The doors had been slamming all night and every time they did, I would flinch and the baby would wake up and cry. The door slammed again and I huddled under the covers with Amanda. She is scared. I kiss the top of her head and we comfort each other. I picked up one of our *Little Ted* books and I read it to her by torchlight. She looks up at me and smiles as I do. I finish the book and hunger soon gets the better of us.

No food was made for supper tonight. Only accusations and recriminations filled the house. I had to be brave enough to go downstairs. Or pretend to be anyway. And that was what I was doing now. I tiptoed down the stairs so quietly I was barely breathing. Fear seemed to rise higher in me with every step. Finally, I make it to the kitchen. The bread bin is within my reach if I use a chair. I push it towards the kitchen top. I use the same chair to open the cupboard to get the peanut butter and jam. I smile. Victory. We would eat like kings tonight. I made two sandwiches each and also grabbed some biscuits. I practically ran upstairs with the food which we then devoured.

Emboldened, I go back downstairs for a drink. When the shouting gets louder, I put the glasses down and head for the door, which is slightly open. I can see my mother crying. Mascara is streaked down her face and her eyes are red.

'Could you give her up?' my mother asks, looking at my father.

'With difficulty,' he replied.

'Oh.'

I look at my mother. It looked like the life had gone out of her in that moment. I wanted to walk into the room and put my arms around her, tell her everything will be okay. But I couldn't. It wasn't safe when the adults argued. I turned to go up the stairs. As I did, a piece of tinsel caught my eye. It was only then I remembered that it was Christmas Eve.

The next day Christmas is cancelled. My mother never leaves her bed. My father storms around the house. Every now and then the ceasefire is broken and yelling resumes. The whole house is tense. I come out of the bathroom to see Amanda crying at the top of the stairs. I take her into my arms, pulling her close.

'Come on. Let's go open our presents.'

Amanda's face brightened at the word "presents" and we almost run down the stairs, excited. We open our presents and I turn on the TV. Our own Christmas.

I make us breakfast: cereal and orange juice. We play with our presents and then open up the massive tin of chocolates and gorge ourselves. Our parents are still arguing upstairs. I could hear the baby crying in the same room. The poor thing. Our parents had been arguing since my brother was born. The door slammed upstairs and we both jumped. We could hear our mother screaming, something heavy thudding down the stairs. We get up and walk to the door. Dreading the drama heading towards us. It hits us both at the same time what the thudding is: a suitcase.

Our father is leaving. He turns to look at us. At a loss for what to say, so he says nothing. Our mother reaches the bottom of the stairs. Shocked. Our father walks out of the door and our mother heads into the front room. I see her watch as her husband gets into his car and leaves, through the window with a baby in her arms. Tear-stained and red-eyed. Her face the personification of sadness. She looks broken, like she has aged ten years. I do not watch my father leaving. I just stare at my mother, transfixed, wondering how I can take away her pain. Which is why I did not notice the door going again.

'Daddy! No!'

Amanda is chasing after our father. As fast as her little legs can carry her. Our father must have looked in the rear-view mirror as his daughter ran after him because he put his foot on the brake. I see my mother's expression change to one of horror.

'No!'

The baby is pushed into my arms and my mother rushes past leaving me in the doorway, staring after her. My mother runs but she is not fast enough. Amanda had too much of a head start. It takes a moment of hesitation before our father opens the door, allowing Amanda to climb in.

'No! No! Stop.'

Our father drives off, our mother running after him until her energy gives out and she cannot run any more. She sits down in the middle of the road, scooped out and devastated. It is a full ten minutes before she stands up and walks back towards the house. She takes her two remaining children in her arms and hugs us while I stare at the road. At the space where my sister had been. Before she had climbed into a car and out of my life. Before five had become three.

Eventually we walked back into the house. To sit and take in the incomprehensible. At some point we go into the living room and watch TV. Every now and then my mother tells me that it will all be okay, but mostly we are too numb to speak. When it is time for bed, I kiss my mother and walk up the stairs alone. Past the artwork we made, past the family photos, past the Christmas decorations, past all of the mementoes of a family that has been torn apart. I get into bed and trace the place where my sister used to be with my finger. I ache for her. Not for my father, only my sister. It is a pain so pure that I can't even cry.

Chapter Two
The Wedding Day

Natalie

I drive to the wedding venue to check things over. It is in a beautiful Georgian mansion in Mayfair. It looks stunning and makes me feel very poor indeed. I head to the room where the reception will happen and I look at my wedding administration list. Or my wedmin list as I like to call it. It feels as overwhelming as ever but I can feel a small kernel of happiness. The planning was not fun but it would pay off soon. Then I will have my weekends back. Thank God. I look at my handiwork. The room looks stunning. Not that it needs much to be honest. The rooms were already magnificent. I just made it look more weddingy. If that is a word.

The pale blue of the room is perfect for a wedding and chandeliers hang from the ceiling. There are white and pink roses on every table, along with some foliage so it fits the colour scheme. The wedding favours are personalised M&Ms along with a CD of the wedding music wrapped in pale green or pale pink tissue paper. Each packet of personalised M&Ms has a brown luggage-style tag with the name of each person as a placeholder.

The chairs are draped in white covers. Shades of white, pale green and pale pink are scattered throughout the room. The plates are white china and the napkins are white with edges of the wedding colours. The entire thing looks elegant and classy. It takes a moment for me to realise that this is all my taste. It is how I would have wanted my wedding. Amanda said yes at every step, of course, but my bias has come through loud and clear. The thought stings. I will never have this for myself. The pain would be too much.

Everything is done now. All I have to do is make it through the day. Out of all of the things a big sister has to do, going to her little sister's wedding must be the worst. I feel a flash of anger and resentment. I have hated the stress of planning this and the room will soon be full of awful things: people I don't want to see, bad memories, drunk people. The worst of it all.

I never hated weddings before but this, and being in my thirties, has changed my mind. Everyone now asks when I will "get a ring on it". Like that was still the most important thing for a woman to do. The thought makes me think of Rob. I wonder if he will come or if he will cancel. No, Rob will definitely come. He hates letting people down. Even if the maid of honour dumps him just before the wedding.

We had been on our way home from a long lunch with Amanda and Neil's family. Rob had been perfect. He always was. Neil's brother's children were running around. Three boys, all under the age of six. Rob had cooed over them, told everyone how he was excited to have his own son one day. Cue everyone looking at me. We were together for seven years and were not married and had no children. People found it suspicious. We talked about marriage a few times. But we never jumped into the deep end. I was never really sure why.

Guilt threatens to bubble up and affect my emotions, but I stop it before it happens. I am skilled at that. Pushing things down so I can get on with my life. I could have handled the situation better, I know that, but what was done was done. There was no point moping about it now. I do one last check of the room. It looks great. I smile and head for the door, confident that Amanda will like it.

After checking on the venue I head to Amanda's. Today is the last day. The big day. Despite everything I can feel myself getting excited for my sister. Happy for her even. Neil is a great guy and I think they will be happy together. He is besotted by her and I can tell she loves him.

I pull up at her terraced house in Clapham. It is a three-bedroom Victorian house with red brick. It does not have much of a garden at the front but someone, Neil I guess, has put some plants there. Black and white tiles lead to the door. It looks like a proper home. They will be filling it up soon enough, I think ruefully.

I knock on the door and Amanda quickly answers. She looks harassed.

'Where have you been?'

'I was at the wedding venue, making sure everything was all right.'

I feel pissed off at my sister's lack of gratitude.

'I sent you a text after I couldn't get through on the phone.'

'Oh okay. Come in then.'

I start to come in but then Amanda stops and runs her hand through her hair, looking worried and stressed.

'Shit. I forgot.'

'What? What is it?' I am worried now.

'Dad is here.'

I feel like I have been punched. I can't remember the last time I had seen my father. It was certainly over six years ago. The thought that he is here now, in the same house as me, makes me feel ill. Worse than that, Amanda did not even warn me. I thought he might come to the wedding, but at least that was a big venue with lots of people. The chances of avoiding him were good. But here? No, I do not think so. I will not put myself through this.

'I don't want to see him, Amanda.'

'Natalie, please. It's my wedding.'

I am even angrier now. I don't like Amanda emotionally manipulating me. I have done everything I could for her.

'That is not fair. I have put my life on hold to plan your fucking wedding and you can't even respect me.'

'You work so that's not a life on hold.'

'I work? Yeah. I work and do your wedding. That has been my life most of this year and now Dad is here and you didn't even tell me and he paid for your dress and you didn't even tell me. Did he pay for the wedding?'

Amanda looks at me and I can see her soften. She will not push this. I can tell she thinks better of it. She only fights when she is one hundred per cent sure she will win.

'I'm sorry. Just go into the kitchen. I will get rid of him. Just give us a little bit of time. I know you two don't get along. You have been amazing. I couldn't wish for more.'

I am happy with her reaction but not impressed. I know it is all fake.

'Okay.'

Damn, for that moment I forgot that my sister is pregnant. I feel guilty, yet again. But Amanda knew how I would feel about my father being here. Just because she is pregnant and getting married does not mean that the entire world revolved around her. There is never an excuse to be selfish and not care about other people's feelings. Our mother had taught her that, but Amanda was more like our father. Not the worst of him of course, but the other stuff. They seemed unable to care about other people's feelings.

I go into the house and head to the kitchen. I cannot close the door behind me, because loads of crap is propped in front of it. Great. A need for a glass of wine comes over me. I am not a big drinker, and now is really not the time, but I need something. I need anything. Maybe a strong cup of coffee would do it. I open the cupboards but I cannot see any. I open all of them, searching. It is all herbal tea and coconut milk. Christ, could I be any less like my sister. What is this crap? As I move some things around, I hear a noise behind me. I do not want to look but I cannot stop my body moving.

There he is. We lock eyes for a moment. Him wary, me defiant. He is about to say something when I turn my back on him and resume my search for caffeine. I hear him shuffle off like the old man he now was and the stress and tension in me starts to lift.

I cannot be certain, but I think I hear him say 'goodbye, Natalie'.

I give myself a moment before I go into the living room and see Amanda. The sight of my father after all of these years has been a huge shock. Even though I knew I would see him today, a part of me still can't believe it. To me he has always been a breathing ghost.

It was only then I remembered Amanda had told me in a passing comment that she was thinking of inviting Father to the wedding, saying it would be too sad to have no one walk her down the aisle. I had known then that it would happen. I did not put up a fight. I had not said it was him or me, because it had not seemed real. But now a ghost had come back from the dead and he was bringing back all of the trauma from the past with him.

37

It was not the easiest thing, for the maid of honour to avoid the best man. But we managed to occupy different spaces in the same room. We never once spoke or met each other's eyes. I wished the same could be said of Father. Who keeps trying to engage me in conversation and smiles at me constantly. I want to punch him. At least he had not brought that bitch he called a girlfriend.

I don't want to upset Amanda, so I smiled and nodded and made polite conversation. All the while I thought about all of the things he had done. How much I hate him. It would have been tolerable if our mother was here, but her absence highlighted the pain and the loss. I am looking at him now, this sorry, old man, wishing he had been someone else. He walked Amanda down the aisle. They looked so happy together in that moment, like partners in crime. The pride on his face cut me to the bone but I couldn't place why.

I never cared about how he felt about his children, but I did care about how Amanda felt about him. He never deserved her love. It pained me to see him get it. And so unquestioning and forgiving that love was. You would think he had been father of the year. Rather than the selfish, awful man he was. He would never walk me down the aisle, that was for sure. I head to the bathroom. I need a break from all of this. It is too much.

I just managed to make it to the bathroom when I feel a huge wave of nausea hit me. I don't manage to reach the stalls before I projectile vomit all over the bathroom. My hands go to my mouth in shock. What the hell? I didn't think I had drunk that much, but of course it wasn't that; it was him, my father who was a stress I didn't need.

I have no idea what to do next. There are no paper towels. It is a miracle that no one else is in the bathroom. I hear giggling behind the door, and in a panic, I look for somewhere to hide. I am too far away from the stalls so I hide behind the door. Thankfully they do not see me as they walk in past me, I am covered by the huge, heavy red door. To stop it closing I hold onto the handle. The girls do not notice that the door doesn't close behind them.

'Oh my God! Someone has thrown up everywhere. Jeez, I think I am going to be sick.'

'Oh vom, you're right. Who would do that?'

'Let's get out of here quick. Before I am sick too. Yuck.'

The two girls head into the stalls and when I hear the locks going, I sneak around the door and walk out as fast as I can. I hope nobody noticed me leaving the bathroom. The lights are dim and everyone is either in conversation or pissed.

Across the floor I see Rob. It feels like a bolt to the heart. Damn, why now? For a moment we lock eyes. The hurt in his eyes kills me. Guilt, shame and embarrassment all build up inside. I am a terrible person. This night is one of the worst nights of my life.

I find the woman who works at the venue to let her know someone has been sick in the bathroom and ask if it can be cleaned up. She looks horrified and promises that it will be dealt with straight away. Again, I feel guilty.

I head towards the exit, as fast as I can go. I need air. When I get to the courtyard the fresh air feels like a cool, heavenly hug. I take a moment away from the madness. I want to leave more than anything, but I could never let my sister down. She made me her maid of honour. I was doubly responsible to do everything I could tonight to make Amanda happy. I look around, hoping to not bump into anyone.

The courtyard is beautiful, with little cobblestones and wrought-iron chairs and tables in an emerald green colour.

I sit down on a chair and just breath in the air. I will allow myself five minutes. I take my compact out of my clutch. I look terrible. Tired and ill.

'Fuck, I look awful,' I said to no one in particular. I take out my concealer and start to reapply my make-up. Putting the concealer underneath my eyes and around my nose, following it with a touch-up of eyeliner, mascara and lipstick. The shadow of another person crosses over me. It takes one moment for me to react, so busy am I trying to fix my deranged appearance.

'Weddings, they are pretty full on, right?'

I jump at the sound of the woman's voice. I look at her and take her in. She seems vaguely familiar, but I have no idea who this woman is. She certainly is not from my side of the family. She must be a relative, or friend, of Neil's. She is in her late forties or early fifties. Blonde, thin, tall and dressed all in black. At a wedding.

She is wearing a very bright red lipstick that is far too obvious. There is a fleeting moment of suspicion, but I dismiss it quickly. It is not that this woman is not threatening, she is just not a danger to Amanda. I warily wait to see how this exchange will play out.

'They are indeed.'

'And you are the maid of honour, so it is doubly hard.'

'I am indeed. Who are you here for?'

The woman is taken aback at the question.

'Sorry,' she splutters.

'What side?'

She still looks confused.

'Bride or groom?'

'Oh.' The woman thinks for a moment. Weighing her answer carefully. 'Bride, I guess.'

The answer is met with silence from me. Now I know she is lying, but I do not know why.

'I haven't introduced myself. I am Dea Thurston.'

'Hi, Dea.'

'You look a little unwell. I wanted to know if I could help.'

I smile at her.

'I'm okay, thank you. It's probably stress or a bug. I better go back in actually. I have to make sure everyone behaves themselves.'

41

'Well, it was great meeting you.'

'You too. Maybe we could chat again later?'

'I would like that,' Dea says as she takes a cigarette out of her purse and lights up.

Hmm. A smoker.

I raise my hand as a goodbye and head back in, hoping Dea is not who I think she is. On the way in I catch my reflection in the window. I smooth my hair down, still not happy with it. Fuck it. It will have to do.

I arrive back right on cue. They are about to do the first dance. I head towards the DJ as quickly as I can. I catch my sister's eye on the way there and earn a stern look. Everyone else is milling around while doing as much damage as possible to the free bar.

Amanda and Neil are preparing themselves. I whisper the instructions into the DJ's ear and wait. My sister is psyching herself up. I have a moment to take in how beautiful Amanda looks. That white mortgage-repayment expensive dress really is something to behold. Her new groom stands beside her, missing her confidence but sharing all of the joy. I can tell Neil is nervous, but he is happy. I like him, but mostly, I love how much he loves my sister.

We are not close. But then again, how could we be? We never spent much time together unless we were at family events, and even then, we hardly get any time to speak. It was just the way of things.

I grab the microphone and start.

'Ladies and gentlemen, the bride and groom will now do their first dance.'

Everybody stops and watches. There is a notable excitement in the air. A frisson of anticipation.

The start of "You're Nobody Until Somebody Loves You" by Dean Martin plays through the sound system. Amanda and Neil look at each other, a moment of 'let's do this', and then they start dancing. Everybody whoops all at once. They are outstanding. Like something out of *Strictly Come Dancing*.

The months they practised have certainly paid off. The song changes to "Black and Gold" by Sam Sparro. I look around at the wedding guests. They all have a look of wonderment on their faces.

As I scan the faces the memories come back, one blast after the other. Some good and some bad. My gaze rests on my father. He hasn't aged well but I guess alcohol does that to a person. It is hard to look at him now, but it is also sad. He looks so small, frail almost. It was hard to believe the power he had over me all my life. He is just a weak, old man now. He must have felt me looking at him because he looks at me and smiles. The look in his eye is as wary as ever, but there is something else there too. It pisses me off when I realise it is hope.

Some of the guests bump into me as they walk past to get onto the dance floor and join in. Almost everyone is, at least, tipsy. Mostly people are drunk. Everybody is happy and dancing. Except me. This seems like a good time to make a break for it. Unfortunately, my brother Paul has other ideas and grabs my hand.

'Not so fast there, sis. This dance is mine.'

I am momentarily annoyed, but I always melt at my baby brother's smile. His happiness always makes me happy. We dance and for just one moment I am happy and carefree. After three songs and impeding breathlessness, I am pleased when his ex, Stacey, cuts in with their son Nathaniel in tow. Things were bumpy when they broke up, but their son is the glue that holds them together. However misshapen that thing may be sometimes. I am proud of how well they have handled things. The sight of my brother dancing with his ex and his son gives me complete joy. I take a moment to watch them and then I make my escape.

Amanda is loved up and dancing with her husband and nothing else needs doing. Rob is the best man and he already agreed to collect everything at the end of the night and pay the vendors. Ah, bliss. My maid of honour duties are over. I head for the door, giving one more look back at the revelry. As I do I catch Rob's eye. He smiles at me and winks knowingly. I am thrown by this and smile back. Unable to help myself.

Then I pull myself away, walking a little faster to the exit. As I am about to leave, I cannot resist it. I look around to see Rob again. He is gone but I can see the woman I spoke to outside, Dea Thurston, dancing with my father. I try to not jump to conclusions but fail. I knew it. She is one of his many girlfriends. He really is a bastard.

I let myself into Paul's house with the keys he gave me. I close the door and lean against it, letting out a sigh as I do. I take off my heels and rub my feet. I hate heels. The Western version of Chinese foot binding. Why do we do it to ourselves?

I am finally free. The house is quiet and dark. I suspect my brother and nephew will be home late. I head to the spare room. Wobbling as I do. I step on a piece of Lego and hold in my swears.

I tread more carefully, expecting an obstacle course of toys. I need a good night's sleep and some time to process everything. When I manage to get to the bed without impaling my foot again, I lie down. I thought I would lie down for a moment and then have a shower and brush my teeth, but exhaustion kicks in. I wake up the next day, make-up caked onto my face and the hairpins still in my hair. My nephew is staring at me from the bottom of the bed like he tends to do sometimes.

'Hey, kid.'

'Hi.'

An awkward silence follows. I must look a state. With my make-up caked on and smudged in. Hair everywhere, still wearing the same clothes I was last night.

'Good wedding,' he says. Then he leaves.

Kids are weird.

Chapter Three
That Moment

Rob

Watching Natalie drive off, leaving me on the side of the motorway, felt like an out-of-body experience. Had that really happened? Hell, *what*, had just happened? Looking around and almost expecting to wake up from a dream, it finally hits me and I snap.

'That's actually my fucking car!'

Out of all of the grand theft auto in history, this one has to be the most vicious. And original.

It feels like I have been walking along the motorway for days. Car headlights blind me. Everything is grey and dour. I keep going over every single detail about today. What could possibly have triggered such an extreme reaction? I cannot think of one thing I could have said to upset her. Never mind get dumped on the side of a motorway. We had not argued. The entire thing was such bullshit. It was just a pre-wedding get-together in the country. Partly to meet Neil's family and partly to just have a get-together. Nothing happened. Nothing I can think of anyway.

I am pissed off and tired, but I am a man on a mission, fuelled by pure anger. Things cannot get worse, I think to myself, but then I hear the thunder. I stop and look up at the sky, wondering why the world hates me so much right now. Then it begins to rain. Slowly at first, but then so heavily that it feels like being hit by sheets of water. It takes minutes for me to be soaked to the bone. I stand there, resigned at first. Nothing is left in me but then I start to walk again. Faster and faster.

'Fuck, fuck, fuckety, fuck, fuck.'

I kick at a bit of rock. Turns out that was a bad idea. A sharp pain goes up my foot. It throbs now.

'Bollocks.'

At this point I stop wondering how things can get worse and just wait for the next thing to happen. I see a sign in front of me. Service breaks. Finally, I can get out of the rain. This will all be over soon.

'Hey, you're a wanker!' Yet another motorist decides to troll me.

Today is making me lose faith in humanity. I am too exhausted to yell back but I flip the third in the direction of the moron. I am not in the mood for taking any shit from anyone. I try to walk even faster. I have had enough and the end is in sight.

I sit in Wimpy. So wet I look like I swam here. The smell of the food is making me hungry, my coffee is slowly getting cold.

My entire life has been swept out from under me. I try to put the pieces of the day back together so I can see the clearer picture. What happened? One minute everything had been fine and then…

'Who is the lucky lady?' The waitress is back, smiling a little less due to the item on the table. I guess it has dashed her hopes.

I don't know what to say so I say nothing. The silence becomes heavy and grows more awkward.

'Thanks for the coffee.'

I smile. Trying to be more social.

'No worries, let me top you up.' The waitress smiles and pours more of the black stuff into the cup.

I will need it. This night will just get longer. I stare at the small, shiny object until the pain gets too much. I snap the box shut and put it back in my pocket. What would I do with this engagement ring now? I am trying to not show my emotions in public, trying to act like a normal human being. I am not sure I am succeeding. The phone rings, breaking me out of this fog of confusion and pain.

'Hello.' Relief follows as I hear the voice on the other end. It was not the first person I called. Normally I would call Natalie. But ha, ha, to that now. Ditto Amanda. Or even Neil at the moment. The humiliation is too much.

Instead, I call a work colleague. The fact I am the boss of the work colleague does make it awkward. But beggars can't be choosers. It would be weird, but she had texted me and I told her my car had broken down. So she offered to come and pick me up. I have no idea if she believes my story. I will have to factor this into her next bonus. It is true dedication. I pick up my coffee and down it. This day will be over soon.

1993
Natalie

The weeks after Father and Amanda left had been tough. Mummy focused on the baby and did what she could. I could tell that she was trying to put a brave face on it, but the sadness seemed to radiate from her. Mummy had thought about calling the police and telling them that Father had kidnapped Amanda. In fact, I had encouraged it, but she said it was something you could not come back from.

I did not agree and tried to get Mummy to call the police numerous times, only dropping it when Mummy snapped at me. I hate being snapped at. She would give it a week, she said. Then if he had not returned with Amanda, she would start calling around the family and sort it out. He just needed some time, she said. He would come back. This did not help me. I did not want my father to come back. All I wanted was my sister. I could not imagine anything worse than my father coming back. He was not the father he used to be. All he did was make Mummy unhappy. In fact, he made the entire family unhappy.

I spent my day trying to make things easier for Mummy in subtle ways. She was a wonderful mother.

She loved her children and was always there for them. She spent hours cleaning the house and cooking every day. She was doing a correspondence course at the moment. Sometimes she would be up until the early hours studying but she always put her children first.

I helped her clean and cook. I even changed the baby's nappy sometimes. The main aim was to make her smile. I could tell that she was missing Amanda. I ignored the fact she was also missing Father; I did not want to think about him. In the evening I helped her give the baby a bath. I loved these moments with Mummy and the baby because these moments made us a family again.

It was a long walk to school and the baby cried all the way. Today was the first day back at school after the Christmas holiday. And I would have to do it without Amanda. We both go to the same school. We walked there together with Mummy every single day, but Father had not brought her back.

It was over two weeks now. Mummy had made frantic calls to every member of the family which had resulted in Mummy managing to speak to Father. He asked for more time but had promised that he would bring Amanda back. I did not believe him. He was full of lies. Mummy had lost a lot of weight and was looking ill. I knew she was not feeling well because she sat down a lot and seemed exhausted all of the time.

'It is just because of the new baby,' she told me and I believed her.

Finally, we were at the school and I would not have to listen to the crying baby any more. It was so annoying and I was sick of it.

'Here we are. I hope you have a wonderful day, my little girl. Goodbye. Give me a kiss.'

I kissed her on the cheek and headed to my first class. This sucked. It all sucked. I had no idea when I would see my sister again. Today would be awful without her.

The morning went quickly. My maths teacher, Mrs Chisholm, who was my favourite teacher, had been as kind to me as she always was. But her niceness made me paranoid. Did she know about my home life? Did she know that I did not have a father any more? The bell signalled break time and I ran out to the playground. And then I see her: Amanda. I stand there in shock. Amanda looks like she doesn't have a care in the world. She is laughing and playing. I slowly walk towards her. Feeling utterly betrayed.

Amanda had not missed me. Amanda did not care about me. Amanda had deliberately left. Here Amanda was, playing and laughing like she did not have a care in the world. I had an urge to kick her. To scream at her. To tell her how I really felt. I hate her in this moment. I had been missing her, pining for her. I had even made excuses for her and she did not even care about me. I was close now. So close that Amanda finally spotted me. Guilt passed along her face. At least there was that.

We both stood there. Looking at each other. Neither knowing what to say or do. I thought about asking her why she left. But I could not find it in me to start speaking. Amanda took a step towards me and then started to talk.

'Natalie...'

But I wasn't listening. I turn my back on her and walk away.

Chapter Four.
Rob

I wake up and my hand reaches to the other side of the bed. Muscle memory. She is not there. Of course she isn't.

I hate waking up alone. For seven years I woke up with Natalie in my bed. Our bed. The one I lie in now.

The one constant in my life. The woman I love. Gone.

None of this had been my choice. The entire thing was so unlike Natalie. I have gone over that night a million times now. I can't do it again. I have to reconcile myself with the fact I might never find out what happened. We were happy. We had always been happy. We talked about the future all of the time. We even talked about all of the things that would have come with that future.

Was she cheating on me? Had there been someone else? Was there someone else now? The thought stabs at me. I did not think I could take that. The love of my life with another man. It did not bear thinking about.

I get out of bed and head to the shower. I can't just lie in bed all day feeling sorry for myself. No matter how much I want to. I have to pull myself together. The house is a mess. I hate mess. So I guess Natalie is not the only one doing things out of character. I do not have it in me to tidy. To clean. To even look at things. I have been ignoring my surroundings. She is everywhere. Everywhere but here.

I should go to work. We have a new campaign we are vying for. Sure, the boss can take a day off, but the work still needs to be done.

The PR firm I started is now one of the top ones in the country. It has won numerous awards. That did not happen by accident. So I have to go back to work. Maybe it will save me. I am dreading having to be around people and pretending I am fine, but I could do with some purpose in my life. I have to bury myself in work and forget about Natalie. Well, forget her until I manage to win her back.

Because I do not know how to survive otherwise.

She had looked at me during the wedding. Numerous times. You can't spend seven years with someone and not know them. I am sure she still loves me. There were feelings in her eyes. Hell, she even smiled at me at one point. Some of it was guilt, but some of it sure looked like love. She looked so sad. And stressed. She was different somehow, but I know Natalie is still in there somewhere. I just have to find out how to reach her.

Natalie

I can feel my phone vibrating. I have just enough time to take it until I have to scrub in for my next C-section. I take the phone out and look at the screen. It is my brother, Paul. Weird that he is calling me. We see each other every night. I love my baby brother so I answer quickly.

'Hello, you.'

'Hello, sis. How is it going?'

'Great. You are aware we saw each other this morning, right?'

'Yeah I am. I just have a question to ask.'

'Okay. I have about twenty minutes until I need to scrub in. I have back-to-back operations today.'

'Sounds like fun,' Paul jokes. He is squeamish and hates everything medical. He once almost puked when he cut his finger cooking. It was only a bloody scratch.

'Yes. That is why I do it. The fun factor.'

I laugh.

'It has been a week since the wedding. Can you believe it?'

I can tell Paul is making small talk with this comment, trying to ease in his question.

'I have loved every single day of having my freedom back. Planning it was so stressful.' I hear myself whining and promise to myself I will stop going on about the wedding planning.

'I can imagine. It feels like it has gone in the blink of an eye. I wonder how Amanda's honeymoon is going.'

'Yeah, me too. Bali would be great right now.' I look out of the window. It is sunny enough, but it has been raining all day.

'They will probably get bored. Three weeks in Bali? A little indulgent,' Paul said.

'Well, that is Amanda all the way. Indulge, indulge.' I stop as I hear the words come out of my mouth and cringe. 'Sorry, I did not mean that. It was rude. I am just a bit annoyed about a few things.'

'That is okay. Siblings are irritating.'

A part of me wonders if he is thinking about his sister who turned up on his doorstep without warning and has stayed since.

'Well, you are being very kind. But I should be kinder. Even when I don't feel like it.'

'Is it because she invited Dad?'

'No, I expected that. Well, maybe. He paid for the dress.'

'Really? I didn't know that.'

'He was also at her house on the wedding day. And I think she gave him my number. It just feels like she lied to me.'

There is silence on the other end of the line. I know Paul is going to ask me for something, and he is finding it hard.

'That was not very nice of her. Anyway, I have a huge favour to ask. Don't get upset, okay? You can always say no.'

'Okay. What is it?' I am sick of doing favours for people.

'See Dad. Just once. With me. For me. He asked me to have one beer with him. I don't want to do it alone, and I don't want to do it with Amanda. You know they are close. I would feel like a third wheel.'

Close. It was true. They were and it pissed me off. I could understand if Amanda was the youngest, if she did not remember the crap Father had put the family through, but she remembered. She was old enough. She was there. A witness to every moment, just like I was. It irritates me how much I am starting to resent my sister. I love her so much and I still want to be her best friend.

I think about what Paul is asking. How he was a baby when the worst of it happened. How he never had a role model or a father figure.

Then I remember that I have made such a mess of my own life. I spent my life fixing other people. Literally and otherwise. I have done enough for my sister and despite the fact that seeing Father is the last thing I want to do, it would be for Paul. When I say yes, I am even more shocked than Paul. But it is the right thing to do. To give my brother a chance to realise just how much of a bastard that man is.

I don't want to tell my brother to hate Father, or that he is a terrible person. He might end up resenting me. It is better he finds that out for himself.

'Call me when you arrange a date okay? Time and place.'

'Wow, Natalie. Thank you so much for this. It means the world to me. You are the best sister in the world. You really are. I just feel like I need to do this, but I did not feel like I could do it without you. You are the best.'

'Okay, okay. Stop now. You do not want me getting a big head.'

'I will stop but know that I love you, sis.'

'I love you too, baby bro, but now I have to go and cut someone open. See you tonight.'

He laughs but it is a nervous one.

As you get older you only see people at funerals and weddings. I think about that old saying while I wait for Paul and Father. Paul and Father. I think about that last part. It must have been a madness that made me agree to this. This was going to be hell.

Covent Garden is its usual blustering self. Street performers of various talents perform for the crowd, the market still has its spark. It is busy and full on. I love it. Paul had arrived promptly. In fact he arrived before me but now he has gone off to get some drinks.

I hope he will get back before our father arrives. I do not want to be alone with him. Luck is not on my side as no longer than a minute later, there he is: scruffy of dress and scruffy of manner.

Father could be called intelligent, as long as his life choices are not taken into account. But he obviously spent no time at all on how he looks. He wears the oldest clothes which always have holes in them and tends to shuffle about. Almost like he is in a dream. He notices me and puts his hand up, the smallest wave. I do the same before I can stop myself. An unconscious politeness.

I am out of my depth socially. This is beyond me. How can I talk to this man? He is coming over now and my heart is racing. The only thing stopping me running is this politeness.

'Hello,' Father said, smiling.

'Hey,' I replied, not.

The conversation hung in the air from there. Father covering the silence by taking off his coat, sitting down, fiddling with the menu.

'How is Rob?' he asked, looking up.

'He's great.' I was surprised he even knew his name.

'Does he still work in PR?'

'Yes.'

'Good. It is a stable occupation. Lots of money.'

'I have my own money. So, it's not really relevant.'

I try to keep the irritation out of my voice so he does not know that he got to me. My father is a dinosaur. He still thought that a woman should marry well. Even though it was our mother who had the money. Hypocrite

'Are you next?'

'Next for what?' I have to force every word out.

'Marriage.'

What the actual fuck? Memories of my parents' marriage come flooding back.

'I hope not, Tim.'

He briefly recoils at being called by his Christian name. A silence follows which feels like it might suffocate me. Where the hell is Paul with the drinks?

'I'm never getting married.'

He stares at me. Hard. Then his face softens. Something seems to pass over him. Was it guilt?

'Not all marriages are like ours was, Natalie.'

At first, I do not know what to say.

'I wasn't sure that you knew how awful it was. You never seemed very aware.'

Despite everything, and my snark, I can feel a small smile pass over my lips. He has never shown any self-awareness about himself before.

'We loved each other. We really did. It's just.' He paused, searching for the words. 'She deserved better than me but when you're in love it doesn't matter. Nothing else matters. You choose this person and you just hope love is enough. You hold your breath and jump in. Sometimes you drown.'

I cannot believe what I am hearing. He has never taken responsibility before. Never apologised, never admitted anything. He has always been defensive. He blamed my mother for everything.

'We have never talked about this.'

'Ah, that is because you are scary, Natalie.'

'How can I be scary? I'm just a kid.'

'Didn't you go to high school? Kids are the worst.'

We both laugh and a moment passes between us. Something that feels like a beginning. We are taken out of the moment with a clang. Paul has returned with the goods.

'I hope you don't mind, Dad, but I took the liberty of getting you a beer.' Paul put the drinks on the table and gave me a wink as he did.

'You okay?' he mouthed.

It irritates me that he is so happy in this moment, that he could tell that a little bit of the ice had thawed. I wonder if that made me a bad person. So much has happened and everyone else has let go. But not me. I am the oldest. I remember. And I know that if I let go, he would win. He wants me to be his daughter again. I do not know if I will ever be able to give that to him.

'Cheers!' I say. We all raise our glasses and even though there is a part of me that resents it, we are acting like a normal family.

'Cheers!' Tim and Paul chorus back to me.

I sink into the chair and drink my wine. As I lean back I watch Tim and Paul talk. They do not know much about each other. At some points it looks like they are on a first date. The awkwardness, the tentativeness.

None of this makes me comfortable, but why should I see my family less, or be cut out of things, just because this asshole decided to be present again? I guess his girlfriend must have left him. Maybe when he got another one, he would leave us alone again. He was good at that. Leaving and finding women.

I watch him as he talks. Analyse him. I can tell he can feel it because he squirms. I look away. Watch the other people who are also having a nice drink on a weekend. I bet everyone here is having more fun than me.

This meeting was about Paul meeting his father properly. I thought about that. None of us were children any more. And here is Tim, trying to make inroads. He has spent most of his life in Spain with the woman he cheated on my mother with. Yet now he is trying to actually be a father. It is ridiculous.

I think about leaving them alone. They seemed to be chatting away happily. But I can't catch Paul's eye to ask him. I guess I will have to sit here and brave this out, hoping my father would not ask me any more questions. He has not asked me about my work. I guess having an obstetrician as a daughter just wasn't a thing. He has always been a sexist. Screw him.

'Do you want another drink, Natalie?'

I look at Tim.

'No thank you. I am good.'

He looks hurt. His ego in play again. He can hurt you a million times and the one thing you do to him is the end of days.

'Okay. Well, I will go and get myself and Paul another drink.'

'Great.'

I try to give a genuine smile. I doubt it works. Tim shuffles off. Paul looks at me.

'He is not that bad.'

I stifle a scream inside and smile again. My jaw is starting to ache. I do not want to be the bitch who ruins everything again. I can only suck it up.

'Do you think it would be okay for me to go now? I will stay if you want. You just seem to be getting along well.'

'Sure.'

Paul gets up as I start to stand. He gives me a hug.

'Thanks for doing this, sis. You really are amazing. I don't know what Amanda is talking about. You never hold a grudge.'

I ignore the barb. I hug Paul back and then let go. I need to get out of here. I do not even mention how much someone with an alcohol problem is drinking. Can my brother not see it? An alcoholic is drinking alcohol and I am the one with the problem.

'Have a good afternoon. Love you, baby bro.'

'Hey, less of the baby. Sure you don't want to say goodbye to Dad?'

'I am sure. See you soon.'

I am grinding my teeth so hard I might be about to chip one. I give an awkward wave and start walking as fast as I can without looking like an idiot. But I know, even if I ran, something has happened that I will not be able to escape. He is here now and I fear this time he won't leave us.

1999
Natalie

I can see the light is on in Mum's bedroom. It is with trepidation that I walk towards it. I never know what I will find. Even though I had seen a lot — tears, tantrums, depression — it takes me a moment to take this in. Mum is unpacking Father's suitcase. She has taken him back. Again. I feel a wave of crushing disappointment. Why does my mum have to be such a doormat? I start to leave but it is too late. Mum turns her head to acknowledge me.

'Hello, Natalie.'

'Hello, Mummy.'

Mum looks at me.

'Did you want something?'

'How can you do it?'

'Do what?'

'How can you let him walk all over you again?'

'Natalie, you are too young to understand.'

'That is so condescending.'

'I know it sounds that way, but you have so much left to learn. Things get greyer as you get older. I am not just talking about hair.'

Mum gives a faint smile at her little joke. She is hoping to see kindness in my eyes, but I don't have any to give.

'You could do so much better.'

'You want the truth?'

'Yes, I want the truth.'

'Fine. The truth is that sometimes you have to love someone more than they love themselves.'

'God, that is lame.'

I can tell Mum is hurt by my words, but she doesn't show it. She has become the queen of the poker face.

'I am sorry that you think that.'

'I can't see this through your eyes. I just can't.'

I leave. Feeling like my world has blown open. I wish I could respect my mother. It hurts that there is no female in my life that I can look up to, but I guess I have no male role model either.

I go downstairs and he is sitting there. Snuggled up with Amanda and Paul like we are a normal family. I give the bastard an evil glare. I grab the remote and start flicking through the channels. Sitting on the edge of the sofa. Not part of this crap.

'Oh look. *Fine line between love and hate* is on. Perfect.' I look around as I say this. Daring father — anyone — to say anything. They turn to look at me, but they do not dare make a comment. They all look away.

Jacqueline

I unpack Tim's clothes carefully. Putting them in the drawers and wardrobes. I only realise now that I never used up any of the space he left behind. I hate being a single mother and even though I know this situation is not ideal, I am hoping for the best. It will be good for the children to have their father back. To get to know him. I am even excited about the thought of having help with childcare and some help around the house. I stop as I feel the presence of someone behind me. It is Natalie. I did not want her to find out like this. I was going to go to her room. It was all so unexpected. I talk to her and nothing seems to help.

I look at my daughter. The harshness of her youth, and the inexperience of it. She doesn't know much about love yet. She has never experienced it. It is incomprehensible to her that you can love someone who might hurt you. Who constantly makes mistakes. That anyone in life could possibly settle, or forgive. But life wears you down. The more mistakes you make in life, the easier it is to forgive other people. We are all so flawed.

I look on as she walks away. I feel like I have lost my daughter. Both of them. Amanda had chosen to live with her father for so long. The pain has been unbearable. It is hard to get through to Natalie. I know she loves me, but it devastates me that she doesn't respect me. It even makes me question if my husband is worth the price, but it is done now. Hopefully there won't be another time. The stakes are so much higher now. That is the worst of it. That I am lying to my children. There is something in me that might take me away from them forever. All they will have left is a father who has never been a father. I guess that is better than nothing. All I have left is hope.

Chapter Five.

Rob

'Just come. It will be fun.'

'To karaoke? I don't think so. It's lame, Neil.' I was not going to be dragged into this. If he wanted to go and embarrass himself then he could do it on his own.

Neil sighed. I looked up at him. Yet again we were the last ones here. I feel bad. He is such a good employee. Hell, I would even call him a friend. I look at the work we have done and the storyboards for the campaign. It all looks great. I am glad he had three weeks off in Bali. He deserved the break.

'That is a shame, Rob. Because Natalie will be there and I do believe you are still smitten with her.'

I look back at Neil so quickly I almost hurt my neck. Shit, I was too obvious. It is now just over three weeks since I have seen Natalie. Every moment has been hell. The thought of seeing her face is worth the price of anything. Yet the thought of seeing her again makes me queasy. I try to play it cool.

It might be a disaster but not seeing her was definitely worse than the risk. I at least want to see how she is doing. Or if we still have a spark. Life without her is empty. I still cannot give up the hope of us getting back together. The thought of her never being in my life again hurts too much.

'Okay, let's go.' I grab my jacket.

'What? Now?' Neil looks at his watch.

'Well, what time is Natalie going to be there?'

'Seven thirty.'

I look at my phone.

'Great. We leave now and go to the pub for a quick beer. Take the edge off. Who else is coming?'

'Amanda,' Neil says. He seems deflated now. None of that "smitten" bravado. I reckon it has dawned on him that Amanda will give him shit for this.

'That is good. Let's go.'

Neil puts his jacket on. He looks like a man heading for oblivion as we head towards the pub.

Natalie

I sit down with my drink next to Amanda. She looks amazing after her honeymoon. It is hard to know if it is pregnancy glow or a good tan. Either way, it suits her.

The journey to Oakey Karaoke had not been fun. A sweaty middle-aged man had tried to grope me and I had to grab his hand and twist it while giving him The Glare. Today was hot and the Tube had felt like the pits of hell. We then had to wait ages to get a drink, elbowing our way to the bar. It was not what I needed after a stressful week bringing children into the world and removing things from places they should not go.

Amanda was unusually quiet now as she sipped her mocktail. She had complained about not being able to drink about ten times already. It was getting old. She had another eight months to go. It always worried me when Amanda was quiet. She always had so much to say. I hoped it was nothing too bad.

Oakey Karaoke is a Chinese restaurant slash bar slash karaoke bar. It is a weird, kitsch mix, but one that certainly worked. it was just on the right side of wrong. The entire place was painted pink, with pictures of old-style crooners like Dean Martin and Frank Sinatra on the wall. There was also pride of place for Elvis Presley who had his own wall. The people on the walls had talent far beyond any of the clientele combined.

'This decor makes me want to wear sunglasses. Turn it down a few notches.'

Amanda stifles a laugh as she looks at me. It was then that I realised that Amanda had seemed unable to meet my eye. This added to my anxiety. What was going on?

'This place is fun though, not like those pretentious, overpriced places you go to.'

'I'm starting to agree with you.'

'Can I get that in writing?' Amanda asked, pretending to be shocked. Then her smile drops as I follow her gaze towards the door.

'What is it?' I ask, head turning.

'He brought Rob.'

'Are you fucking kidding me?' I feel the panic rising in me. I cannot even bring myself to turn around. I look at my sister and wondered exactly what emotion is crossing her face. Then it hit me. Guilt. It was guilt.

She could have warned me. I turn to the door and there he is. Rob. My ex-boyfriend. Looking as beautiful as he always does. He is wearing my favourite tailor-made suit. The electric blue one that looks as expensive as it is. All the emotions hit me like a bomb. I feel like I am going to throw up. Trailing behind Rob is Neil, looking sheepish but with a wicked glint in his eye. I try to hide my emotions.

'Great, this is all I fucking need.'

'Sorry,' Amanda said

'It's fine. It's not your fault. I can handle it.'

The men came into my peripheral vision and we both stand up to greet them.

'Hi.'

'Hi,' Rob replied.

Fuck.

We just stare at each other for a moment. Then the moment becomes an uncomfortable silence. It breaks and we try to give our attention to something, anything, else.

'So, who is going first?' Neil asks.

I look at him, knowing this is all his doing and want to punch him.

'Nobody until you two get a fair amount of alcohol in you. I have to do this sober, you guys don't,' Amanda said.

'That is my cue. What does everyone want?' I ask.

'A beer. Peroni,' Neil said.

'Me too,' Rob said.

'Amanda?'

'I'll come with you.'

I head to the bar. Amanda in tow. The bar was much clearer now and I get the order in quickly.

'Do you need any help?'

'No, I'm fine.'

'I'll stay and help you take the drinks over, save you doing two trips.'

'Are you okay?' Amanda asks.

I smile at Amanda. I know she is worried. I look over to where the men are sitting. They are deep in conversation.

'I'm good, stop fussing. What do you think they are talking about? What do you think he has been saying about me?'

'Nothing I reckon. I mean they are friends.' Amanda paused. 'But we are all still friends.'

I look at my sister. Hard.

'Well, we will be.'

'Will we? Maybe. If we manage to not kill each other.'

'That's a healthy thought.'

I roll my eyes. Whatever.

'You never told me what happened between you two.'

Out of all of the times she could have asked me, she asks now.

'I don't want to talk about it.'

I don't even look at her when I say this. I grab the drinks and leave.

Rob

I look over to Natalie. She is beautiful. Easily the most beautiful woman in the room. It kills that I still love her. After she left me on the side of the road and stole my car. It blindsided me. Hell, it would blindside anybody. And I still have no idea why.

In that moment I realise: I have never asked her. We had never even officially broken up. There was no "it's over". One moment we were driving down a road and then it had become this. Barely meeting each other's eye, giving in to the assumptions. The assumption that it was all over between us. That we didn't love each other any more.

I could tell my presence was having an effect on Natalie. What was she thinking? I couldn't tell. But I could tell that she was rattled. That she was having a tough time. Although I was angry with her for tearing us apart so viciously, I still wanted to go up to her right now and put my arms around her. To love her and tell her everything would be okay.

'I think that will work.'

I snap out of my thoughts. I have not heard a word Neil has said. I just smile and nod. I want to sort this mess out, but it is beyond me. How can you fix something when you have no idea how it had broken? That was the real question. In the corner of my eye I can see Natalie and Amanda returning. I don't want Natalie to know I have been thinking about her.

'I can't believe you brought me to such a naff place. I hope no one I know sees me.' I say to Neil, ribbing him.

'If they see you, they are in the same place so, no worries.'

Hm. Neil could be a cocky little shit sometimes, but he was a good guy. He seemed to be enjoying this, but I wasn't sure why. Was he enjoying the awkwardness between Natalie and I? It was irritating if so.

'Anyway, don't knock it. I have had some of the most fun times ever in this place and nobody I know goes here. You just get to be the most embarrassing version of yourself. It's a win-win.'

Amanda and Natalie are back now. They put the drinks on the table and sit down. I notice that Amanda has put some weight on during their holiday. She looks tanned though. And blonder. The complete opposite of her sister with her gorgeous dark brown chestnut hair. I always thought Natalie looked a bit like Winona Ryder.

'I got some shots too. We are all probably going to need them,' Natalie said.

'I can't have any, but you all go ahead. So, who's going first? Who wants to be the karaoke winner?' Amanda asked.

She looks excited. Jesus, is this actually a competition? You can win at this crap? And what about the comments about the drinks? To make Natalie feel bad? And why wasn't she drinking? This girl never met a party she did not like.

'I think me,' Neil said.

'You are delusional,' Amanda replied.

'You?'

'There we go. That's the right answer, honey,' Amanda said, smiling at Neil and stroking his cheek. God, he was such a wet dog around her.

'I will throw my hat in the ring,' I say.

I hate things like this, but I do not want to come across as boring in front of Natalie.

'I think Natalie might win,' Amanda said.

'I'm hurt,' Neil said, feigning indignation.

'Natalie? Are you kidding? I have never heard her sing.'

It was true. Seven years and I had never heard Natalie sing. I just assumed she was tone deaf.

'Yes, I can.' She looks indignant.

'Really? Let's hear it then.'

'Fine. I am certainly going to beat you.'

She downs two shots and heads towards the stage. I watch her as she goes and as she chooses her song.

After she does, she takes two steps into the middle of the stage. The spotlight hits her just so.

The song starts. It is "Love is a Losing Game" by Amy Winehouse. I flinch as the song starts. I can't understand why she would choose that one. I look at her, in her red shoes and her navy dress. She looks stunning.

It is then that I realise that a part of me really truly hates her. It had been there for a while now, but this was the first time I had acknowledged it. I am surprised that I want to leave, get away from her. If I never see her again it would be too soon.

At least the song was mercifully short. Natalie finished. Her voice was better than I thought but nothing to write home about. I had envisioned a Cameron Diaz *My Best Friend's Wedding* scenario but she had managed to hold a tune. Amanda and Neil clapped passionately but I just rolled my eyes. Neil nudged me.

'Clap!'

But I would not budge. I stare at Natalie, something solidifying inside me. I keep staring at Natalie as she walks off the stage and back to her seat. Natalie looks back at me. Almost like she is daring me. Neil got up next and had already reached the stage. The strains of "Wonderwall" filled the room.

We are still staring at each other. Something inside me snaps. I stand up and march to the stage. When I get there, I grab the microphone off Neil. Neil is confused at first and he just looks at me. He is a bit taken aback and bewildered. I do not care.

'No one wants to hear that nineties shit, Neil.'

I change the song to The Raconteurs "Many Shades of Black". I sing with gusto, aiming my performance straight at Natalie who sits there with her poker face. Stoic as ever. She was a rock with the sea underneath, making waves. She was always like this. She seemed fine on the outside but like a duck, her metaphorical feet would be paddling away under the water.

Neil finally gets sick of standing around like an idiot and walks off the stage and sits down. I see Amanda rub his back and stroke his hair. When I finish everyone apart from Natalie claps.

I walk off the stage and see Amanda stand up. Excited that it is finally her turn. Before she even gets to the stage Natalie overtakes her and she barges onto the stage.

'That was great, honey,' Natalie says to Amanda who goes and sits down dumbfounded. It is on now.

'This is all your fault,' I hear Amanda say to Neil.

'I know. I'm sorry.'

On the stage Natalie takes her hairband out and runs her fingers through her hair. Literally letting her hair down. She starts to sing Abba's "The Winner Takes it all". I glare at her and then drink some more. What the fuck is her problem?

'We may as well eat,' Neil says opening a menu.

'Yeah! I'm starving. You want anything, Rob?' Amanda asks.

'A beer.'

'Any food?'

'No.'

Natalie was perfectly in tune now. In fact, she was great. She sang the song perfectly, with passion and she matched my gusto.

As the song finishes, I stand up and head back to the stage. There is tension throughout the entire place. I do not care. Natalie throws the microphone to me. As we pass each other, electricity passes between us. But is it hate, love or both? I think we both know we have feelings for each other but with every song they get more muddled.

But Natalie doesn't go to sit down. No, she heads to the dance floor as "Ride On, Baby" by the Rolling Stones starts. Natalie reaches the dance floor and starts to dance. She doesn't care who might be watching. She doesn't even notice when I stop singing. Or that the whole restaurant is watching. I watch as she dances. Knowing that all the bravado in the world will never hide the truth: she was the love of my life and now I have lost her. I put the microphone down but I can't move. I can only stand there and watch her, sure that everyone can hear the sound of my heart breaking.

The song finishes and Natalie stops. The trance breaking. She looks at me for the longest moment and then she heads back to the bar. I am still on stage. Microphone in hand. My heart has been torn out. Finally, I move and head back to the table. My legs feel weak and I am surprised I get there before collapsing.

'Hey, Rob, maybe you should go back up and sing "I Will Survive". Neil starts to laugh as I look at him with pure hatred. I get up and leave this shithole. I don't look back.

Chapter Six

Natalie

It feels like I have stepped into a darkness. My life was steady, moored to happiness. Now that stability is gone. I scrub harder at the kitchen counter. I have cleaned and tidied almost everything in my brother's little house. I hope he won't get upset when he arrives home with little Nat. The house was fine before and yet I have been cleaning and tidying for hours. Trying to make order out of chaos. This is what I do when I am at sea. Rob always teased me about it. The flat is messy, let's have a fight.

Seeing Rob was awful. I broke up with him for him, but I could never tell him that. To see the hate in his eyes — it killed me. I love him so much. To be responsible for his hurt is one thing, but for him to hate me. I guess I shouldn't have expected anything else.

I had left him by the side of the road and then not spoken to him for weeks. I just drove to my brother's house and that was that. I would have been devastated if he had done that to me. I should have seen it at the time, but it seemed like the only way.

Maybe it was best that he hated me. It left no door open to step through. The strength I needed every day to not call him or go to him. The strength to not love him, that was all easier if he hated me.

The problem was the link to Neil and Amanda, but there was not much I could do about that. While he was in their lives, I would always hear his name, and probably bump into him occasionally. The thought of him finding a new girlfriend and going on double dates with Amanda and Neil came to me in a sharp, painful burst. One of those false memories that makes you flinch.

I always fuck things up. Unless it is my career. It is the only thing in my life that I excel at. The rest of my life is a mess. A mess of my own making at that. Luckily, I will be going to work tomorrow. I can compartmentalise. I would not be able to be a doctor and do my job otherwise. No one wants an emotional doctor.

I put the cloth in the sink and take off the Marigolds. No need to scrub a hole in the counter. I hear the door and I feel happy. My boys. Just when I need something consistent in my life. And some love.

'Aunt Natalie!'

Nathaniel is running fast towards me, his arms outstretched and looking the picture of happiness. I was never a kids' person, taking small people on a case-by-case basis. But Nathaniel has my heart. He also has a variation on my name. The sight of him melts me. He is just like his father, only pint-sized.

'How is my favourite young man?' I stretch out my arms for a hug.

'Oi, you said that was me!' Paul said, pretending indignation. Then he looks around. 'What is that smell?'

'I think it is called clean.'

'It looks like a bloody showroom in here. Is this really how you waste your time?'

'Ahem,' I say, gesturing to Nathaniel.

'Dad says "bloody" all the time. I got in trouble saying it at school.'

I give Paul a "really?" look. He gives me an "I don't care" look back.

Nat is in my arms. The love I have for him feels like a drug. The highest high I have ever felt. I kiss his soft hair and bury my face into his neck. I love this kid more than life itself. I look up and see Paul watching and smiling.

'Let me make you tea. You look like you probably worked up a sweat.'

'Thanks, bro.'

'Daddy, can I go and watch some CBeebies now? You said I was allowed a little.'

'Of course, son. On you go.'

I watch my nephew go and I smile. He is adorable.

'You can't steal him. Stop thinking about it.'

I laugh.

'We will see.'

As we wait for the kettle to boil, I notice it is raining outside.

'Looks like we got back just in time,' my brother says.

'Yes. It does.'

I watch as the rain hits the window. Becoming so heavy it looks like pouring water. The rat-a-tat-tat is comforting. Being inside when it is raining outside is one of life's small pleasures. There is just something about it.

'So how are things going?'

I startle and look at Paul. I had been lost in thought.

'Great. The job at the hospital is rewarding. I like the people I work with. I have been getting your house in order. I even looked at a few flats online. I do not want to outstay my...'

Before I can finish, Paul interrupts me.

'Why do you always do that?'

'What?'

'Always rounding off every achievement and never giving yourself a rest. Mum is dead and to you, Dad may as well be. Natalie. You're free.'

'God! Don't say that.'

'It's the truth.'

How do I answer that? I think about it. My brother has got to the truth of me. He always does.

'I still want Mum to be proud of me.'

'Okay, but please take some advice from someone who has a child.'

'Okay.'

'All a parent ever wants is for their child to be happy.'

I look at Paul. All of this prodding at the parts of me I do not want prodded. I want to run away again and yet I am sick of doing so.

'So, are you happy?'

Bullseye.

I somehow manage to get a no out. Paul is dishing tough love out in spades today.

'What are you going to do about it?' He smiles at me and I cannot help myself: I smile back.

'Something.'

'Good.'

Paul has shifted the sands. Bringing up something that I wanted to keep just where it was, buried deep, away from my thoughts and emotions.

'Rob hates me. We are really broken up now.'

'Is that a good thing?'

'I don't know.'

'Because you still like him?'

'Yes, but I know everything. I knew what he was going to say and do before he did it. I knew every promise. He made me feel like a chick.'

'You are a chick.'

I give Paul a stern look.

'I needed more than what was happening. He was so predictable. He always put his career before us. He was such a workaholic. I don't want to end up like my mother. I need more than a few memories.'

'That's what a relationship is. Memory. Marriage is memory. It's having somebody along for the ride. To witness and to care. You are not going to be happy if you get scared every time someone loves you. Tell him to be more romantic, more spontaneous. Tell him to put you before his job but for God's sake don't just give up.'

'I broke his heart. He won't forgive me.'

'He'll forgive you.'

As I consider this, I realise that I have finally lost the ability to talk my way out of being happy. But now a wave of panic and pain is hitting me. What if I have blown it? I consider Paul's words.

'I stole his car.'

Paul is taken aback by this piece of information. He thinks for a moment.

'What kind of car?'

'A BMW.'

'Jesus. The BMW parked on the street is his? Yeah, that one is a deal breaker. You might not be able to fix that.'

I laugh. I love my brother. He is witty and always said the right thing. Then I feel the stab. The real crux of the matter. I have to find the strength to tell my brother this.

'I can't get pregnant.'

Paul looks at me, comprehension not catching up immediately.

'I mean, there is nothing specifically wrong. It just didn't happen. And we tried. A lot. I gave up everything: caffeine, alcohol, sugar. I ate organic food, I exercised. I lay on my back for fifteen fucking minutes after we had sex *every single time* because of some stupid superstition. It just. I couldn't. He deserves better.'

Paul comes and puts his arms around me.

'I didn't even know you guys were trying.'

'We didn't want to tell anyone in case we jinxed it.'

The thought makes me laugh now. One of those bitter ha ha ha ones. Then I feel the tears coming. A sob I couldn't keep down. I have never cried about this before but now I have started, the tears keep coming. It becomes a wracking grief that seemed to be coming from my entire body. A pain of children unborn and wants that had not been given. A life that could have been so different.

'How long did you try for?'

'Three years.'

'Are you kidding? Three years is nothing. You are probably just being unlucky. Have you checked an ovulation calendar? How regularly were you having sex?'

'Ew. I don't want to talk about my sex life with my little brother.'

'Did you go to the doctor?'

'Yes'

'And?'

'Nothing was wrong. It is "unexplained infertility".'

'It can correct itself. It doesn't mean anything.'

'Can we talk about something else? It doesn't matter anyway. I am sure Rob has moved on with someone who has a more hospitable womb.'

'Don't be silly. He really loves you. You should see how he looks at you.

We stand there for a while. Me thinking, Paul stroking my hand.

'Thank you. I feel better.'

Paul smiles at me.

'Now come on, let's hang out with your awesome nephew.'

'Yes, let's do that.'

I grab my tea and we head to get a hit of Nathaniel and CBeebies.

Lying in bed that night I felt more at peace than I have in a long time. The past few months had come with a persistent niggling of anxiety. Of memories that should have been left where they belonged. Buried deep away from emotions. But the biggest secret had been the one of my desires. A part of me had always been too scared to even tell anyone I wanted a child. I thought telling people would jinx it, and then it did not happen anyway.

It was too much to even admit how bitter I have been. How jealous of any woman who had not been burdened with the utter devastation of multiple negative pregnancy tests. Then the positive one that had been so full of hope. Yet it had only led to loss. The cruellest hit imaginable. An ache that still clawed at me to this day.

Each one the end of a dream. I had seen it all in my job, Women, and men, with a deep need to be parents. I witnessed the pain first-hand too many times. Now I feel better. I was unburdened by my secrets and regrets. I drifted off to sleep quickly.

The next day I felt happy for the first time in weeks. I have a feeling that everything just might turn out all right. I walk into the living room. Paul and Nathaniel are watching TV in their pyjamas. I sit down on the sofa beside them. Nathaniel turns and smiles at me as he snuggles up and then puts his head on my lap. I stroke his hair. Loving the sight of him, half wishing I could drink him up.

'You look better. How did you sleep?'

'I had a good night's sleep. First time in a long time.'

'I can tell.'

'I feel refreshed. It's awesome.'

'Good, I am happy. The house looks great by the way. Thanks for cleaning.'

'No problem, I stress clean.'

'Yeah, I know. Why do you think I was so happy when you came to stay?'

I laugh. I may have been an emotional wreck but I was a clean and tidy one.

'I hope you are going to sort that problem out. The one that begins with R.'

'Robot? Has Aunt Natalie got a problem with a robot?'

'Not quite son.' Paul laughed.

'Oh. You mean Uncle Rob, don't you, Daddy? Why is he a problem?'

I catch Paul's eye. He looks suitably sheepish. Great. Now I will get a thousand questions.

'I am going to get some breakfast.' I tell Paul and quickly leave the room.

'Remember Amanda's birthday party tonight,' he calls after me. Shit. I had forgotten. I hope HE will not be there. That he will have slithered off from whence he came. I don't let it get to me. As I make myself some porridge, I feel re-energised. Being amongst family has left me feeling comfortable and loved. Safe. I used to have that with Rob too, but I screwed it up. The thought makes me feel overwhelmingly sad. Why can I not just get out of my own way and be happy? Maybe I will never know. Or, just maybe, I could stop being self-destructive and allow myself to be happy. Yes, that is what I am going to do.

We drop Nat off at his mother's and then we head to Amanda's. It feels good to have my baby brother as my partner in crime.

'The invite said dress up but most of my clothes are still at Rob's.'

'Yours and Rob's.'

I roll my eyes.

'Technically.'

'Uh huh.'

Paul glances over. 'You look fine.'

'Thanks, that is what a woman wants to hear. You look "fine".'.

'If you want more, I suggest you win your boyfriend back.'

'And I suggest you become more articulate or you will stay single forever.'

'Ouch!'

I smile. Paul and I always tease each other. But somehow it never hurt. Well, hardly ever. You need that one person in life who will always tell you the truth. No matter how brutal.

'Do you think he will be there?'

'Who?'

'The bastard.'

'Maybe. I think things are a bit rocky with Sheila right now.'

I wince at the name of that woman.

'Great.'

'He said you had a nice chat at the pub.'

The hopeful note in his tone annoys me.

'You do realise he was drinking.'

'What do you mean?'

'He is an alcoholic and he is always drinking.'

'He is not an alcoholic. He never had a problem. Did he?'

If it was not for the last question and the doubt in Paul's voice, I might have punched him.

'Are you kidding? He drank, he smoked, he dabbled. He is a full-on addict. Women, drugs, alcohol, the lot.'

I look across at Paul and he looks sceptical. It pisses me off. Why can no one else remember this shit?

'We are here.'

Yes, we are indeed. I get out of the car and I try to not slam it. I do not knock on the door. I just go in. I am sick of being the outsider in my own life, the only one who saw the monster without the mask.

I am taken aback as I head in. Amanda's hall and living room have been covered in gold and silver balloons and streamers. It looks like a retro disco. There are thirty people here at least, all dancing to Motown classics.

It does not take me long to find Amanda. She is dressed in gold lame. She looks like a trophy. She has a gorgeous tan from her honeymoon and she is glowing. Literally. I thought it was a myth that pregnant women did that. I have seen hundreds, if not thousands. They were mostly just sweaty. Or tired.

'Natalie!'

I head towards her.

'You look great,' I tell her.

'So do you,' she replies but she looks and sounds surprised. She is hilarious.

'Come and get a drink!'

She leads me to a table which has actual bowls of alcohol. Amanda puts the ladle in and pours the contents into a paper cup. I think about asking what it is, but I think better of it. She hands me the cup and I take a sip. It is okay actually. But it is strong.

'I am still on these mocktails, but you have fun.'

'Thanks. I will.'

'Come on! Let's dance.'

This is Amanda sober. Still full of energy and up for a killer night. I never let go this much. Not even when I am steaming drunk. We dance to song after song. Until our feet hurt and we are tired.

'Come on. Let's go and catch up,' Amanda says as she leads me by the arm. It is impossible to resist her. She is fun and vivacious. We walk past all of her narcissistic friends and hordes of people I do not know. Then we pass Tim. Who, I notice, is drunk. Again.

We find a quiet spot on the stairs. I take my shoes off and rub my feet, happy that I rarely wear heels. Amanda rests her head on my shoulder. I lean my head towards hers. Feeling loved and happy.

'How are you feeling?'

'I'm okay. I don't have much morning sickness. Which is great.'

Of course, Amanda did not get bad morning sickness.

'How are you?'

'I am good.'

'You are staying at Paul's?'

'Yes. I like it.'

'Yeah, you two were always close.'

I ignore the jab.

'And I see a lot of my nephew.'

'Yeah, he is getting big now, isn't he?'

Amanda has never shown much of an interest in Nathaniel. Although I have no doubt that she loves him.

'Sorry about the karaoke and Rob thing by the way.'

'It's okay,' I lie.

'Paul said you all met up with Dad and had a great time.'

'He said that?' I do not even try to keep the surprise out of my voice. She ignores it, of course.

'It would be nice for us all to be a family again.'

'That is not going to happen, Amanda.'

'Why not?'

'Do you really want to get into it on your birthday?'

She gives me her classic glare. The one that lets you know you have not met the queen's demands.

'Let's forget about it for now.'

'You realise he is a drunk, right?'

'What?'

'He is a drunk. He is always drinking. He did the same with me and Paul.'

'Oh, for fuck's sake, Natalie. He is only having a bit of fun.'

I put my head in my hands. I cannot help it. It was always this: him and her against me. Then Paul on the sidelines. Unsure what to do or believe. Christ. He ruins everything. He always has.

Amanda takes my hand.

'Come on, let's forget about it for tonight and have some more fun.'

So I do. Because it is the easier path to take. I am so exhausted trying to get people to see the truth.

Rob

I high five Neil. This is the moment that makes it all worth it. The elation of winning a big campaign. It is huge and we both know it. We headed to the pub to celebrate, and the rest of the team gradually tailed off one by one. Now it is just the two of us.

'Well done, Neil. You can take a huge amount of credit for this. You have done so well since you came here. We would never have got this campaign without you.'

I raise my beer to him.

'Don't be silly, you would still have got the campaign. Just maybe not for as much money.' Neil laughs and raised his beer back at me.

'Do you have to get back to Amanda?'

I don't want to get him into trouble. I have a feeling she is pregnant. Why else would she not be drinking?

'No. It's fine. She always works late on Tuesdays. She does not mind me going to the pub every now and then. She has a lot of friends and goes out with them — a lot.'

I nod. I am trying to not ask him about Natalie. He is my only connection to her, but I do not want to put him in the middle. The night at the karaoke still plays on my mind.

Over a month has passed and there is still no reconciliation. Part of me still can't give up. She is the only woman I have ever truly loved.

I try to think of something to say to fill the silence, but I come up blank.

'So, you and Natalie breaking up was a huge surprise.'

Clearly Neil had read my mind.

'So how are you doing?'

'I'm okay.'

'You two seemed solid.'

"Yeah. We did, I was surprised too.'

'It was awful the way she did it. You did not deserve that, mate.'

I can tell Neil is being tentative. I am touched that he cares.

'I am sure she had her reasons. Maybe one day I will find out what they were.'

I try my best to stop feeling the sadness that is creeping up on me. Natalie is my sore point. Dumping me on the side of the road was an open wound. It was so unlike her, but she had done it. You could not argue with that. Neil was right, I did not deserve it. No one did. I wasn't sure if I could ever forgive her for it.

'Maybe she didn't want to get married. Or have kids.'

I look at Neil. What he said has struck something in me.

I just didn't know what.

'Maybe. I guess. I don't know. I would be surprised. We talked about it. A lot.'

Neil nods his head. I can tell he is thinking.

'She seemed edgy about it at the rehearsal dinner.'

Now I really am interested.

'Really? What did she say?'

'She did not say anything to me, but other people kept asking her when it was her turn to have kids and if she was married. She seemed really irritated by it.'

I thought about it. Could that really be it? Could she just not want to settle down? I doubt it. She always said the only reason we were not married was because we had not got around to it. We both wanted kids. No, there was something else. Or at least I hoped. Something that could be fixed.

'Thanks for telling me that, Neil. It was very helpful.'

'I will go and get us another beer.'

Neil goes to the bar and I sit back in my chair. I am still trying to put the pieces of my life back together, but I just did not know how to do that without getting closure from Natalie.

The night at the karaoke had given me nothing. I thought we would have a reasonable conversation. Or even get back together. Realising how much I resented Natalie had been a surprise. It did not stop me loving her, but my anger was still growing.

'Here you go.'

'Thanks.'

'That night at the karaoke was something.'

'Yeah, I'm sorry.'

'That's okay. Y'know, usually when two people seem to hate each other that much. It can mean something else.'

'Don't.'

'I'm just saying that the opposite of love isn't hate. It's indifference.'

'She has slept with double the amount of people I have slept with.'

Neil blinks and doesn't saying anything. He is taking it in.

'Okay. Not sure how that is relevant, but that piece of information is going to stay with me.'

'That's the problem.'

'What? She likes…' Neil stops. He looks like he is searching for the right word. One that will not get him fired. 'Men?'

'No, idiot. She can't fucking commit. We got a plant, it died, we got a dog, she gave it away.'

'She gave the dog away?' Neil tries to hide his shock.

'She said it went for her asthma.'

'She gave the dog away?'

'Something has happened. I just have to figure it out.'

'I never knew you guys even got a dog.'

'It was for two weeks.'

'Two weeks! Fucking hell.'

'Do you want to get over it? It wasn't a fucking child.'

'Nearly.'

'She's all bravado. Always.'

'Yeah, she is a bit tits and teeth.'

I shoot Neil a look.

Sometimes Neil seemed to forget that I am his boss, and mostly I liked that. I am not a fan of status and bureaucracy. Then there were days like this. Where I wished Neil had the common fear of bosses and losing your job that everyone else had. Yet I could not help but admire someone who just didn't seem to give a fuck.

'Come on. Let's go somewhere else. Make a night of it. You said Amanda is working late anyway.'

Neil looks pleased.

'Great! Let's do it.'

Chapter Seven

Natalie

I can feel him there as I look out of the window. It has been incredibly hot all summer. It was thirty-four degrees yesterday. Today the heavens opened up. The air had to be cleared. The thunder was deafening, the lighting came in short, sharp shoots.

I can feel him hovering. He wants something but he is still searching for a way to ask. I would put him out of his misery, but it would ruin the fun. Finally, he coughs, clears his throat. I wait with an impending sense of doom. Anything that takes him this long to ask me is going to be a kicker.

'Hey, I was just wondering.'

Then about a minute of silence. Christ, this is too painful. Time to be kind.

'What were you wondering, Paul?'

'Well, we were just wondering.'

We? Fuck. This really was going to be horrendous.

'Paul, just say it.'

'Amanda and I…'

He stops for another moment. I try to not roll my eyes. I fail and it spurs him on.

'Amanda and I want to have a family dinner.'

'Jeez, is that it, Paul? Really? Hardly worth such a preamble.'

'With Dad.'

I inhale and breathe out.

'Please, Natalie. It is time to put the family back together.'

'What family?'

'Natalie.' Paul sighs. A sigh of exasperation. I want to slap him.

'Do not Natalie me, Paul. You wanted to meet him with me. I did that for you. I hated it but I did it. Why do you have to bully me?'

'I am not the one being a bully, Natalie.'

His words sting. The unfairness chocks at me.

'Did Amanda put you up to this?'

'No. I can make my own decisions.'

I snort. He gives me daggers in return.

'Did he put you up to this?'

'No.'

'He is so manipulative, you know.'

'He is not the problem, Natalie. You are being the problem. Everyone else wants to get along. Be a family again. You just dredge up the past and hold your grudges. Why are you so unforgiving?'

I am too surprised at his comment to get as upset as I should. Paul and I have had some arguments in our time, but all of this sounds like Amanda.

'Where is this coming from?'

I ask this question, but I already know.

'Me. I have always thought this.'

'Wow. Really? Did you just miss your entire childhood then?'

'I was there.'

'You were not really though. You were always away with relatives, at school, or, and let's be really honest, playing computer games in your room all day.'

'You do not get to just dictate the narrative of our entire childhood. You were not the only one there. Human beings are complex.'

'Or maybe as the youngest, you were just protected, Paul. Maybe I spent my childhood protecting and raising you both! So much for gratitude.'

'So that is what this is about? You resent us?'

'Where is Nathaniel?'

'What? Why?'

'Just answer the question.'

'He is at his mother's. Why?'

'So I can tell you how much of an arsehole you are. I will not be bullied, Paul. Fuck you, fuck Amanda and fuck him. Fuck you all.'

I start to leave but it is not over yet.

'Don't you want a father, Natalie?'

I look at Paul. His comment stings like a cut.

'Yes, Paul. I always did, but we do not always get what we want, do we?'

I leave the kitchen, the anger in me looking for an outlet. My stomach cramping.

I gather my stuff as Paul's shadow creeps across the door. He stands just outside it, visible and yet, not.

He stands in front of me as I walk into the hall, blocking me. He thinks about trying to stop me, but he knows me enough to know that I will not be cowed down. He moves to the side and I leave the house.

'Family is family, Natalie. You cannot change that and you cannot choose them. It is time to move on.'

He has to stand in the doorway and have the last word. I can count on one hand how many times my brother and I have fallen out like this. I do not reply. I will not give him the satisfaction. I have to go to work now.

In the car, I keep thinking of Paul's words. They find their way in and place doubt. I have to pull over and I cry. Should I let everything go? Am I just holding grudges? Maybe Tim has changed. I do not know who I am any more. It feels like my world has been blown apart. I have no family. I am completely alone.

2000
Tim

I look at the pictures of my wife from our wedding day. The frame feels heavy in my hand. For some reason it is comforting. I put the picture back down and look at the other pictures on the mantlepiece. It seemed like yesterday that we got married, and today I buried her. I felt nothing but disbelief as they had lowered her body into the ground. How could this now be reality?

My beautiful wife who was not even forty-six. She didn't even have any grey hairs. I feel the stab, the pain of my wife being taken when she was still so young. I am a single father now. I have no idea how to do that. Life without my wife is terrifying.

I wish I had known that when I left her. Or any of the other times I hurt her. She had done so much, and I had never even noticed. My heart was full of regret and guilt. I had been a bastard and now she was dead. It was so unfair. She deserved so much more. I knew it and so did everyone else. I could never make it up to her now.

A sound in the next room catches my attention. It is my children. I go in the direction of their voices and I stop in the doorway.

They look so small. They are sitting on the floor and holding each other's hands. They are beautiful and sad. A mixture of incomprehension and grief is on their faces.

I try to stop the feeling of terror that overcomes me, but I cannot. I have to raise these children alone now. I may have lost a wife, but they have lost a mother. I do not even know what to say to them. How to even begin to make this better. I do not know them or how to raise them. It is like we are strangers living in the same house. Our DNA barely binding us together.

I can never fix what has been done. Being a single father was never in my game plan. I was terrible enough at being a father when my wife was there being a full-time mother. Now I am solely responsible for these human beings. Products of my own making. Their anger was the worst. I could feel it. Sure, Amanda didn't direct her hate at me; she was just angry in general, but Natalie hated me. I always felt it. Pure and powerful. Like a laser.

Paul had always been indifferent to me. It was like he saw how both his sisters acted towards me and decided to split the difference. I have a feeling that only Amanda loved me. I think that is unfair.

Sure, I have made mistakes, but I am still their father. I did not deserve to be treated like a monster. I came back, didn't I? Done the right thing in the end. Today has been awful. Almost all of my in-laws practically spat out my name. I saw their contempt for me in their eyes. I have been widowed for God's sake. Where is the compassion?

You would think I was the only person in the world to ever have an affair. I guess my wife told them numerous stories about me. I do not even think it would help to put my side across. Yes, my wife's death had been unbearable for me too, and being public enemy number one would never help matters, for anyone.

I look at my children again. The responsibility feels like it might kill me. I had never given much thought to having children. It was just what you did in those days. You got married and then you had kids. I do love them. I don't regret having them, but I have only ever been able to sacrifice so much. But now it is sinking in that I will have to sacrifice much more, and the thought fills me with dread. An overwhelming dread that feels like it might consume me.

Present Day
Natalie

I am feeling groggy. I managed to book a Travel Inn on a rare break at work. I got there in the small hours and only managed to get a few hours' sleep before I had to head back to the labour ward. The disorientation is a bit much but at least I have somewhere to put my stuff. I felt like a hobo taking it to the hospital yesterday. A few colleagues made cracks about me being homeless. They meant no harm, but the sad truth was that they were right.

Yesterday just seemed like wall-to-wall Caesarians and instrumental deliveries. I was thankful for the blood, gore and babies. Anything to get my mind off my fucked-up family and an impossible dinner. It was hard to think about the argument that Paul and I had just hours before when new life was coming into the world.

I have no idea how I managed to become the villain of the family. I almost called Amanda and gave her what for. I decided that was what she probably wanted. So I could get told what a bitch I am again.

I let out a sigh. I need to get a drink. Get caffeine in me before the next human being enters the world or the next gynaecological emergency happens. I forgo the tea and coffee in the on-call room and I head to the cafe in the hospital. They do a great coffee.

I order my coffee and I sit down and close my eyes for a moment. The argument with Paul was horrendous. I am not sure if there is a way back from it. Something has been irrevocably changed between us. I never thought my brother would be capable of that. Hell, I did not even know what he really thought. He had always taken a neutral stance against our father. Winning a scholarship and going to private school also meant that they had barely spent time together. Paul had always avoided him. Now he was running towards him with open arms.

The pain of being accused of ruining the family hurts like a bitch. I am so sick of all of the family politics. Sick of the fighting and the effort to stay on friendly terms with people, just because you share their blood. I am starting to question if it is worth it at all.

The only thing I have is my compartmentalisation. I have always been able to manage my emotions at work. I have been called cold by family so many times but never by my friends. They only see the surface. It is not my fault they are so superficial.

'Hi, Natalie.'

I look up. It is the anaesthetist, George. He is a really great guy. Funny and decent. He has three children of his own. All blonde and gorgeous. We got along well from the get-go.

'Hey, George.'

'You okay?'

I laugh. George is so intuitive. He always knows when something is up.

'Just some family problems.'

'Worse than a mother-in-law from hell?'

'Much worse. A father from hell and two siblings to match. I am outnumbered.'

'Jeez, sounds awful.'

'It is.'

Then to my horror I start crying. So much for compartmentalising. The mortification somehow fuels my tears. I am a female consultant crying in the cafe. In my scrubs. In a public place. This is doing nothing for gender equality. This is doing nothing for anyone.

George looks shocked initially, but then he gently puts his arm around me and leads me to a more private area of the hospital, in a corridor only accessible with our key cards. I hide in the corner and he stands in front, blocking people's view of me.

'Come on. Tell Uncle George all about it.'

I laugh. Everyone calls him Uncle George when he is sharing his wisdom. He has lots of it because he is a grown-up with his life together.

'My brother and my sister want our father in our lives again. They say I am a bitch holding a grudge.'

'Okay. Let's talk about it.'

I let out a sigh. It is all so complicated.

'My father never had good timing. There are few moments in his life that he can be proud of. He tore our family apart on Christmas Day. He left my mother for another woman and my sister went with him. Choosing him over us despite everything.'

'Christ, what a bastard.'

'Thank you!' I almost yell. 'Finally, someone who admits it. Anyway, months later he came back. but when the ship has hit the ice, it can never be brought back to its former glory. I never truly loved my father after that.'

'At least you have your boyfriend.'

'We broke up.'

George put his head in his hands.

'Christ, you are having a tough time. Well, here is my opinion. Your father was a complete bastard, your mother was very unfortunate to have him as a husband and I do hope she got some joy in her life other than him, and as for your siblings, they are just lashing out. Maybe have this one dinner and then you have done your part. I am sure you will make up. It will be okay.'

'Thanks, George. You are a great friend.'

'I know. Now let's help more babies be born.'

I laugh as I follow him. Feeling lighter and happier. I forgot how great it felt when you just talked to a friend. As I walk, I look out of the window. It is lightning again. It zigzags into the ground. It feels like the thunder and lightning will never stop.

Chapter Eight

Natalie

I look down onto the busy street. It is July and the height of summer. It was thirty-six degrees yesterday. Today looks like it might be the same. I can see mothers in summer dresses and sandals pushing prams. Daddies wearing cargo shorts and various little cherubs dressed for the weather. You do not always get a decent summer in London, but when you do it is glorious. The view from my hotel room is beautiful indeed. I could stand here for hours and watch the world go by.

After that one night, I had not found it in me to go back to Paul's after our argument. I just need space. A break from always being the outsider in my own family. I do not doubt my brother loves me. Or even my sister. Hell, even my father loves me in some way, I guess. But is love ever enough? I guess the theme of my life at the moment is no. But maybe it is enough for other people.

Summers with Rob were always perfect. We would have picnics and drink wine in pub gardens. He had a way of making everything fun. It was now five weeks since we broke up and we had only seen each other once.

What a disaster that was. Now I am a thirty-seven-year-old woman with no home and no boyfriend. I had thrown a grenade into my life then just watched passively as it blew up. Even I was unsure why sometimes. Paul had sent text messages.

Sorry but you had to hear it.

What was that? Not an apology. More like a further fuck you.

Amanda also sent messages.

We are not trying to hurt you. Just think about our point of view. xx

Kiss kiss on the end. They were a team now. How had that happened? I just knew it had something to do with him.

I would be a grown-up. I would go to yet another family event. A carousel of them. All spinning around. The exhaustion is so much. But I would give this Saturday to family relations. What was left of them.

I love my family but sometimes that love was best felt from a distance. Especially when your sister is pregnant and she reminds you of everything life probably wasn't going to give you. I am happy for my sister. I really am. Another nibling is exciting and I will love that child with all my heart, but I just wished I could have those things too.

I was fast realising that I was going to become one of those women with an excellent career and not much else. I know it does not make me a feminist to think I want the kids and the man, but I do. I want a family of my own. To right all of the wrongs that happened in my own childhood. I would do anything to make my own beginning.

Yet I know I am making my own difference in the world. I look at my phone. I have to head off now. Prepare for doomsday again. It is just a picnic in the park I tell myself. I can walk away at any point. It would be childish to not accept Neil's birthday invitation. I sigh and leave the room.

Green Park on a weekend is as busy as it always is. There have been many family picnics in this park so it does not take me long to find them. They are all already sitting there. Laughing and giggling as a family. I feel like the loneliest person in the world. He is front and centre. Tim. Dad. My father. God, what a prick. He always was a narcissist. He is telling a joke and everyone is laughing at him. The king of the court.

I am looming over them. My shadow on the blanket before they spot me. Why do they all look a little surprised? Even though I told them I would be here.

'Natalie! You are here!' Neil gets up to greet me and hugs me. It feels nice.

Amanda gets up and gives a lukewarm hug to go with her lukewarm smile. Paul does the same. Nathaniel is not here. He must be with his mother.

Then to my horror he stands and starts to walk toward me. He is going to touch me and I don't feel like I can say no or complain. Because then I would just be the bitch again.

'Natalie. My beautiful and smart daughter.'

He opens his arms wide and envelopes me in a hug. I try to not be too rigid. His smell makes me nauseous. A mixture of alcohol and some old-fashioned aftershave. It is cloying and overbearing. I think I might throw up.

He finally lets me go from his bear-like embrace and throws his arms out.

'Come, come, sit down. We have a feast here. We are so happy you could come. We know you are so busy saving lives.'

I see the jab. The 'we', but now I do not know if they are real or if I am being oversensitive. Maybe this is all me. Then I remember how he reacted when I told him I was going to be a doctor. He told me I was 'beautiful with decent tits'. Why bother working? 'I am sure you could find someone to marry you, love.'

I paste that smile back on and I find a gap. I reach into my bag and pull out a bottle of champagne for Neil. He looks happy to see it.

'Thanks! This is a good one. I will open it in a bit.'

That is classic Neil. He is always generous. Like Rob.

I look at my sister now. She is beautiful. She is going to be a great mother. I almost want to embrace her again. Pull her close and tell her that I have missed her, but I don't. The closeness between us has been like waves for years. Something always got in the way of us staying close. We went through periods of being like best friends. Then the ghosts would come.

I sit near Amanda on the blanket and they all continue with their conversation. To my horror they are talking about some reality TV show that Amanda loves. Apparently, Tim has been watching it with her and is now really into it. It takes everything I have to not roll my eyes. I must behave.

'What do you think, Natalie?'

I look at Tim.

'I have never watched it, Tim, so I can't comment.'

I see the flinch. The flicker of anger he always gives when I use his Christian name. He smiles but it is not a real smile. I see him. I know who he is.

'Where is your boyfriend, Natalie? I met him at the wedding. Seems like a nice chap. What is his name again?'

'Rob. I invited him. He could not come,' Neil says mournfully.

Tim and I just look at each other. He is baiting me. I know he is.

'Rob and Natalie broke up. I told you that, Dad,' Amanda chimes in. At least she has the decency to look annoyed.

'How old are you now, Natalie?'

'Thirty-seven, Tim.'

'You should crack on, love. You are not getting any younger. I am telling you this because I love you. I am your dad after all.'

Paul clears his throat. The awkwardness hangs heavy in the air. No one knows what to say, but at least other people are seeing this. How much of a twat this man is.

'You know, Tim, I don't have to worry about that. I don't think marriage or children are for me. None of that seems like a lot of fun.'

'Oh, don't be silly, love.'

'Silly? Did you enjoy it?'

'What?'

'Being a parent?'

'Of course. I love my kids.' He looks around and smiles at his three grown-up children. 'And now I am getting a grandchild! How wonderful. Family is so important.'

'You already have a grandchild.'

Tim turns and looks at me. Surprised.

'Yes, of course. I meant a new baby. A baby is always so exciting.'

I think about asking him what he remembered about Paul being a baby, but I decide against it. I do not want to become the villain again. Surely they can hear this crap?

'Time for some champagne, I think!'

Neil pops the cork and hands out the plastic cups. His timing was always good. Not that I had forgiven him for the comment about Rob. Why did everyone have to make me feel so guilty and awful all of the time?

We all take our cups and have our cheers. Except Amanda. Who has apple juice and looks pissed off about it. Ha. You cannot have everything, dear.

Everyone grabs a plate and we help ourselves to the food. I start with the olives and sandwiches. It is quite a spread. Amanda did well.

I bite into my cheese and chutney sandwich and I look around the park. It is beautiful and vast. There is a family of four near us. A couple with a child around six and a four-year-old. The children are colouring in and the couple are holding hands and looking at each other adoringly. I smile. Not every family has to be like this. So deeply fractured that the wound will never heal.

'You know what, Tim. Let's have dinner next week. Wouldn't it be great to catch up properly?'

Everyone stares at me a little too long. Paul almost chokes on his food. Finally, Tim recovers himself.

'I would love that, Natalie. Let's make it a date.'

'Wonderful! You two can come too if you would like,' I say to my ungrateful siblings who I pretty much raised.

Neil looks put out.

'And you of course, Neil. I would never forget you. I would love to have you all.'

I have no home to have this dinner in so I will have to find a restaurant. Anyway, screw the logistics. The more people see of this twat called our father the more they will see how horrible he is. I am sure of it.

Then
Jacqueline

I am almost done putting sunscreen on my daughter. Natalie hates it. I guess all children do, but that is what has to happen. I cannot let that cute, dimpled face and soft skin get burned. Natalie is squirming around. She cannot wait to get in the water, I can tell. My beautiful daughter has always loved water and her squeals of delight whenever she is in it make my heart burst.

A moment of queasiness comes over me. My second pregnancy is proving to be a difficult one. My morning sickness when I was pregnant with Natalie only lasted two months. After that the pregnancy had been a good one. The envy of all of my friends actually. But not this one. This baby was giving me a tough time.

Finally, the little one is smeared and safe. I let go and she runs towards the water, squealing as she does. I almost laugh as I follow her. I give a quick look at Tim who has taken up residence on a blanket, with a parasol over him. He is sipping a beer as he watches the ocean.

I love him. It hits me every time I look at him. He is handsome. Tall, slim and tanned. His eyes are an aquatic green and he has a strong nose that gives him a beautiful profile. He has a good jaw too. Hell, he has a good everything.

But he has disappointed me. Repeatedly. When we met he swept me off my feet. We had an insane, lustful connection that blocked out the rest of the world. For the first few years anyway. Then we moved in together and his bad habits had come to the fore.

He was selfish and hard to live with. He expected me to be a traditional woman. He didn't cook or clean. He drank beer every night and went out with the boys a lot. I soon found out that he was not the man I thought he was.

I had considered leaving, but then I got pregnant. And that was the end of that. I liked to think it would have brought us together, having a child, but that was not what happened. At first, he had been overjoyed and treated me well. He even cooked sometimes and made me tea. He was convinced we were going to have a boy. That he would have a son. Then we had a little girl and he was disappointed. That hurt. Put me in a tailspin even. As time had gone on, I was realising more and more that Tim had this other side to him. A darker, scary side. He was selfish and being in a relationship with him was exhausting.

Now I was trapped. I mean, sure I could leave him, but then I would be a single mother, and my children would grow up without a father. The thought of that was more than I could bear. No, I would stick this out. We were getting married soon. Before I started to show he said, even though we already had one child. Despite everything, I am excited about my wedding day. I have dreamt about it since I was a little girl. Pictured the dress, the flowers, everything. It was an obsession. And maybe that was it. Maybe I just wanted to be a wife and mother so much I was willing to put up with his bad points. Everyone is flawed.

I watched Natalie dip her toe in the water and then run back. She did this a number of times. It was so cute. My daughter melted my heart. There is nothing I would not do for her. She is perfect. Every inch of her. I put my hand on my stomach, protecting the little baby growing in there. Two children. Soon I would have two children. It was more than I had ever hoped for and the happiness was all-encompassing, but along with it was an uneasiness. An anxiety that just always sat there. Sometimes it was a little buzz, a bee flying past your ear, and other times it was huge: a tonne weight that took away my breath and made me feel like the world was about to end. I pushed it down and counted my blessings. This is my family. I have more than most, and I am grateful for it.

Present day

Natalie

'So, how are you feeling?'

'I am feeling okay. I am a bit sore, but I am so happy. I cannot believe I have a baby!'

'Most people feel that way. It is a little miracle.'

I look over at the baby. It is a little boy who is only a few hours old. I see babies this small all of the time and yet it still amazes me.

'Can I have a cuddle?' I ask the mother, Kirsty, a friendly redhead who has lived in London for five years. She gives me a huge smile.

'Of course! You brought him into the world, go ahead.'

'Ah, you brought him into the world. I just helped.'

Mothers never give themselves enough credit. The human body is amazing. I wish more women knew just how amazing they were. I pick up the baby. He is so tiny and so cute he takes my breath away. I have delivered hundreds, no, maybe even thousands of babies and I am still not immune to the miracle of life.

'Do you have any?'

I look at Kirsty. This question does not hurt when it comes from patients. This is my safe space. I matter here.

'No, I don't.'

'Not yet. You should though. Look at you. You are such a natural. You would make an amazing mother.'

I smile, touched at the words. Maybe she is right. If I could just take the heartbreak of trying. A leap into the unknown. I guess it is too late now anyway. I no longer have him. The only one I would want to do the whole shebang with.

The baby starts to cry and I hand it back to Kirsty for a feed.

'He is beautiful. He is lucky to have you as a mother. What is his name?'

'William.'

'William. I love that name.'

I leave Kirsty to feed William. I need to eat something before the latest baby decides to be born. I almost walk into George on the way out.

'Hey.'

'Hey.'

'How was your weekend?'

'Just took the kids to the park. Tried to relax. How was yours? Any more stories about your difficult family?'

'God, yes. We had a picnic for my brother-in-law's birthday and my dad was there and he was such a sexist dinosaur to me. Kept going on about how time was running out for me and my ovaries.'

'Hmm.'

'What do you mean "hmm"?'

'Well, how old are you?'

'Screw you, George.'

'You are a doctor. You know better than anyone. Facts are facts.'

I think about this. A woman's biological clock does screw her over.

'I tried with my ex and nothing came of it. Nothing medical. It just never happened.'

The words just jump out. My candour surprises me. I never talk about this stuff.

'Well, there is still a shot. You just have to take it. Then at least you will have no regrets.'

'True.'

'It is time for you to get back on the horse.'

'What are you talking about?'

'It is time for you to start dating again. Just let me set you up with someone. I know this really great guy.'

I feel mortified and wonder how I can let George down quietly. I have no interest in dating. I just want to focus on my career. But then I remember little William and the loud ticking sound in my ovaries. But mostly I think of Rob. Where he is? What is he doing?

'George, I am not interested in dating at the moment. A lot has happened and also, I want to focus on my career. Men are just a distraction.'

I know he will understand.

'Look, he is a great guy. It won't be a date. Just have dinner. I will make it clear to him. You need to get out more. The only people you see are your siblings. That is not healthy.'

'Oh okay. But I resent this. A lot.'

'Wonderful! Also, I hope you can come round to ours soon as well. It is barbecue season. There are few things that are better than a barbecue.'

'Yeah, except maybe something less carcinogenic.'

George looks at me.

'Sorry, I was trying to be funny. That sounds great.'

'See you later, Natalie.'

George leaves, raising an eyebrow in a jokey way.

As I go to get some food, I wonder what the hell I have let myself in for.

I cannot believe I am on a non-date date. I let my insecurities and politeness overcome my rational brain. I know he was just trying to help. I know nothing about the man I am supposed to be on my non-date with other than the fact his name is David and he works at the hospital, even though I have never seen him before. He must be in another department at least. Still, talk about messy.

The place David has chosen is the "in" place to be, and the price of the menu reflects that. Rob and I have been here before. Just to make this worse.

It is high end, but I do not mind. The food is always great. I had spent a lot of my time in these "see and be seen" places. It went along with Rob's job. He knew everyone. A number of well-known people surround us. An actor I watched in a film the night before, a journalist that seemed to be in every magazine and newspaper at the moment. And me. And David.

He is not my type, but he does not seem like a jerk either. So that is something. He is nervous. I can tell. At least that is endearing. I told David that this was not a date. That I did not have it in me for more. He seemed okay about it and agreed. I felt guilty that I am having dinner with someone who I have no intention of seeing again. I know despite ending up in this situation that I need to be single. My life is a mess and my heart is somewhere else.

'I heard about this place from a friend. I hope it's as good as they say.'

'I'm sure it will be.'

David looks really nervous. He really did think this was a date. He would not be this nervous for just an informal meal. How the hell can I get out of this?

I look at the menu, wanting the ground to swallow me up. I feel angry at myself for being so naive. I have to be firmer with people.

'George says your family are a bit much.'

I laugh.

'Yes. They are.'

'Families are all difficult, aren't they?'

'Yes.'

I laugh again.

'I completely agree.'

I relax. This might be fun. I could do with having someone else to talk to. Then he puts his hands on top of mine and gives me a flirty smile.

Then I am not smiling any more. I move my hand. Everything is awkward now. Neither of us know what to do. Thankfully the waiter comes to take our order.

'Drinks?' the waiter asks.

'Yes. I will have a white wine, thank you.'

'I will have the same.'

'Would you like to order food now?'

'Yes,' I say as David says no almost in unison.

We look at each other.

'I will have a caprese along with some bread and olives to start.' I tell the waiter.

I have had this before. Sometimes the best foods are simple.

'I'll have the same. That sounds ace.'

'And I will follow that with the sea bass with rosemary potatoes on the side.'

I look up at David, half-expecting him to choose that too. He seems a bit wet to be honest. It is almost like he knows what I am thinking.

'I will have the steak and chips. With peppercorn sauce. Thanks.'

The waiter nods as he writes it down. Then he takes our menus and leaves. I smile at David's choice. Until I feel something touching my leg under the table. David is playing footsie with me. I pull my leg away, but he puts the other one forward. Oh, screw this I think as I kick him.

'Ouch.'

'Oh, are you okay?'

I have to repress a smile.

'Sure.'

He is annoyed but he is trying to not let it show.

My smugness only lasts for a moment because in the next moment I am obliterated. A man walks into the restaurant with a beautiful woman in a blue dress. It is him. It's Rob. My Rob.

I watch as Rob and the woman are seated. David notices me staring and follows my gaze.

'Someone you know?'

It takes a moment for my brain to catch up.

'Just a friend.'

'Maybe we should invite them over?' David says, but then I can tell he regrets it. I think about it. If it was anyone else, I would want to be rescued. Asking Rob and whatever bitch he is with would be weird.

'No.'

I see the relief in David's face.

'Good. I want it to be just the two of us.'

David leans in and tries to take my hand again.

Christ, this is hell. There is no good way out of this.

'You know what. I will go and get them. It has been ages.'

I practically ran over to Rob and stop right in front of him, facing the worst of two evils.

'Hi.'

Rob looks up, shocked and puts his hand up to say hello back. The exchange is followed by an excruciatingly painful silence.

'Hi, I'm Natalie.'

I put my hand out to Rob's date.

'Hi, I'm Claire.'

Claire. How long has he known her?

'Can I help you?' Rob asks. It is clear by his aggressive tone that he is pissed off.

'Rob!' Claire and I say in unison.

'Now that's not very polite, is it? I was just wondering if you would like to join us.'

I gestured over to David. Rob follows my hand and stares. There is a flicker of jealousy, which is followed by more anger.

'I'm sorry. What do you want?'

I ignore Rob.

'Claire! Would you like to join us?'

'Sure.'

It occurs to me as Claire says this that she actually seems to mean it. I can feel a niggling guilt which gets worse as I note that Claire has hair that could do with a good conditioner. I have an inkling that Claire may end up as a casualty of war tonight. It makes me hate myself.

'What?'

Rob sounds stunned and agitated.

'Are you kidding me? Just go away.'

Claire looks at Rob, embarrassed. She gets up and follows me to my table. Rob stares after us. He looks thrown. After a beat he follows, shaking his head and clearly wondering what the hell I am on.

I get two more seats for the table. Claire sits on one of them. I am pretty certain this is going to be the worst meal of my life.

'David, this is Rob and Claire. Rob and Claire, this is David.'

'Great to meet you both,' David said, still looking a bit put out.

'Do you know what you are having yet? We have already ordered.'

'No, we haven't ordered. When would we have got the chance, Natalie? We had just sat down.'

He has a tone to his voice. I return his tone with a stern look. I signal the waiter who comes over with a smile. Menus already in his hand. The sign of a good waiter. He already knew what I wanted.

'I see you have guests. Let me just get more settings and then I will take your orders.'

With that the waiter handed Rob and Claire the menus and then went off to get more napkins and cutlery.

Rob opens the menu. He is clearly fuming.

The table has broken into an uncomfortable silence. David starts tapping his fingers on the table in a very irritating way.

'I am having the steak,' David said.

'Sounds good,' Rob said, closing the menu.

'So how do you two know each other?' Rob asked David.

'We work together at the hospital,' David said.

Rob let that sink in.

Shit. This was not good. Rob was going to get the wrong idea.

'Are you enjoying your date?' Rob asked David. Punching the word "date" and looking at me in an accusing way when he did.

'Yeah, it's going great,' David said in a happy way. I cannot look. It is like a lamb to the slaughter.

'So how long have you two been dating? Weeks, months, years even?'

Rob is interrogating David. I am angry at him. He is implying that I cheated on him. I kick Rob under the table. It has no effect.

'Actually, this is our first date,' David replied.

'How lovely. Your first date.'

'It is not a date. This is the first time we have met each other. Now it would be great if you could stop interrogating poor David now, Rob. Surely there is something else we can talk about?'

I give Rob a look that says quit it. He gives me one back that tells me where to go. I look at Claire. I am jealous of her, but I feel sorry for her. She seems so nice.

It is not fair on her to have her date question his ex's date, or non-date in this case. And it was all my fault. Again.

'Really?' Rob said, surprise in his voice.

'It is actually a blind date. George set us up,' David said. Not ready to give up yet.

'I am surprised Natalie agreed to that. She is a bit of a commitment-phobe,' Rob said.

David laughed.

'That is what George said, but I am sure I can win her round.'

David turned to me and said the last part with a smile. It even took me a moment to realise he had taken my hand again. I want to be sick. I pull my hand away. I will also have to punch George for that comment. What did he know? Rob and I had been together for seven years. That was a pretty long commitment!

'Excuse me. I have to go to the bathroom.'

I head to the bathroom. I can feel Rob watching me as I go.

As soon as I am in the bathroom I head to a stall. I put the seat down with a piece of tissue and just sit there and breathe. This meal is a car crash. My life is a car crash. I am a woman in her late-thirties and my life is a mess. I take a moment and gather myself. Then I leave the stall and look in the mirror and touch myself up. Game face on. Let's go.

'What the hell are you playing at? Are you trying to ruin my life? Have you not done enough damage already?'

I jump. It is Rob and he is angry.

'Oh relax. You know what. Take your grudge, plant it in the best soil you can find, make it grow as big as a house. I don't care. I am happy with my life.'

'I don't care that you hate me.'

'Don't flatter yourself. I don't hate you. The opposite of love is not hate. It's indifference.'

'What did you say?'

'You heard.'

Rob has the weirdest reaction to this. His anger immediately disappears and he looks happy.

'Why are you grinning like an idiot?'

'I'm not.'

'Debatable,' I reply and then walk away. Rob stares after me, smiling as he does.

The rest of the evening is covered in pleasantries and small talk. David mercifully keeps his hands to himself, and as long as he does, I am nice to him. When the food comes Rob and I both realise we ordered the sea bass at the same time. It is awkward as we look at each other's food.

At the end of the evening David and I excuse ourselves. To my horror David asks me for a lift home. I say it will be fine but if he does not keep his hands to himself, I will stop the car and throw him out into the road. He laughs and agrees, apologising as he does. Maybe he is not such a creep after all.

Rob

I squint as I watch them go. Yes, indeed. That is my ex-girlfriend driving off with her new date in my car. It was the perfect kick-to-the-gut ending to one incredibly weird evening. I cannot believe I love that woman. She is bat-shit crazy.

'I am really sorry about all of that, Claire. I am very embarrassed.'

'Don't be. It is fine. I am just glad I got to meet the famous Natalie. She really is something.'

'Yeah. Something is the right word.'

I realise that Claire is stroking my back. I stand up, uncomfortable. I do not have any feelings for her. Not that I would act on them if I did. It would be inappropriate.

'She was nice to me. Genuinely nice to me even though she thought I was on a date with you.'

'Maybe that means she has moved on.'

I do not want it to be true.

'No, she was jealous. I could tell. There are definitely feelings there. And the thing with the man she was on a date with, David. Well, I think she just wanted to be rescued. Did you see her face when he touched her? She did not like it.'

'Yeah well, they left together. They even drove away in my car.'

Claire laughed. 'Yes, you told me she had stolen your car. Is it wrong to find it funny?'

I laugh.

'No. It is pretty funny.'

'Let me pay for this, for my food. It was so nice of you to take me out to cheer me up. It certainly was an entertaining evening.'

'I won't have it. Not after you were subjected to an evening of torture.'

We both laugh again. I also noted that Natalie had insisted on paying for her and David. Something David had initially been annoyed about but he had given in easily. I hoped that was a good omen.

'Let's go,' I say and stand up. Claire stands up too.

'I would drive you home, but I don't have a car at the moment.' Claire laughs.

'It's okay. I live close by.'

She kisses me on the cheek and then we go our separate ways. I feel a bit uncomfortable. Tonight has made me think, that Claire might have feelings for me. There were supposed to be two other people coming along tonight and the optics of me and her alone were not great. She recently broke up with her boyfriend.

Hopefully she was just looking for a friend. You can never be too careful in this climate.

I decide to walk home and sort my head out. It is a forty-five- minute walk back to my part of Wandsworth but it will help me clear my head.

I am glad it is night-time. The temperature has dropped. The weather is too much at the moment. I walk past the nightlife of South West London. Guys on a night out, drinking beer and bonding. A hen party passes me and I am encompassed in balloons. The women are happy. The bride-to-be is wearing a tiara and a white dress. Her entire life is about to start. I think about the ring I have, or had, for Natalie. It came from my grandmother's engagement ring. She had raised me, my parents incapable of doing so. But she said the ring itself was too old-fashioned. I promised her I would take the stone and reset it for the woman I would spend my life with. It broke me that my future had been taken away from me just as I was about to do that. All I wanted in life was to make my own family. To have what I never had.

My ex really was a riddle. A riddle wrapped in an enigma. I went through every single second of the dinner. From the moment I first saw her to the moment I watched her drive away in the car she stole from me. It was called ghosting, Claire had told me. When someone just dumps you and ignores you. I had to trust my instincts. That was not what happened. I could not see a future where Natalie was at least a friend. As painful as that thought was, I needed to know our relationship would continue in some way.

I know this is not healthy. Maybe I am just deluded. In the weeks that have passed I have been in limbo, hoping that something would happen and the woman that I love would tell me what was wrong and come back to me. I could be wasting my time. But it was not a waste. Because I had to do anything I could. Otherwise, I could never live with myself.

Natalie

Boy, do I have a bone to pick with George. What the hell was going through his mind? David behaved himself on the car ride home. I soon realised why his behaviour had changed so much, from a charging rhino to a meek, little dog.

'You are in love with that guy, aren't you? Who is he?'

That question threw me. Was it that obvious? I guess so. I ducked the question. Instead mentioning how good the food was at the restaurant. He had seemed quiet. When I dropped him off at his place in Tooting, he just thanked me for the meal and then walked away. Looking sad as he did. I did not feel sorry for him. He had been too predatory. Finally, I see George. He sees me coming.

'What? You don't look happy.'

'Are you kidding? That David guy was so full on.'

George looks concerned for a moment.

'No, not like that. Nothing happened. Well, only to my hand and foot.'

Now George looks confused. I burst out laughing and so does he.

'He kept trying to take my hand and play footsie. I did not like it.'

'Oh dear. He sent me a text saying it went okay but that he was not into you.'

I keep as straight a face as possible.

'We bumped into my ex. It was a bit weird.'

'The one you are still in love with?'

'Why does everyone keep saying that?

'Isn't that obvious?'

I sigh. I have no time for this.

'I have bigger problems than this. So, whatever.'

'Like what?'

'Like being a homeless thirty-something. I said I would host my father for dinner and I have nowhere to do it. Unless I take everyone to a restaurant. Which I could do, I guess.'

'I thought you were staying with your brother.'

'Not at the moment. I need space from home.'

'Where are you staying?'

'In a hotel. An inexpensive one. Until I plan my next move.'

'Come and stay with us.'

'Are you kidding?'

'No, it is the summer holidays so just be aware. As long as you are not scared of teenagers. We have a guest room. We all love you. Come on. Just until you get yourself sorted.'

I am so touched. George and his family are the perfect family. They are all lovely people. Sure, they make you feel inadequate by running marathons and being perfect at everything, but everybody has some fault.

'Okay then. Mostly because you owe me for the awful date.'

George laughs.

'It is a deal then. You can host your father there too. Then you won't be outnumbered like last time. Bethany and I will back you up.'

I have to do everything I can to restrain myself from hugging him. Oh, sod it. I hug him. He seems surprised by the intensity. I might be about to break a rib, but he hugs me back. It feels good.

'Thanks, George. You are such a lifesaver.'

Chapter Nine

Natalie

Today is the day. I can handle pressure. I am a strong person. Yet I feel like a wreck right now. They are all coming. I am barely talking to my family. All we have done recently is exchange faux-polite text messages. He will be here. They will all be. I will be outnumbered again. But I have George and his wife Bethany. Their three teenagers are off with friends. I do not blame them. It must seem strange for them to have this grown woman here. Taking up the guest room, bringing her family around for dinner.

I cook lasagne. It is my fail-safe and my comfort food. I will need all of the comfort I can get tonight.

'Everything is going to be fine, Natalie,' Bethany says.

She can tell I am nervous.

'It will be,' George reiterates.

I nod. It just might be.

'I am just going to finish setting the table,' Bethany says as she leaves.

Then the bell rings. Here we go. I go and answer the door. There is Amanda, Paul and Tim. I look at them all together. Feel a stab of pain. I note Neil is missing.

'Hi,' Amanda says. 'Neil had to work. He sends his regards.'

I am sure he does. Lucky bastard.

'Come in. Thank you for coming to George and Bethany's house. They are going to join us. I hope that is okay.'

'Of course,' they all say.

I step out of the way.

'Come in.'

They walk in one by one. Amanda first then Paul who says hi and then kisses me on the cheek, followed by Tim. It makes me squirm when he touches me.

'It is so nice of George and Bethany to let you use their home, Natalie,' Tim said.

'It is. Just go through the door. The food is ready. What can I get you to drink? All okay with wine? Apart from you, Amanda. I got you some lemonade if that is okay.'

Amanda looks pleased. She likes lemonade. Maybe she is getting used to not drinking.

'Wine is great, thank you, Natalie,' Tim said.

'Yes. Thank you,' Paul said and looks and smiles at me. I wonder if he is feeling guilty. He does look uncomfortable.

They all go through. George and Bethany greet them.

'Please sit down. Natalie has cooked a lovely meal,' Bethany says and looks at me and nods encouragingly.

Everyone sits down. I am glad Neil is not here. Even numbers are good.

'I will go and get the drinks.'

I go into the kitchen to get the wine and lemonade. I can hear everybody getting to know each other. Tim is making a comment about how much their house must be worth. He always has an eye on other people's money.

I walk in with the drinks and put them down on the table, going back for the rest.

'Natalie must make a lot of money too.'

Tim looks at me. Who the hell does he think he is? It is none of his business how much money I make.

'We don't do it for the money, Tim. It is very low paid for years. Do you remember when I started? I was so broke.'

I see a flash of anger. He knows what I am referring to. Long ago, when I was the parent and he was the child.

Bethany stands up. 'I'll help you bring the food in, Natalie.'

She is always so intuitive.

We go into the kitchen together.

'He seems a bit blunt.'

'He is. He has no manners. It is one of the nicest things about him.'

Bethany laughs and gives me a supportive look. Then she puts her hand on my arm. I smile, appreciating it.

'The food should be ready now.'

I take the lasagne out of the oven. I have also cooked carrots and broad beans. I baked an orange and almond cake for dessert. So much effort for a bunch of twats.

We dish up the lasagne and put the vegetables in bowls so people can help themselves.

'It smells great,' Bethany said.

'Let's hope it tastes as good.'

We go through and dish everything out.

'Oh, your lasagne. I love it. It's the best,' Amanda said.

'Me too. One of my favourite dishes,' Paul agrees.

'I like lasagne. I am sure it will be great,' Tim chips in.

I appreciate the compliments. Good to see they are making an effort to be nice. We all sit down and start eating.

'How is the pregnancy going?' George asks Amanda.

'Great, thanks. We are really excited.'

"Any morning sickness yet?' I ask Amanda.

'Some, but it is not too bad.'

'Good.'

'It is so wonderful having a child, Amanda. I am so happy for you. I can't wait to be a grandfather again.'

There is a silence and then I realise everyone is looking at me.

'You made a noise, Natalie,' Amanda says, her eyes boring into me.

'Did I?'

'Like a snorting sound.'

'Sorry. I didn't realise.'

Amanda rolls her eyes and drinks some of her lemonade. Tim is still looking at me. He never likes being called out on his bullshit.

'I made a lot of mistakes as a parent. That makes me feel sad. My broken relationship with Natalie is the biggest regret of my life. I would do anything to fix it. I hope we can be friends in the future, Natalie.'

Everyone is looking at me. I give a little smile.

'Thank you, Tim. Your honesty means a lot. I am also happy you have learned to take responsibility and apologise.'

'You could be nicer, Natalie.'

'How was that not nice, Amanda?'

She is thinking about saying something, but the presence of my friends, stop her.

'Building relationships takes time, I find,' George says.

'Very true,' Tim agrees.

Paul just sits there. I wonder what he is thinking. I wonder if his dad is living up to his expectations. If he was worth the damage done to our relationship. He used to be the only safe anchor in my life. After I had thrown away the only love I ever had. It is almost like he can read my mind.

'How is Rob?' Tim asks.

'We broke up, remember?'

'But you must still speak to each other?'

'She just cut him out, Dad,' Amanda said.

'Ah, you really are a surgeon.' Tim laughs at his own joke. My siblings do not dare.

'It is called ghosting,' Paul said.

'Actually, I had dinner with Rob this week.'

That throws them. Amanda and Paul practically choke on their food.

'Really?' Amanda said, unable to believe it.

I think about responding but I am not done yet.

'Anyway, how is Sheila?'

My aim is true. Tim's fork stops midway to his mouth. Lasagne falls from the fork, his mouth stays open. He gathers himself.

'She is well, thank you, Natalie.'

'Who is Sheila?' George asks.

'My dad's long-term girlfriend,' I tell him, punching the "long-term".

'How long has it been now, Tim? Thirty years? Thirty-three? Something like that. Well done, though.'

'Actually, she is my ex-wife, but lately we have been trying to make things work again.'

For some reason this feels like a punch to the gut.

'Wow. Good for you.'

'Amanda came to the wedding. Didn't you, darling?'

Wow. I look at Amanda. Who at least looks sheepish.

'When was that then?'

'Oh, I don't know. About ten years ago. Maybe a little more. Sheila still lives in Spain. We have lived there on and off.'

Tim says the latter for George and Bethany's benefit.

I look at Amanda again. I had no idea they were in contact then. I guess they have always been.

'Were you there, Paul?'

'No.'

'Any children?'

'Natalie!' Amanda scorns me.

'No. Natalie. It is just you three. Sheila couldn't. All very sad for her.'

'Probably why the relationship lasted so long though, right?'

Tim smiles wearily.

'It doesn't have to be like this, Natalie.'

'Yes, it does. I have been bullied into participating so here I am. But I don't like you and I never will. I will not be bullied into faking.'

'Okay.' Tim sighs. It infuriates me.

'Do you ever think of her?'

'Who?'

'My mother.'

'Of course. It takes two to ruin a marriage.'

'It takes one to stick his cock in someone else.'

My family recoil. Paul rubs the bridge of his nose. His classic stress gesture.

'Natalie, this is not fair on your friends.' Paul finally says something.

'You are right. Sorry, George, sorry, Bethany. Let me top up everyone's glasses. Enough of this chat.'

'Don't worry about it, Natalie. Family is complicated,' George says.

'We are not upset,' Bethany adds. She is such a lovely and sweet person.

'So, what is it that you do, Tim? Or did? Maybe you are retired.'

'I am in property, George. I have been my entire life.'

I manage to not snort at this. Most of his "work in property" was my mother's money and wealth.

I fill up everyone's glasses and then bring dessert. It is the home stretch. This evening will be over soon.

The conversation stays on safe territory for the rest of the evening. We talk about possible names for Amanda's baby. Tim thinks "Tim" for a boy would be a great name like any true narcissist. Paul goes for Graham for a boy or Jennifer for a girl. George and Bethany think Jennifer is a great name, but if they had another son, they would have called him Phillip.

'You can have it if you like it,' Bethany says. 'We are not going to have any more.'

'Thank God,' George replies. We all laugh.

Soon I am showing them to the door and I can finally breathe. George and I watch them walk away.

'You did really well,' George tells me and smiles.

'Thank you. You and that wife of yours are the most amazing people.'

He pats me on the back and then starts to walk away.

'I am also really sorry about the cock comment.'

George laughs.

'Don't. It was funny. Anyway, he deserved it.'

I am about to get ready for bed when I get a text.

Come and meet me and Dad in the pub on the corner. He wants to say sorry. So do I. xx

It is from Paul. Against my better judgement I decide to go.

The pub is full. This is a surprise to me. I cannot remember the last time I went to a pub in the evening. It is a Sunday. Do these people not have to go to work tomorrow? I look around, trying to find their faces. Finally, I see them in the corner. They are drinking beer and laughing like old buddies. It hurts. Another little stinging cut to add to all the others. Paul catches my eye. There is a fleeting moment of something — guilt — I hope. Then he waves and beckons me over. I walk over, dreading this. I feel like I cannot breathe. I reach them and smile. Social conditioning. I did not even mean it, but the smile stays there. Then I realise there is nowhere to sit.

'I will go and get you a seat.'

Paul dashes off and comes back with a chair.

I sit down. I do not know what to say. It feels like it was all said at supper.

'Thank you for joining us, Natalie,' Tim says and smiles. He almost looks sincere.

'Yes, thanks, sis. We didn't want to leave things like that. We love you so much.'

I try to not vomit in my mouth.

'No worries.'

This is followed by the most uncomfortable silence of my life.

'Can I get you a drink?' Paul looks at me hopefully.

'Sure, I will have a small Sauvignon Blanc.'

Paul goes off to help medicate this situation. I need that wine more than anything.

'Natalie, thank you for coming.'

'You already said that,' I reply with an edge to my voice. So he knows. I am always bravest when I have him alone. He flinches. That look of hurt that he specialises in. People who dish it out are always the worst at taking it back.

'Is there a reason I am here? I'm really busy at the moment, so if we could get to it.'

'I just wanted to say sorry.'

'Okay. Thanks.'

'I mean it.'

'Fine.'

'I don't just mean for tonight. I mean.' Tim pauses and wells up. I have never seen him cry. It makes me uncomfortable. 'I mean for everything. I know you did not have a good childhood. I know you pretty much raised your siblings. That you cared for your mother. I know you were there when she died. I know this. It has been so tough for you and I'm sorry. I should have been a better father.'

I am surprised and I take a moment. He seems to mean it. I smile, properly this time.

'Thank you. I appreciate that.'

Tim smiles back but I can tell he expected more. A parade or something. Where the hell is Paul with my drink? It has been ages.

'So, I'm hoping this repairs our relationship.'

I try to not sigh but it happens too quickly.

'I think it is great you finally apologised, but I think our relationship will always be what it is.'

'And what is that?'

'Non-existent.'

It is Tim's turn to sigh. I can tell he is annoyed.

'I think it is time for you to let go of your grudge.'

'There is no grudge.'

Tim raises an eyebrow.

'Really?'

'Yes, really. I just don't like you and I don't want you in my life.'

'Well, I'm here and I will not be bullied out of it.'

'I am not bullying you, Tim. I am perfectly civil. My siblings can do what they want.' I decide to not add that I am the one being bullied.

'Okay. I guess it is what it is.'

'Yes, it is what it is.'

'But maybe you could work on being more forgiving.'

I feel a short, sharp burst of anger. He always has to have the last word. Always has to be an arsehole. Whatever. I will not let him get to me.

'I'm just going to check on Paul and that drink. He seems to be taking a long time.'

I make my way through the mass of people and finally see him. Just standing there.

'What the fuck?'

'What?'

'Does it really take this long to get a drink?'

'I thought it would be good for you to bond.'

It is at this point I see the drinks on the bar. All ready to go. I am livid.

'I have no idea why I came here. You are all such horrible people. I am so sick of being bullied. Tell Amanda to fuck off and you can too. You just keep trying to force something that is never going to happen. None of you care about me. You can all go to hell.'

'Natalie.' Paul stops and wisely so. Only the word "sorry" could make any of this okay.

'You are all out of my life.' I turn and walk away. I walk towards Tim to tell him the same thing.

I reach him and he looks at me. He looks breathless. He looks *not right*. Something is off. He looks pale. He is trying to talk but he cannot. He puts his hands to his face and his face drops. It is then that I know. I know.

I reach for my phone in my pocket and I call an ambulance. Then I go to him, full of fear, the seed of panic growing at an alarming rate. I hope for the best. But it is too late. I can see it. Like so many times before. I know I am right.

I get him from his collapsed position on the chair to flat on the floor and then Paul is beside me.

'What is happening?'

'You are going to be all right, Dad. Everything is going to be fine.' I say this for Paul's benefit and I almost choke on the words. It is a lie. He is already dead.

By the time the ambulance arrived he was already fixed and dilated. I had hidden that from Paul. Ignorance wasn't always bliss, but some days it was just easier. I had put him in the recovery position and kept saying everything would be all right. Maybe if I had said it a hundred times more it would have made a difference. I never thought that this would devastate me, my father's death. I thought it would only bring closure, but now it has happened I can feel my entire world explode into a million different pieces.

He was the last of our parents. We are only three now. Three adult orphans. Can adults be orphans? I guess so. At least it happened quickly. One moment there. The next moment: gone. But then I remembered that it had happened so quickly I didn't even have time to do CPR. To take him to the hospital. To stop the haemorrhage. And now it was all over. The timing of it, I thought ruefully. He always had to fuck up my life. Cause as much damage as possible. I would never fix my relationship with my father now and in knowing that, I am surprised that a part of me even wanted to.

Chapter Ten

Natalie

I sit beside my father's corpse unable to comprehend what has happened. I just want to go home but guilt stops me. I turn as the door opens. It is Amanda and Neil. I take a sharp intake of breath. I know she loves him. This will be worst of all for her. She looks at him in disbelief. Then it happens. She starts to cry. It does not sound normal. Or even human. It is a wail of pure grief. Neil comes and tries to hold her, but she pushes him away and puts her head on our father's chest. I cannot watch this. It is too private. Too awful. I stand up to leave and walk towards the door.

'Natalie.' My name is just audible through the tears and snot and pain.

'Yes, Amanda.'

'Did you do this?'

I recoil at the accusation, but I do not answer it. I walk through the door instead.

I sit in the hospital waiting room with a cup of tea in hand. One of the punters for once. I am numb and my tea gets colder by the minute. I cannot manage to move my limbs. I think if I stand up I will faint. So I just sit on an uncomfortable chair, my legs not feeling like they belong to me. It dawns on me that I cannot stay here forever. That soon, I would have to put one foot in front of the other and walk back towards what used to be my life.

'Hey, you.'

It is Paul.

Finally, my legs work and I run into my brother's arms and sob.

'It's going to be okay,' Paul said as he nuzzles my hair. More lies, I thought.

We stay like that for a while. My brother comforting me. At last, there are no more tears to come. We both sit in the waiting room. Watching the BBC news and not knowing what to say.

'I will deal with all of this. Okay? I am here for you. I don't want you to have to deal with all of this on your own.'

'Paul. Don't be silly. I will help.' I mean it when I say it. I have been the head of the family for a long time. Even when I was a child.

'Natalie, I mean it. I will deal with this. I want you to get in a taxi and go home. I want you to take some time and do some self-care. You have just been through an awful experience. You are always there for everyone else, solving problems and clearing things up but not this time. Go home and stay there. I will call you and update you. I mean it.'

I listen to my brother. It is all getting too much. I need a moment. Hell, I need a holiday. I kiss my brother and thank him. As I am leaving the hospital, I walk past Dea Thurston. She does not acknowledge me, but I cannot help but wonder.

Tonight's events keep replaying in my mind. The doctors had done everything they could, but it was too late. He died before he even arrived. I feel around in my coat pocket for my ancient iPod shuffle. "She Talks to Angels" by Counting Crows starts. I walk. The wine I drank earlier at supper is taking up residence in my skull and kicking it gently.

I pass surgeons in their scrubs, nurses with kind faces and rushed manners, doctors walking around with purpose. Most of them I know but I manage to be invisible to them. It makes me happy because I feel invisible and I could not take their sympathy. I see families sitting together silently with the weight of not knowing. A hospital porter passes me transferring a patient as I head towards the exit. Fresh air hits me. A welcome relief. I take a deep breath in when I go out of the door. For a moment it feels exhilarating and sharpens my senses but then suddenly I violently throw up against the wall. My stomach contracting together so strongly I feel like it might go into a permanent knot. I look up when I finally manage to stop.

'Sorry,' I say to the horrified onlookers.

I go back to George's and I just lie in the bed and stare at the ceiling. I go over the events of the evening a million more times. What I wanted was to never see my father again and now this will be a reality. But this is not what I wanted. Not like this. It is too much to see my father again after all of these years only for him to die in my arms. It is cruel. But then maybe I will be free now. Free from the past and free from his actions. The thought makes me hopeful but only for a moment. I will not hold my breath. I have a feeling that freedom will be as elusive as ever.

Chapter Eleven

Rob

I sit around our large oval conference table. It is far too big. I wish we had bought something smaller now. The air conditioning is cranked up. A welcome relief from the summer we are having.

My mind wanders and I start to look around the table. There are six people here. The client, the daughter of a prominent businessman looking to clear up her partying image, and two people who work for her. Then on my side we have Claire, Neil and me. Neil looks tired. I wonder what is keeping him up. Maybe things are not going well with Amanda. She has always been high maintenance.

I try to listen to Claire. She is saying something about our strategy. How it will be easy to turn this young lady into a respectable member of society. Despite her past drug use, partying and copious amounts of Instagram nudity. She had an overdose and finally realised that she had to clean up her life.

I feel sorry for her. Born into wealth and fame: the pressure of it all, and the expectations of her domineering father pushed her over the edge. The overdose did not hit the headlines. She would talk about that in her own time in a magazine of our choosing. Crisis management. This is my favourite part of the job. Being thrown into an impossible fucked-up situation and fixing it.

When people are having the worst day of their lives, they call us. We do PR. We fix reputations. If only I could do the same thing in my own life. It was now over four weeks since Natalie and I broke up. Four long weeks of summer. I still had it bad which is why I was finding it hard to concentrate. Finally, it is all wrapped up. I leave Claire to deal with this. If she needs my input, she will let me know. We get up and leave the conference room.

'You look tired.'

Neil looks at me.

'Yeah, I have been up all night with Amanda.'

'How come? Married life not going great?'

Neil gives me a funny look.

'God, you do not know, do you?'

'Know what?'

'I guess, well, how would you?'

'Know what, Neil?'

'Her father died.'

The information makes me feel nauseous. Natalie is not close to her father. She never has been and never wanted him in her life. But I do not think his death will leave no mark.

'Natalie was there when it happened. Paul too, I think.'

'What?' I cannot believe what I am hearing. Why the hell was Natalie there? She hated him and only saw him when she had no other choice.

'Why was Natalie there? They never hung out.'

'Amanda was trying to get the family back together.'

I feel anger. Of course she was.

'Paul too,' Neil said quickly, panicking, knowing what I was thinking.

'How is Amanda taking it?'

'Badly. She was a proper daddy's girl. Natalie hasn't taken it well either. Apparently, she's a mess. But then she's been a mess for a while now.'

I think about that. Let it sit there.

'When is the funeral?'

'Tomorrow.'

'Text me the details. I want to show my respect.'

Neil looks at me and smiles, cocks an eyebrow.

'Okay. It will be great having you there.'

Neil walks away and I stand there with my thoughts. This will only be the third time I have seen Natalie since our brutal break-up. This time I am not going for answers, I am going for her.

Natalie

I am sitting in my family home. The home I grew up in. It feels strange and awful. It holds no happy memories. This terraced house in a part of London that had "potential" when my grandparents bought it decades ago. It has reached that potential now. God knows how much it is worth. A four-bedroom terraced house in London. Few of our generation could afford that. No one else seemed to be thinking about this. They are thinking about the thing I am doing everything to not think about. Him. His death.

I look around the house. It has not been kept to a high standard, but I am surprised that it is reasonably tidy and clean. I wonder who cleaned it. Does he have a cleaner? Is Sheila back from Spain? The mistress, wife, ex-wife.

I stand up and look around. He has never thrown anything out. The same books, the same paintings, the same furniture. There is a painting of New York. What artist painted that? I could not remember and the signature is not clear.

I walk to the garden. It is huge and unkempt. I look at this garden and our house. How impossible it seems that someone could have an unhappy childhood here. I walk to the middle of the garden and take it all in. This had been my childhood home but there had never been an actual childhood. That had been taken away by infidelity, alcohol and death.

I spent my youth on tenterhooks, in a permanent state of anxiety. I did not want to give away the rest of my life to the past, and mostly I had not. Seven years of studying had made me a doctor. Further years of study had made me an obstetrician. It had been deliberate on my part. It was easier to get on with your life when you were always busy. Hardcore studying, working, exams, Rob.

I filled my life to the brim. Well as much to the brim as I possibly could. All to avoid moments like this: the quiet moments when the silence comes to get you, carrying the ghost of the past with it.

I worried about the amount of hate I had inside of me for someone who was related to me. With his death I knew that it had lessened. That was the thing about someone dying; it just seemed wrong to constantly point out what a jerk they were. I had even tried to think about the good times, but I was human, and the things that hurt, the wounds that caused the most scarring came first. Sometimes I thought that maybe he wasn't that bad after all. Then I remembered him leaving, and it came hot and heavy.

My father was not a good man. No amount of twisting the facts could change that. Not even Rob with his entire PR company could. He had been left wanting. As a father, as a husband, and as a human being.

I feel like I cannot breathe and the tears come. I hear a noise behind me. It is a dog. I assume the neighbour's. It pisses in the garden. I shoo it away and it turns and gives me a defiant glare.

'Yeah, fuck you too.' I glare back.

I hear a whistle. It is the neighbour. I look at them and wonder if they know.

'Are you the other daughter? I was so sorry to hear about your father. He was such a lovely man '

Turns out they do.

'Keep your dog off our grass. Thanks.'

I head back into the house and bang the door loud enough for them to hear. Lovely man? Fuck them. Fuck every gaslighting person who tried to make my memories something else. My childhood was awful. No one gets to tell me it was happy and that my father was decent. No one.

For a moment I feel guilty. I was rude. But the truth is I am too exhausted by constantly pretending.

I do not want to go back into the living room. Amanda and Neil are in there. Amanda is being very pregnant and having her feet rubbed. She is tired of course. I wish I could handle it better but, actually, so much of me hates her right now.

'Does anyone want tea?'

'Yes please. Decaf.'

'I doubt Tim had decaf.'

'He does. Top shelf.'

Of course.

'And I wish you would call him Dad. That always upset him.'

I think about saying something, but she is pregnant and her father just died. So I leave it. Paul will be here soon. Usually this made me happy as it would even out the numbers. Now I am not so sure.

As if on cue the doorbell went.

'I will get it,' Neil says.

In bursts Paul, Nathaniel and, surprisingly, Paul's ex-wife.

I greet them all with a hug and a kiss. Laying it on extra thick for my nephew.

'Lovely to see you, Stacey.'

I mean it. Stacey and Paul had a terrible break-up, but at the minimum I would like them to be friends.

'I'm just making some tea. Would anyone like some?'

'Yes please, sis.'

'That would be lovely, Natalie. Thank you.'

'And what about you, my little one. Is there anything we can get you?'

'I am not so little now, Aunty Nat. I am a big boy.'

'Ah yes, I am sorry. You are indeed.'

'Can I have some juice?'

'Of course.' I have brought some for him.

Nathaniel gave a sly look at his father, asking for permission. 'And maybe a biscuit?'

Paul looks at him and gives a little laugh. 'Of course you can.' Then he kisses him on the top of his head.

'Amanda and Neil are just through there. You go in, I will make the tea.'

I take Nathaniel by the hand and lead him to the kitchen.

'I hear you are about to join the mummy club, Amanda,' I hear Stacey say to Amanda.

I just want today to be over.

I go into the kitchen and open my bag. I came prepared for my nephew. I take out his favourite smoothie and some biscuits.

'There you go.'

His eyes light up at the sugar on offer. Today will be tough on him but, hey, at least he will be buzzy.

'How are you feeling?'

'I'm okay.'

'Good.'

I look at him. He is so pure and innocent.

'Do you miss Grandad?'

'No. I never liked him.'

I laugh. I love that kid.

I boil the kettle and get on with the tea.

'What do you think happens after we die, Aunt Nat?'

'We go to Heaven.'

Nathaniel looks at me, surprised. I guess he was expecting me to be cynical. The truth is, a huge part of me even believes it. Medical science had not completely stripped me of faith.

I make the tea and bring the first of it through. The room is sombre. Mostly, they are all still in shock. Paul goes to say something but then stops.

The funeral is not for hours but we, as in Amanda, decided we would meet up here and sort some stuff out before. As if the day was not awful and stressful already. Turns out being pregnant gave you carte blanche to do whatever you wanted for nine months. Like some blessed hippo.

Tim did not leave a will, of course. That would have made things easy on his family and he had never been very good at that. Luckily, I did not want any of his crap.

I go back in to get the rest of the tea. Nathaniel is playing with a little yellow toy car, vroom vrooming it around the kitchen counter.

I get the rest of the tea and take it through too.

'This is the decaf, Amanda.'

She looks at me with a serious look. 'Are you sure? You didn't get them mixed up, did you?'

I resist the urge to slap her.

'No and even if I didn't, one cup of caffeinated tea would not do anything.'

She gives me a look and I give her one back. I go back for my own tea. I lean back on the kitchen counter and take a moment just to breathe. I think I will stay here and look after my nephew.

'Natalie, can we get started please? We are on the clock.'

Or maybe not. The mourner-in-chief has given her orders.

'Come on, kid, let's go in.'

Nathaniel looks up at me, a look of sadness in his eyes. He follows me through. To the gallows we go.

I sit in a chair and Nathaniel climbs on top of me and cuddles in. I put my arms around him and bury my head into his hair. This is what true, uncomplicated, love feels like. I try to not smell him. He hates it when I do that. He always smells so good. From the moment he was a baby. I wished I could soak him up.

'Fine, first thing first: everyone has to go through the house and put stickers on the things they want. We have colour-coded stickers here.' Amanda holds them up; they are little dots.

'Natalie is red, Paul is blue and I am green. Any disagreements about what people want will be sorted out amicably.' She gives Paul and I a look.

'What about Nathaniel?' I ask Amanda.

'He can share Paul's stickers.'

'And what about the house?'

Amanda turns and looks at me and blinks.

'What do you mean?'

'I think it is clear. The stuff is easy, hopefully. I mean. I doubt I will want anything. But the house and any money is another. It should be split equally.'

Amanda's expression changes. She looks harder, angrier. I look at Paul. He is uncomfortable and will not meet my eye.

'I took care of him, Natalie.'

I manage to not laugh.

'How could you take care of him? He wasn't ill.'

'I think we know that is not the case now.' She is raising her voice.

'He had a catastrophic stroke. There was an autopsy. It was quick and without any obvious prior illness. As in: he was independent and did not need taking care of. Hanging out with someone is not the same thing as being their carer.'

'I still can't believe it. He died so suddenly. One minute there and the next just a heap on the floor. He looked like his life had been scooped out of him,' Paul said. He looks sad and Stacey puts her arm around him. I look back at Amanda. I can tell she is building up to something.

'I was his carer.'

'He did not have a carer, Amanda. He wasn't ill.'

I look down and Nathaniel looks like he might cry. I was almost shouting and now I feel bad. The poor kid does not need this.

'We will do this at another time, Amanda.'

'It is Dad's money and I was the one in his life.'

She will not let this go.

'No, it was Mum's money.'

'Bullshit.'

Paul coughs.

'Sorry for my language. She is always so difficult.'

My mouth must be hanging open. I just got called difficult by Amanda. She has gone mad, clearly. I decide to tell her the truth.

'And my money.'

Amanda looks at me, confused and then angry.

'You probably make the most money out of all of us and you want it all to yourself? You really are such a selfish bitch. The NHS pays you a fortune.'

'The NHS does not pay anyone a fortune, Amanda, and it is my money. Your father borrowed money off me my entire life. Well, until I cut him off. I paid tens of thousands towards this house to keep the creep above water. Not for him, but for you, Mum and Paul. Nice to know it was the right thing to do.'

There is no more to say. I have never seen Amanda so quiet. Then she starts to cry. Wracking, inconsolable sobs. Oh, for fuck's sake.

I look at my siblings.

'Regardless, the house should be sold and the money split three ways. I am fine with that. As should any other assets he might have. I doubt he has any, but we will see.'

Paul smiles at me. 'Thank you, Natalie. You are always incredibly generous.'

I smile back. I really needed to hear that. But mostly I just needed some kindness.

'Come on, Nat. Let's have a look around Grandad's house and see if there is anything you want.'

We get up and walk out of the room. Amanda is still crying and being consoled by Neil. Poor guy. I do not know how he puts up with her.

Putting stickers on things had been surprisingly fun. Not that I wanted anything of his, but a lot of my mother's stuff was still here. I looked at the clock on the wall. It was still an hour until the funeral. This day was moving so slowly. I head to the bathroom and try the door. It will not give.

'One moment,' came a voice from the other end.

'Oh, sorry, Amanda, I didn't realise you were in there.'

I head upstairs to take another look around. This is a good Victorian house. The decor is old-fashioned and dated but it is solid and beautiful. I try to imagine what it would look like refurbished. I hope we sell it to a family and they grow up happy. Then this house would not feel so cursed.

I feel the threadbare carpet on my feet and I remember all of the other times I walked up and down these stairs. The shouting and yelling. The thump of a suitcase ending a childhood. Then I started to think about the end. When my mother was too weak to even climb these stairs. Her entire life had been lived on the bottom floor. The pain is almost too much. I just want to stop feeling. That is why I never wanted to live in this house. I never particularly liked visiting it either. It had been a long time since I was last here. I wish I could have stayed away forever.

I reach the landing and look around. It looks like he never changed anything. I cannot believe he just left everything the way it was. Everything from the decoration to the furniture is the same. This entire house is like a museum. All of the pictures are still here too. Me as a child, all of our first day of school pictures, Amanda winning a swimming competition, all of us getting various degrees and awards, a big one of Paul graduating. There were even pictures of the entire family. We look normal. And happy. I look closer at one of the pictures. The men are in suits and the women are in dresses. I try to place what occasion had caused us to dress up so much, but I couldn't. In one picture Paul did not even exist yet.

We looked like the perfect family. As if the world hadn't even touched us. I guessed it hadn't yet. It was during a time when a facade of happiness was something we all bought into. When our parents were still indestructible and not just ordinary human beings who failed most of the time. A door slams shut behind me and I jump.

I open the door and see an open window. I go and close it. Then it hits me: this used to be my room and, like the hall, he had not changed anything. All of my old things were still here. I had not taken them with me when I left. I did not want anything of my old life. I still don't.

The draught that followed seemed to touch my soul and for a moment I see myself there. A frightened little girl with dark hair and wide, scared, green eyes. Frightened and crying as her parents argue downstairs. Playing her music box on her lap, winding it back up when it stops to hear "Twinkle, Twinkle, Little Star" again. She is hoping the noise won't wake up her sister because then she won't be able to feel her emotions. The scared little girl will have to pretend to be a grown-up and comfort her sister, stroke her and let her know that everything will be all right. Inside she is terrified and hiding her anxiety will only cause the stress to worsen inside of her. She doesn't know what will happen to them. I almost reach out to her, the pain in my heart breaking for her.

A loud noise downstairs brings me back to reality. I turn around and close the door without looking back.

I think about my younger self. All that she went through. And the saddest thing of all is that if I could go back, I couldn't tell her that everything will be okay. Or that it will get better. Sure, when she becomes an adult, her life became her own and she was finally happy again, but that was far off.

I head to the second bathroom and try to push the memories of my past from my mind, even as they try their best to find their way back in. I breathe in and out but as I sit there trying to be calm, I know that it is a plaster on a waterfall. A thread has been pulled and I will now slowly unravel.

Chapter Twelve

Natalie

The car ride to the church was stifling. I could barely breathe through the heat and oppressiveness of the people next to me. It was one of the hottest days in history. Even the breeze was hot. There was no escape from the pressing heat. It felt like standing in front of an open oven. Neil had hired a seven-seater to follow the casket in. They had decided to not hire a driver to "save money". It enraged me because I know how much Rob paid Neil. They were not poor. The entire thing was manipulation. It was pretend poverty to steal more than their fair share.

Finally, we arrived. To my surprise the church is packed. But I guess drunks are popular. Sociable creatures that they are. Always propping up the pubs. I look around at these people. Most of them I do not know. There are a few faces from the past. Drinking friends from long ago, friends that enabled him again and again. Over in the corner I can see the man who lied to my mother numerous times to cover my father's many affairs. Somewhere I see a flash of mahogany hair. Is that her? Sheila, the woman who slept in my mother's bed.

I look at these people. They all seem to know me and keep saying hello and how sorry they are for my loss.

To be brutal, I don't care. All of these people in black to pay their respects. I doubt they knew just how much of a bastard my father was. If they did, they were just as bad as him.

I didn't even know why I was here. People had started to hand me condolences cards. I didn't even know they were a such a big thing. I had never sent one. I counted the ones in my hand. Twenty. Twenty cards of condolence and sympathy. I doubted if I died people would send that many cards.

'We shouldn't have left so early. It was hot as fucking hell in the car and the church is not much better. Who the hell are these people? Oh my God. I can't take any more.' Amanda put her head in-between her knees after her uncharacteristically sweary outburst.

I turn to her, surprised. It must be so hard being pregnant in this heat. Everyone heard and they were looking at Amanda now. Some looked shocked. I look up at the sky. It is the lightest, happiest blue. There is barely a cloud in sight and the few clouds there are fluffy and white. Life not only went on; it was more beautiful than ever.

'Are you okay? I know it is hard being pregnant, especially in this heat,' I tell Amanda while rubbing her back. Amanda recoils and gives me a filthy look.

'Amanda, you are pregnant. That is wonderful news. I thought maybe you had just put on weight, and quite a bit at that.'

It is Lily, a family friend. Or, more accurately, someone the family has known for a long time. Friend is too strong a word.

'How lovely,' Lily says while she rubs Amanda's bump. Then she leaves.

'We did not want anyone to know yet, Natalie. Thank you so much for that. You really are on form today.'

I purse my lips and will myself not to cry.

'We aren't telling anyone yet, Natalie. It hasn't been twelve weeks,' Neil said, looking angrily at me.

I can still feel Amanda's glare.

'What? Do you want people knowing you are pregnant, or thinking you are a raging bitch?' I ask Amanda. Matching her glare look for look.

This does not help the situation, but if I just take this shit over and over again it will destroy me. I start to leave then. I do not need an answer. I just had to locate my spine.

'I think maybe the worst timing ever is telling people at my father's funeral. So, thanks for that,' Amanda shouts at me. I stop.

'That was really inappropriate, Natalie. You really need to work on not being such a bitch,' Neil said, anger in his voice. I am surprised at his outburst. Neil is usually quite a meek, little soul.

'That's your opinion, Neil? I thought it was just posh twat whinging.'

I walk towards the other side of the church. The part reserved for friends. Then I sit down. I can see Paul talking to Amanda and Neil. He comes over.

'Come on, back to the family side.'

'No, Paul.'

'She is just hormonal.'

I give Paul a look.

'Don't be one of those men who go on about a woman's hormones. It's sexist.'

'Sorry, sis. Trying to be funny.'

I stand up. Toe to toe with my brother.

'I am going to go over but only because it will not look good if I don't. I want you to know I am sick of all of this. I am sick of being treated like crap and I am sick of being gaslighted by you all. I just want to get this over so I can stop pretending to care that bastard is dead.'

I walk not to the other side, yet. I go out one door and down the hall. I walk to the little room the viewing has been arranged for and I look at him. My father in his coffin. Open casket. What was Amanda thinking? I hate open caskets. I hate viewings. So morbid and gross. Seeing someone who you loved, or in this case, was merely related to, dead in a coffin. I do not get it. Was it supposed to give closure? A dead body was a dead body. There was no comfort that could ever come from it.

I let out a sigh. There are so many emotions and I do not know how to process them. Maybe I should go into therapy.

I go to walk out just as Amanda and Neil walk in with Paul tagging along.

'I can't believe it. That's him,' Amanda almost wails. She really is playing this to the hilt. So much for being British and stoic.

We all stand there. Looking down at the man who was our father. Or father-in-law in Neil's case. It does feel unbelievable. Life can never understand death.

'Can I be alone for five minutes? Do you mind?' Amanda asked. It was not really a request though.

'Of course,' Paul said.

'I will just be outside, let me know if you need me,' Neil said, rubbing her shoulders and kissing her on the top of the head. Paul touched her arm as he walked past too, giving it a reassuring squeeze.

The princess of the family. We all go outside and wait.

'He looked so peaceful. So like himself. But also somehow not,' Paul said. I nod and so does Neil.

'I didn't like his make-up,' I said.

I can tell Paul and Neil are trying to not laugh but the effort of keeping a straight face is too much and they start giggling. I cannot help it either. I join in.

The door opens and Amanda walks out, staring daggers at us all. Then she looks at Neil with an iciness that could plunge the planet immediately into an ice age.

'I would have thought better of you.'

With that jab at Neil, she goes out of the other door and into the body of the church. Chin up, shoulders back.

'Oh dear, we are all in trouble,' Paul said. Then we all giggle just a little more.

'We should go now,' Neil said to Paul. They are the pallbearers.

Paul nods and follows him. The service is about to begin so I walk fast towards the front of the church. Amanda is ignoring me. I look around at the church and I see Rob. The sight of him is a dagger to the heart and yet somehow it makes me happy. This family was his family for so many years. Of course, he was here. It was so like him to always be there when needed. To be respectful. Then I realise why I am so sad. Why I truly feel like I am grieving. It is not just for my father. It is for Rob. I miss him every day.

I can feel eyes on me and it makes me uncomfortable. I hate my father's friends just as much as I hated him.

'All stand please,' the priest said.

Everyone stands and looks toward the entrance of the church. It takes my breath away for a moment. None of this feels real. I notice that Rob is also a pallbearer; the other three are friends of my father's. Rob looks handsome and strong. He met my father once, I think. At some family gathering. He hated him as much as I did. I look at my sister and see her tears. They are so pure. She really has lost a father. I take her hand and squeeze it.

'It will all be okay.'

She looks at me and squeezes back, forcing a small smile as she does.

The coffin is at the front and the ceremony starts. I zone out through the service as the priest talks about love and family and God. Oh, ha, ha, ha.

I try to not sneak peeks at Rob but I cannot help myself. He is sitting on the second row. I noticed Paul shoving him to the family section. Rob looked uncomfortable, like an errant schoolboy who was going to get caught.

Soon we have to stand for hymns and as we do, I hear a loud bang. Some cousin to our left has hit his head on the speaker as he stood. He is almost knocked over by the blow but instead ends up back in his seat. Embarrassed and rubbing a sore head.

I think about going to offer him medical aid but he seems fine. Conscious, not throwing up, that sort of thing. He is swearing and looking grumpy now. Yes, he is fine.

Then I hear it through the singing. It is muffled at first, so I am not so sure but then it is unmistakable. It is Amanda. Laughing. She is trying to make it sound like a cry, but I know my sister. Slowly, other people turn as they sing. Some try to be discreet about it, others openly gape. The poor guy who nearly concussed himself just stood where he was, trying to look dignified, ignoring the laughter at his expense. The man's girlfriend turns to look at Amanda, but she seemed to find it amusing too.

Neil grabs Amanda's face and buries it in his chest. I can tell he is also trying very hard not to laugh. He strokes Amanda's hair to make it look like he is comforting her.

'There, there, it will all be okay. It's okay. Your dad is in a better place,' Neil says as he continues to stroke Amanda's hair. He looks around at the people who are staring.

'They were just so close,' Neil says to them.

The song ends and we all sit back down. From my angle I can tell Amanda is laughing so hard that tears are streaming down her face. I look at Rob and Paul. They too are laughing and trying to make it look like crying. Unlike Amanda they are succeeding. Through it all I manage to keep a straight face. I have no idea how.

An aunt from my father's side leans over from the second row to say something to me, her face full of concern.

'Oh, it's such a shame. You were all such a close family.'

This almost sets me off, but I nip myself hard to stop the laughter coming.

Finally, we are burying him in the graveyard. Feeling somewhat closer than before. At least planning a funeral was much easier than planning a wedding. Less expensive too. I am holding Amanda's hand and I put my hand on Paul's back to comfort him. This is our family. Well, what is left of us. I try to not think that this graveyard is full of my parents' friends and extended family. People that I would gladly never see again. I may be sick of them and their toxic memories but not my brother and sister. Despite our differences, we have to fight through. We are all we have.

I watch as they lower my father into the ground. I try to stop the tears coming but I can't. A part of me hates myself for that. What happened the few times we had seen each other had only been a glimpse. I held onto that glimpse with all of my might, but the bad memories never went away. They just lived there, with that last look, those last words, side by side. Now I can never repair anything. Or fix anything, nor get any closure.

My siblings put their arms around me. I love them, my fellow musketeers. Through my tears and the rain, I look out at the graveyard, at all of the tombstones giving the briefest information of a life lived.

Then I see her. Like a bullet to my heart. The woman who started the unravelling of our family. The woman who had stolen our father and broken so many hearts. I feel myself harden. Everything comes flooding back. The pain, the hurt, my mother's broken heart. Before my head can catch up with my anger, I walk towards her. I want to ask her why, ask her about their relationship or if she ever thought of my mother but she backs off. This irritates me so I walk faster. I only want to ask her a bloody question, but she starts running so I run too.

I can hear people shouting after me, see their faces as I race past them, yelling. Sheila does not stop. She runs for all of her might. Not bad for an older woman.

At some point I stop running and just collapse, lungs aching, into the wet mud and grass. Tears and rain becoming one. I just stay there. Unable to move. After a while I feel someone come up behind me and cover me with an umbrella. I look up to see that it is Rob.

Chapter Thirteen

Natalie

The death of my father brought up the memories of my mother dying. Every time my mother was upset, she would smoke and every time my father cheated on her or lied, she would chain-smoke. Most of my memories of my mother were of her smoking. Smoking while looking out of the window, smoking while looking at the telephone, waiting for it to ring.

The only time my mother drank was when my father upset her. Or when he made her. My father always had a drinking problem and to make himself feel better about it he made my mother drink as much as him. She was only forty-five when she died of lung cancer and I always blamed my father. At the funeral I would look at him and think about how much I hated him. I was certain that he knew that. The day of the funeral he looked sombre and terrified in his black suit. He stared into the eyes of his tiny daughter, but they showed no emotion other than blame and hate before I would turn away. I know he needed me to forgive him. Or even just to love him a little.

He was surrounded by family and mourners, but he looked like the loneliest person in the world. To this day

I cannot find any sympathy for him. Not only did he not deserve my mother, but I always wished that he had died instead. I have no parents now, I thought at my mother's funeral.

My father and mother were like two strangers in a house, thrown together because of circumstance, counting down the days until they didn't need to be in each other's lives any more. My mother was not strong enough to withstand him. I do not blame her for that; I blame him for making her weak. She was the most compassionate and loving person in the world. She deserved the world but all she got was him.

Then

I waver before I put the crisps in the lunchbox. He bought the wrong ones again. Now Amanda would be upset. I try to ignore the resentment for my father that bubbles up but it is no use. Every moment of every day. I resented him when I was cooking dinner and when I was making breakfast. When I was making up the lunchboxes as I was doing now, and when I would take my younger siblings to school, sometimes even stepping over him in the hall where he had been all night. Passed out and drunk.

I did the housework, put the kids to bed. I did almost everything. My father, meanwhile, drank. Occasionally he would be lucid. At those times he would make a meal or take us to do something fun. Or Amanda's idea of fun.

He still had his job working in construction, but I could not figure out how. He didn't need to work of course: my mother's life insurance, and family money, made sure of that. And then there was her. The woman he had never let go. He thought no one knew about her, and the other two probably didn't, but I knew. I had seen them together. But worse of all, sometimes I would smell her perfume. In the kitchen, in the living room. In my mother's bed. It enraged me. That they should live and my mother should die.

Sometimes the only thing that got me through the day was that one day I would be a grown-up. Then I would be free and my life would be my own. I finish making the sandwiches and cut them in half. I put them in the lunchbox with an apple, the crisps and some juice. I shut the boxes and then go to get my siblings.

'Paul, Amanda. It is time to go. We will be late.'

I hear them both coming down the stairs. Paul gave me a big hug.

Then just as I predicted it came:

'This is the wrong kind of crisps,' Amanda said, irritation dripping from her.

I sigh. It took her two minutes to complain.

'Take it up with Dad. He is the one who bought the wrong ones.'

'You should tell him which ones to get.'

'I don't do the shopping, Amanda. It is not my fault if Dad doesn't know you or care what you like.'

Amanda shot me a look but didn't say anything. A first. I was sick of her and her moods.

'We need to leave now or we will be late,' I said. Signalling them to the door. Amanda rolled her eyes and went first. Then we followed. As we all walked down the street, something caught my eye. I turned towards my father's bedroom and noticed that the curtains were twitching. I stopped for a moment, trying to see who it was but it stopped.

The person knew they had been rumbled. I wondered if it was my father, too drunk to get out of bed, or his whore hiding away in my mother's bedroom, lacking the guts to face the children of the women whose life she had ruined. I hate cowards, but mostly I hate her. That woman. The other woman.

I continue walking with my siblings who were looking at me, wondering why I had told them to rush but was now just standing there and they knew no reason why. I swallowed the lump in my throat and smiled at them.

'Sorry, I just thought I had forgotten something. Let's go,' I said.

Amanda rolled her eyes. I looked at my watch, feeling like all of the stress of the world was piling on top of me. Great, we are going to be late.

Now
Natalie

Pink and blue. That is the problem here. There is far too much pink and blue. The moment we are born they just start separating us, telling us who we are and how we should act. I was surprised actually; I thought gender-neutral was a thing now. I guess this overpriced cashmere and dry-clean your baby clothes shop must have missed the memo. It may be "independent" but it was not inclusive. The price tags were eye-watering.

I had been excited about having a Sunday to myself, but Amanda called. She actually said sorry. I was so surprised that when she said she wanted to go and buy baby stuff I said yes. Now here I am.

We had spoken on the phone a few times since the funeral. The phone calls were tentative things. Both of us trying to connect to the other but scared to set the other one off. It was something and I was thankful. I love my sister and I know I am too hard on her most of the time.

I pick up a little pink onesie. It is hard to believe that a human being would ever fit into this. It is even harder to think that at some point I had managed to fit into one of these. Sure, I saw babies all day, but my life was a conveyor belt of them. Out of their mothers and then out of the hospital.

This was cute. I could buy this for my new nibling. But then again, everything was cute when it was in miniature. I touched the softness of the cotton. It was beautiful. I picked up two of the Babygros but then put them down again and sighed. I could not stop thinking about my ovaries. How they had let me down for years. In seven years, Rob and I had probably had unprotected sex thousands of times. No baby. Amanda got pregnant immediately.

Yet my jealousy had mostly subsided. I was glad that she was pregnant and that it was easy for her. I would never have wanted my sister to go through what I have been through. To get that positive test and then be told by a doctor that your pregnancy had been "flushed away" and that it was "normal". Nothing felt normal about it. I wonder how many times I gave a similar speech to a woman? I push the thought away. It is easy to deal with these things until you go through them yourself. Then you know: that words matter and yet now nothing does. The things that hurt me only make me harder.

I hate shopping but this kind is even worse. Helping Amanda shop for baby stuff. It is hell for many different reasons. I have started to wonder if I maybe I was some kind of genocidal maniac in a previous life. I must have been because here I am, looking at tiny little outfits. For babies I would never have. Fuck, this hurt.

I look at Amanda. She has always had curves where I have only lines. Now those curves are blossoming in all of the right places. She looks like a goddess.

'Why can't you just shop online like a normal person?'

'That ruins the experience.'

'No, it takes away the experience. That is why it's good.'

'It's really hurting my feelings that you are not even pretending to enjoy yourself,' Amanda snaps.

I feel guilty but I am also wondering what happened to our truce. We said we would try to be kind.

'I should have gone with Paul. At least he would have known what he was doing.'

The last comment stings. She really has no clue. I stand there, filling up on my latest dose of resentment. I was not going to say anything until the moment I hear the words come out.

'You don't know anything. You never know anything.'

'What does that even mean, Natalie?'

I look at her but I cannot do it. Not now.

I try to not be angry at her. Her pregnancy is saving her from a lot of that. But I have to say something. She is looking at me with her eyebrows raised.

'You have always been obsessed with the fact Dad came back, like it cancelled out him leaving in the first place. You have no idea.'

Amanda rolls her eyes.

'God, Natalie. Not again. How many times can we argue about this? It is such bullshit. How many times

186

can you pick at the same scab? Just leave it alone and it will stop bleeding.'

'No, I don't think so. I will say this and you will listen. Dad came back because Mum was ill.'

'That is not true; she got ill later.'

'Amanda, I mean it. Dad came back the first time Mum got diagnosed with cancer. That is why he came back. And the entire time he was still fucking his little whore on the side. He came back out of guilt. He came back because Mum didn't have enough energy to take care of us. He came back as a carer and a piss poor one at that. But don't blame yourself too much. Because I didn't know and I was so mean to my mother. I thought she was pathetic for taking him back and I let her know it.

'I spent too much time being angry at her and thinking she was a doormat when she was the most beautiful and strongest person that I have ever known. So don't you tell me he came back and he sacrificed and he was some kind of saint because he was an arsehole and right now you are being one too.'

'You are being a bitch, Natalie.'

'Yeah well, it is my default position to extreme bullshit.'

I can feel the eyes of strangers on us, but I do not care. Let them have their entertainment. I am sick of taking it. I stare at her. I dare her.

'We are all sick of your behaviour, Natalie. You need to grow up.'

I have a lot to reply to that, but I don't. I walk out.

Rob

A weekend. Since I became single, they were funny things. Initially I hated them. The loneliness crept in. Being alone with my own thoughts was not healthy. All I thought about was her.

Today was different. I would do a bit of housework and read a book. Work was intense this week. I just needed to decompress. I put a pod in the Nespresso machine and wait for a hit of the good stuff. Natalie bought the machine for my birthday a few years ago. Most things bought in this house were bought by Natalie. She had gone a bit mad, buying throws, cushions and various other things I never knew even existed. We had done every single room one by one. We even painted it ourselves. This house was the story of our lives together.

I need to move. Living in a house that is a relic to the life you used to have is an interesting kind of torture. Natalie and I bought this house in Wandsworth only a year into our relationship. We were supposed to fill it with babies but as the years went by and the babies did not come, the house seemed to mock us with its empty rooms and large garden. I guess it was for the best if our relationship was not going to last. Or maybe, if the children had come, it would have held us together. If only by a thread.

I had boxed her stuff up in a fury one night three weeks into the ghosting. Filled with confusion and hurt. All of my questions were still unanswered. I was finding it hard to believe there was not someone else. Seeing her on a date with David was awful. The worst betrayal I could think of. How could she move on so fast? After we had built so much together. She said it was not a date, true, but it clearly was.

Then there had been the funeral. Watching my family be a family while I was just in the peripheral. Watching them laugh and cry and be together. I just stood there like an idiot at a funeral for a man I hated. For her.

The house would need to be sold, I guess, and we would dismantle what we had built over seven years. Yet the way she had looked at me at the funeral stayed with me. She had even smiled and looked happy to see me.

When she had gone running after Sheila, I followed her because I could never help but love her. She had looked up at me, thankful.

After a while I walked her back to the car. I hugged her and kissed the top of her head. Then Paul had taken over, led her into the car and whisked her away. She left my life again. If we had been alone, I wonder if she would have opened up. The thought of us getting back together was moving further away every day. Even if she wanted to, would I? I always thought yes, but then I thought I knew her. I never thought for one second, we would break up. I certainly never thought she would break up with me this way. In such a cold and cruel manner. I would have staked everything that she did not have that in her. Yet I was wrong. It was a hand grenade to my entire world. How could I trust my judgement again? When clearly, I was so blind.

I make my coffee and I open the French windows and step out into the garden. It is another beautiful, sunny day. The kind that should be enjoyed with family. Yet here I am all alone. I cannot even fathom dating again. Maybe I will just spend the rest of my days as a bachelor. It would save a lot of heartache.

I start to think about my day. Maybe I should do some work in the garden too. The grass is a horror and the weeds are taking over. Yes, that is what I will do. Anything to take my mind off her and all of the problems she brings. I finish my coffee and head to the shed to get the lawnmower, but I stop as I hear my phone ringing. I head back into the house to get it. I do not recognise the number.

'Hello?'

Natalie

The coffee shop is full. I look around the room but there is nowhere to sit. I am about to leave when someone stands up and gestures to me. I smile at them and walk over.

'Thank you.'

'No worries at all. I was just leaving. It is so annoying when you can't get a seat.'

The woman looks about twenty-five. She is slim and beautiful. Dressed in skinny jeans and a casual T-shirt. She gathers her computer and leans down to put it in her bag. Her long, black wavy hair covers her face as she does.

'Bye,' she says.

'Bye. Have a great day.'

'You too.'

I put my bag on the seat, take my phone out and then go and order an espresso, keeping an eye on my bag the entire time. I usually order a latte, but the espresso reminds me of him. The man in Wandsworth that I miss so much. I wonder what he is doing right now. He is probably in our house, feeling a bit overwhelmed at the amount that needs done. Cleaning was always how I relaxed. But Rob cooked, did the food shopping and did the garden. It worked. We worked. And I threw it all away.

I am not even sure I did it for him any more. Over the summer I had lost my boyfriend and my father. It also felt like I had lost my siblings, as they ganged up against me and decided I was the problem. I was alone now and although George would never say it, I felt I was becoming a huge burden. No one likes an adult couch surfer cramping their style. I needed to think long term. I would also have to contact Rob soon about the house. All of my equity was there. I could not afford to move forward without it. Especially not in London. Here I was, a woman in her late thirties who had fucked everything up. Amanda was right. There was something wrong with me.

I paid for my coffee and sat down. I go over the fight with Amanda. Maybe I was being unfair on her. But then again, Amanda has always been given an easy life. Being told to grow up by a princess like that was infuriating. Nothing in her life had ever been hard. She had never had to date and find a man. Neil had always been there, enabling her.

Neil had found her a cushy job in a tech company that makes apps. She got paid a lot of money for barely any work. The company gave generous flexible working. Most days she even worked at home. The food was even free there. Then there was the pregnancy. Wham bam thank you, ma'am. Just like that. Of course. But I was the one who had to grow up. I had raised two children, dealt with my parents' awful relationship and worked my arse off to get where I was. No one helped me. The only good thing I had in my life, other than my career, was Rob. She had even managed to destroy my relationship with Paul. The only family I had left.

I felt guilty as I drove around, but not now. I am glad I left her. I am done with it all. I am done with her. Finally. I feel relieved. If I know anything in life, I know that you should never put up with someone just because you share DNA with them.

I take a sip of my espresso. Ah. A caffeine hit. Joy.

I used to love the rare weekends I had off. Now I am single they feel empty and hollow. I do not know how to fill the void Rob has left. Or the one my father has left, though that one was more complicated.

I finish my coffee and head out. I will go to the supermarket and get lots of nice food. At least then I can pay George and his wonderful family back. If even in a small way.

Waitrose seems much busier on a weekend. Rob always did the food shopping. Even if he did it mostly online. I would just pick something up when I could. I fish around for a pound in my bag and find one. I put it in the trolly and start. At least I do not have to shop for one at the moment. That is one small thing.

I look down at the trolly. Pasta and bread. My comfort foods. I pat my stomach. I have definitely put on some break-up weight. I need to go on a health kick. Obviously not this weekend, I think ruefully as I head to the alcohol aisle and put a few bottles of wine in.

Soon the trolly is filled to the brim. I walk towards the checkout, keeping an eye on the offers on the end aisles.

As I walk down, I see a blonde woman in one of the aisles crying. I slow down and then stop. I wonder if I should go and see if she is okay. I look around. Either no one else has noticed or they are ignoring her. Just walking on does not feel right so I head towards her.

'Are you okay?'

The woman turns and looks at me. I realise that I know her.

'Susan?'

Susan wipes her eyes and looks confused. Then the realisation comes to her.

'Oh hi.'

I can tell she has recognised that she knows me, but she does not know where from.

'I'm Natalie.'

'Right.'

'We went to school together.'

Suddenly it dawns on her: 'Oh yeah. I remember now. You got dumped by Dale Matthews.'

I try to hide my irritation. This is what I get for being a good Samaritan.

'Yes. That was the highlight of my educational years.'

'You were also quite...' She is searching for the word, 'plump.'

Wow.

'Sorry. It's just.' Susan doesn't finish her sentence as she starts crying again. This time even harder than the last time. I am unsure of what to do.

'Are you okay?'

'I am so sorry. It's just my mother died a few weeks ago. It hit me hard. We were so close.'

'I am so sorry to hear that. My father died recently too. I know how it feels.'

'God, how awful for your mother,' Susan said.

'Actually, she is dead too,' I replied.

With that piece of information Susan looks like she is drowning, her mouth open, catching flies.

'Oh dear. I'm not sure what to say now.'

'It's fine. It was a long time ago.'

I put my hand on Susan's arm and give it a squeeze. She looks uncomfortable.

'You will be okay. It gets better with time. I'm sorry for your loss.' Sensing now is a good time, I wrap it up.

'Thank you. You too,' Susan says and pushes her trolly off with a wave.

I head back towards the checkout and as I do, I see trifle like the kind we used to have when my mother was alive. I see the end aisle full of alcohol. The kind he liked. As I walk, everything seems to remind me of my childhood. It hits me and a wave of nausea follows. I am kidding myself. The world is full of reminders of people I will never see again. The more I try to pull down these emotions, the more they come back to the surface. Like a volcano just waiting to erupt. I let go of the trolly and race from aisle to aisle. Finally, I see her: Susan.

She has two ready meals in each hand and is looking at the nutritional value of each, comparing them.

I rush up and grab her arm. She looks alarmed. I guess her old school friend is looking a little unhinged.

'Susan. I have to tell you something.'

'Oh. Are you okay?'

'Susan, I lied to you.'

Susan is embarrassed now, I can tell.

'That is okay. We don't know each other that well.'

'This is important.'

'Well, okay then.'

I know I am breaking social codes. I know I am showing emotion in public. I know I am not okay.

I let go of her arm and I try to compose myself a little. Susan just stares at the neurotic, unstable woman in front of her, wondering what is going to happen next.

'I lied to you because it never gets better. I am still numb. Every day it hits you again that they are dead. Things remind you of them. You always miss them. Time doesn't heal, it just blunts the edges a little. I never really forgave my father and now I can't. My youth and pride stopped me. Everybody has these happy stories of him. I don't. I would like to have one. All of mine are awful. My father may have been a bastard but maybe I never gave him a chance.

'Maybe my siblings are right. Maybe I really was the problem all along. Maybe he was capable of more than I gave him credit for but now it is too late. I have never had a father and now I never will. Not even a bad one.'

I stop. I can tell other people are watching. I am making an idiot of myself, yet again. Everyone probably thinks I am mad. The embarrassment creeps in to begin with but then it engulfs me. The shame is pure.

'Sorry. I have to go. Sorry for your loss,' I said to Susan, trying to act as normal as possible. I walk away with as much dignity as I can muster.

Susan smiles at me and nods. I remember now that she was the school bully. Always a complete bitch. I just unloaded myself onto the school bully. It is almost more than I can take. She will tell everyone about this and what I know most in life is that many people are not kind. I walk out of the supermarket. Fast. I start to well up as I walk. I have to hurry before the tears come thick and fast.

I make it into the car park, my hand shaking as I press the button that unlocks the car. I get in and drive off.

My tears turn to wracking sobs that feel like they are going to overcome me. I start to drive but I do not have anywhere to go. Not really. The light ahead turns amber and I put my foot on the break — too hard. I am hurtled forward not by my braking but by the car behind rear-ending me. The airbag goes off. It feels like a punch to the face. I can taste blood and feel pain.

I stay there for the longest time. Feeling numb as strangers knock on the window and ask if I am okay. The tears have stopped now. Everything has stopped. I try to block everything out. The pain, the blood and the people. No, I am not okay. I am not okay.

Chapter Fourteen

Natalie

Somehow, I end up in the back of the ambulance. They patch me up gently and with kindness. I gave my statement to the police.

It took a bit of persuasion to convince them I had not stolen the car. I kept telling them it was not mine, true, but I was on the insurance. I assume they had called Rob. Out of all of the things I have done to that man, now I have even destroyed his car. There is no end to me. I am truly the gift that keeps on giving.

I am certain that I am about to be arrested any moment. Not for stealing a car, which I have actually done, but for causing a car accident.

Somehow my nose is not broken. It is bleeding badly and I am pretty certain I will have a black eye. The paramedic says I am 'remarkably unscathed'. It does not feel like it.

The police officer walks towards me. I hold my breath. Here it comes.

'Good news, all of the witnesses say the other driver was tailgating. You may have been slow to realise the lights were changing, as you said, but it was not your fault. It is in the Highway Code that you should not tailgate and take emergency breaks into consideration.'

I breathe a sigh of relief. This has been the worst day ever, but at least I will not be arrested. I feel a strange version of happy. That kind when you thought you had nothing left to lose, but then you get to keep what you did not realise you had.

'We have notified the owner of the car. They seemed very concerned about your crash. What is their relationship to you? I don't think you said.'

I open my mouth to say something, ready to wing some more but then I see him. Rob. Here.

I try to stay strong, but I cannot. I start crying again. For the second time in a week, Rob comes up and puts his arms around me. I put my arms around him and bury myself in his chest. It feels like home.

'It is all okay. I am here,' Rob says as he strokes my hair and then kisses the top of my head. I know now that I would do anything to have him back in my life. I let him go because I wanted him to find someone to have a family with. I wanted him to have it all. I still do but I do not have that sacrifice in me any more. I love him. I cannot live without him. Now I am crying because I do not know if he will ever forgive me. If these kisses will last forever.

'You need to come to the hospital. You have taken a blow to the head. We just have to be careful. One of the doctors will want to look you over.'

Rob moves away.

'Okay, I understand.'

I look at Rob and smile. He smiles back.

'So should I put "boyfriend" then?' the police officer asks.

Jeez, this is awkward.

'Yes, thank you, Officer,' Rob tells him.

'Please sit in the seat and I will strap you in,' the paramedic says.

I do as he asks, only I strap myself in. To my surprise Rob follows. He sits in the other seat. He looks insanely handsome.

'Thank you.'

He looks up.

'It's okay. Don't want you getting arrested for grand theft auto.'

'No, I mean, for coming down.'

Rob smiles.

'And for not shopping me to the police.'

Rob laughs.

'You are on the insurance.'

'I know.'

I feel vulnerable and awkward. I glance at the paramedic who is filling in forms and pretending not to listen. Some colleagues who were tending the other people in the car come over. They all start chatting to each other. I look over at the other paramedic who is sitting in the front of the ambulance. She is taking a well-earned tea break.

'I am sorry.'

'I told you, it is okay.'

'No, I mean, for everything.'

He looks at me and purses his lips. I can see the hurt in his face.

'It's okay,' he tells me, but I can tell it is strained.

'I have been really awful and I will probably never be able to make it up to you but please know I am truly sorry.'

I almost tell him I love him but I manage not to. I am not feeling brave enough. He is so close, I do not want to push him away.

'Is there someone else?'

'No. God no. There never has been.'

I hope he hears the last part for what it is. *There is only you.*

'Sorry. I'm not trying to imply anything. It is just that it was very sudden and I would like some closure.'

Closure. I hate that word now. I try to think of something to say but I can't. There is just the word closure going around in my head.

'Did you just stop loving me?'

'No.'

He looks frustrated.

'Then what? Nothing makes sense.'

Rob looks at me, searching for something. I am trying to think of the words. How do I tell him? Should I tell him?

'I guess I just thought you would be better off without me.'

He laughs.

'Why? That is insane.'

'I just felt I was dragging you down.'

He looks pissed off and sighs.

'Look, you have been injured, and I know you have been through a lot recently, but please do not bullshit me. We do not need to talk about this right now, but maybe at some point a proper explanation would be great.'

'It's the baby.'

Rob looks nonplussed.

'What?'

'You know, the baby.'

His face softens as he realises. He comes over and takes my hand.

'That was ages ago.'

'I know, but...' I cannot finish the words.

Rob kisses me again and strokes me. He wraps his arms around me while I cry into his arms.

'You are so silly. We talked about this. We could even adopt.'

I look up. The paramedics are doing a good job of being respectful. The one who patched me up is still filling in a form. I look back at Rob.

'You deserve your own children.'

'I would rather have you and none.'

'At the rehearsal you said you wanted loads. That you could not wait to be a father.'

Rob's jaw drops and he puts his head in his hand.

'Oh my God. So that is it. Natalie, honestly. All of this out of such a little thing.'

'It is not a little thing, Rob.'

'It is to me.'

'Sure.'

Rob rolls his eyes.

'Amanda is pregnant. Did you know that?'

Rob thinks for a moment.

'Neil hasn't told me yet, but I thought she might be. It was weird she stopped drinking, then there was the weight gain. It explains a lot though.'

'She got pregnant immediately.'

'Of course she did.'

I lay my head back and let out a huge sigh. It is a good job this head injury is not serious because clearly the paperwork is important. I need to lie down and rest. I feel so exhausted by everything.

'Is that really it? You broke up with me because you wanted me to go and have babies with someone else?'

'I thought I was being selfless and honourable. Turns out I just always end up being the bitch.'

'Hey.'

Rob takes my head in his hand and looks right at me.

'You are not a bitch. You are the greatest person I have ever known in my life. I love you and I will love you until the day I die. I do not care about having children even an iota of what I care about you and having you in my life.'

There is not much left to say. All I can do now is leap in with hope in my heart.

'I love you. Will you please forgive me?'

'Of course I will. Our house is so empty without you in it.'

Rob stops to kiss me on the lips. It is beautiful.

'I am never letting you go again, Natalie.'

'Good because I want to stay with you forever.'

There is a clearing of the throat. The paramedics are ready and obviously feeling uncomfortable. I can feel my checks flush.

'Sorry, are we ready to go?'

'Yes, all ready. Please strap yourself in, sir.'

Rob goes and sits back down in his seat and does as he is told. We head to the hospital, grinning at each other like a couple of idiots.

Then
Jacqueline

Another baby. I am surprised for some reason. I guess there is no reason to be. Tim hates condoms and I have never been able to tolerate the Pill. The babies have always come. But this one surprised me because it was not made out of love, I guess. We barely had sex any more. When we did it was just two people with needs. To the outside world, Tim and I still looked like a happy couple, but really, we were just going through the motions. The whole "staying together for the children thing".

The truth is, Tim has always wanted a boy and I have a feeling that I will be having babies until one came along. If I stayed that is.

I was trying to study. Trying to carve something out of my life that was something other than a servant for others. It was not that I did not enjoy being a mother; it was the best of my life. Everything I always wanted, but being a wife was not what I thought it would be. Or, more accurately, my husband was not what I expected him to be.

I could not figure out whether he had changed, or if I had just been blind to his faults. I had loved him so much. And when he chose me, it made me feel so special. He was six foot and gorgeous. Blonde hair, green eyes, a great body that he clearly took care of. He was charming. Whatever that "thing" was, he had it. He could have had any woman he wanted, and as I thought of that I laughed because in the past few weeks he had.

Maybe he had cheated throughout our entire marriage. I liked to think that he hadn't. I wanted to believe my husband, but now I know that is not possible. There was no trust any more. But there was another baby. Just as the other two babies were becoming more independent. I felt like I would never be free. The thought made me feel guilty. I love my children and yet I feel so guilty the moment I want anything for myself.

I already love the one growing inside of me. But I have no help. Tim is just a liability.

Tim had turned out to be such a mistake. My family were horrified when they met my new boyfriend. They even threatened to disinherit me. That had partly happened. My mother gave me some money, knowing how tough things were, but a lot of it had stopped. And if only I had more support and could study, it would not matter. Because then I could earn my own money and be independent. It was all I ever wanted.

It would have to be put off now. For more baby years. I knew when the baby was in my arms it would not matter. That I would give myself willingly and wholly. That the only thing that would matter would be that little squidgy face.

Now that I thought about it, it made me happy. To have more love in my life rather than less. Maybe after Tim's confession he would be there for the children more. He might even start watching them for a few hours a day, or on a weekend so I could have some time to myself.

I was happy being a mother, happier than I had ever been, but I was not as fulfilled as I thought I would be. The secretary did not help. Tim said it was just an innocent kiss. A moment of drunken madness at the work party, he said. The emails and obscene pictures I discovered were just her pursuing him. He was innocent, he said. A victim in all of this. He had not kissed her back.

I had smelt her perfume that night and it made my heart sink. It felt like a hand grenade going off in the middle of the life we had built together. Despite everything, I trusted him. I never thought Tim would cheat on me, and now knowing that my family were right about him, it's more than I can take. I thought he was just a flirt and I was fine with that.

It was not his fault women threw themselves at him. That was what he always told me, like it was a curse. Despite the nagging doubt I decide to believe him. I decide to believe even though I do not really believe because if you seek you will find. I know I would not be able to take it right now. I do not have the strength to be a single mother. I choose the benefit of the doubt because that was all I had at the moment, as this new baby grew in my belly; the hope that everything would be okay. That we would finally be a happy family.

Present day
Rob

Natalie is lying in our bed sleeping. The sun blazing a trail across her beautiful face. I wonder if she noticed that nothing has been touched. After she left, I never had the strength to come back into this room. I could not sleep in our bed without her. Three dresses that she had tried on and dismissed for the rehearsal dinner were still on the floor. As were four pairs of shoes zigzagged around the floor. The room was dusty and the bed had remained unmade. It was my shrine to her.

I wonder what I would have done if she had not come back. I push the thought away. It is too painful to contemplate. She is here now and I am happy again.

The call from the police had terrified me. They had said she seemed fine but the words "head injury" were never going to make anyone feel calm. I rushed down there as quick as an Uber could get me. When I got there, she was in the back of an ambulance, bleeding and looking pale. I had taken a look at my car. The damage did not seem that bad considering. It was the least of my worries. I felt like an idiot approaching her. Like an interloper in her life. Would she think I was stalking her? But she was there alone and I had to try. Then her eyes lit up when she saw me and she gave me that smile.

I feel silly now, not putting all of the pieces together. Natalie found it hard to talk about her feelings. She had spent a lifetime surpassing her own needs and caring for others. I had managed to get her to open up a lot more but there was still that little bit of a shell left. Sometimes it was up, sometimes it was down. Despite this, Natalie was the opposite of cold. That was what made me angry about her siblings. She was forced into a parental position and cared for them their entire life. Natalie was warm and caring. She was the best a human being could be.

I kiss her on the cheek and then I go to leave. She probably needs the sleep.

'Hey, you. Where are you going?'

I smile.

'Hello, you.'

'Come in here and snuggle me.'

'Snuggle?'

Natalie rolls her eyes, not in the mood to be made fun of.

'Yes, miss.'

I climb into the bed and spoon her. Breathing her in.

'Thank you for being so amazing. I was such a bitch to you.'

'It doesn't matter now. You were being very silly, but it is in the past. We should just move on.'

Natalie turns to face me and takes my face in her hands and kisses me.

'That is very magnanimous of you.'

'I am not saying you should not make it up to me though.'

'Is that right?'

'Yes.'

'What did you have in mind?' she asks with a naughty glint in her eye.

'Well, we will let you heal first and then we can think of some stuff.'

'Spoilsport.' She looks disappointed.

'What did I miss? What has been happening?' I stop myself and think about the obvious. 'I know he died.'

'Yeah, he died.'

'How do you feel about that?'

She looks away for a moment and I can see the pain in her face. She hated her father and always said she would never care if he died. But reality is often different.

'Well Paul and Amanda kept making me see him.'

'Paul as well. I am surprised at that.'

'So was I. They ganged up on me.'

'Well, they knew I was not on the scene. Let's see them try that now.'

'I was there when he died.'

'I know, I am so sorry.'

'I couldn't save him.'

'It is not your fault. There was nothing you could do.'

'I know but it still hurts. I think Amanda blames me.'

'Of course she does. She always blames other people.'

'It is just awful because I always wanted to have a father and he never was one, but he was the closest I had. Now he has died, the hole is permanent. I know that was the case when he was alive, but death makes it final.'

'Well, we should talk about it. It heals. No more of this bottling stuff up. We can talk about that and the baby too. You have been struggling for too long.'

'You are right. I am sorry. It has been unfair on you. I just tend to do the stiff upper lip thing.'

'I know but you need to stop.'

'I will. I promise.'

We look at each other. It has always been easy being with Natalie. When I am with her it feels like home. I stroke her hair.

'Are you sure you are okay about the baby thing? That it might not happen?'

'Please stop being such an idiot. Also, you do not get to make decisions for the both of us. Leaving me for me just does not cut it. I am an adult, I make my own decisions. Life is hard, sometimes people do not get what they want.'

Natalie smiles at me.

'Okay, but let's actually try.'

I have wanted to try IVF and go all out but I did not want to pressure her. The things that women have to go through are awful.

'Do you really mean it?'

'Yes. I know a really good clinic. I will make an appointment.'

I kiss her, trying to not get too excited, but also meaning every word I have said to her.

'I have to go and help Amanda sort out our parents' home at some point this weekend. Paul will be there too so I am hoping it will be quick.'

'How is Amanda?'

'We are not really talking to be honest. There was an altercation in a baby shop.'

'Oh dear.'

'She has not cancelled though and I just want to clear out the house and get it on the market.'

'Do you want me to go with you?'

'If you want.'

'Great, I will. You might need backup.'

I squeeze her in a bit tighter. Feeling light and happy, knowing that I will never let her go ever again.

Chapter Fifteen

Natalie

I am in a big house and as I walk around, I realise I am wearing a wedding dress. I walk into a ballroom. The room is huge and decadent with chandeliers and expensive paintings on the walls. In the air I hear the start of a song. I twirl around and laugh. To my surprise someone takes my hand. It is my father. He is younger and is wearing a suit. He looks handsome. He puts his other arm around my waist as he puts us in the starting position. We look at each other and smile.

Then we begin to dance. We dance around the entire ballroom. I am twirled and dipped. I laugh, not remembering the last time I was this happy. As I look around, I see the rest of my family. My mother is looking on, clapping. Looking beautiful and happy. I look at my father. At the crinkle in his eyes, at the face I could never bring myself to love. Not even as he was about to die.

I look around for my mother. She is gone and I start crying. I run into the hall to look for her. I go into another room and there she is. My mother walks up to me and brings her hand to my face and wipes away my tears.

'Natalie, why are you crying?' she asks. 'I never died.'

I wake up, startled. I am in my own bed. I am not sure where Rob is so I go downstairs. He is cooking. I can feel my stomach rumble. I am starving. I look at the time. It is noon. Jeez, I never sleep this late. Ever.

'I just had a weird dream.'

'Want to talk about it?'

'I was just dancing around a ballroom with my father while wearing a wedding dress. Then my mother was there and she told me to not be upset because she had never died.'

'A wedding dress, eh?'

I sigh a mock sigh.

'You always just hear what you want to hear.'

'Well, we have talked about it loads.'

'But you have never actually proposed.'

Rob looks nonplussed for a moment as he searches his memory.

'That cannot be true.'

'And yet it is.'

I see Rob smile and put some eggs on a plate with sausages, beans, toast and cooked tomatoes. I really did miss this man.

'Well, then I apologise. How silly of me.'

'Yes. How silly indeed.'

'I will get you a coffee.'

'Thank you for my breakfast, and the coffee.'

'Anything for you, darling.'

Rob brings my coffee and I eat and drink. Happy as anyone can be.

'Natalie.'

I look up. Rob is on one knee, a ring in his hand.

'Will you marry me?'

I jump up and launch myself into his arms, knocking him over. He is flat on his back now, laughing.

'Yes, a million times, yes.'

Rob puts the ring on my finger. It is gorgeous. White gold with a huge round diamond in the middle. I cannot remember what they call that cut.

'The diamond or me,' Rob teases.

'Hmm, the diamond is pretty, but it can't cook breakfast,' I tease him back then I kiss him. That feeling is back. The chemical feeling that loves gives. All my cylinders firing at once.

I stare at the ring the entire drive to my parents' old house. I cannot believe I am engaged. Somehow it feels different. I look out the window and watch London go by. I grew up in Ealing and it is completely different from when I was growing up. I do not recognise it at all.

Through my buzz of joy, I can feel a dread the closer I get to our old house. I know Amanda is already there. I had texted her to let her know I am on my way. I receive a curt reply.

great see you soon.

No capitals or punctuation. I can only assume she couldn't be bothered. I think about my relationship with my sister as we go. I have always found her highly strung and difficult; she has always found me judgemental and cold. I guess both of us are right in a way. So many things have happened over the years that were never addressed. Now all of that stuff had built up like scar tissue. How do you fix years of resentment?

Maybe I didn't try hard enough but the fact is that he was always there. Amanda always came with her agenda. She said I was the only one not letting things go, then why could she not let it go that I did not like our father and wanted nothing to do with him? I never asked her to stop seeing him. That was not my place. Yet I was framed as the bully, the one with all of the issues. Even civility was not enough. She wanted total surrender.

I was unfair in the children's shop. I was projecting on to her. It was not her fault I didn't have children yet. I had never even told her. I thought telling people would jinx it. I kept the pain to myself because that is how I have always preferred my pain.

Now we were here.

'Well, I didn't end up on the side of the road. Yeah.'

I laugh. I would not be so good-natured about it.

'You were the one who drove.'

'Yeah, we should keep it that way. Even if the replacement car feels funny.'

'I promise to never dump you again.'

'Good,' Rob says and leans in to kiss me.

'Because I never want to give back this ring.'

I laugh but Rob doesn't.

'Oh, you never liked being teased back.'

'No, I don't. You go in and have fun. I will go and find somewhere to park.'

'Okay.' I kiss him again and I head towards the door, hoping this goes well.

I knock on the red door of the beautiful Victorian house we grew up in and Amanda answers. She looks amazing. Her belly and her breasts are huge. She is wearing a yellow shift dress and a pair of gold sandals. Her curly blonde hair is thick and shiny and she is wearing minimal make-up. I am awed by her.

'You look great.'

'Thanks,' she said but then frowns. 'What happened to your face?'

I had forgotten.

'Oh. Car crash.'

'Oh my God, are you okay? That is awful. You should have called me.'

'No, I am fine.' I am about to tell her Rob came and rescued me, but her phone starts ringing and she answers it.

I am still standing in the doorway. At least it is August and the weather is still hot and balmy. Her call finishes.

'That was Paul. He is going to be late. Great.' She walks into the house and I follow her, closing the door behind me.

'I have spent the entire morning sorting things into piles. It is so tedious and boring. There are no words. It feels so emotional being here. The house we spent our childhood in. I feel sad my children will not grow up in this house but, oh well.'

Ding dong, dig number one.

'Well, it is probably haunted to be fair. It does not exactly have lots of happy memories.'

'Not for you, Natalie.'

I let that one go.

I look at the piles. At all of the stuff. Christ, this is going to take a long time. Memories and possessions of someone who no longer existed. I see his shoes near the television. I get a wave of nausea when I realise he will never wear them again. Each time it surprises me that I even care.

Amanda follows my gaze.

'He will never wear them again, but I cannot bring myself to throw them out. I just feel like he might need them.'

For a moment I think she is going to cry and I go towards her, but I see her tense up and I stop.

Amanda sighs.

'Let's get on with this, Natalie. The sooner it is done the better.'

I never noticed how much Amanda sighs before. She does it all of the time.

'I agree. Do we have a plan?'

'The British Heart Foundation is coming along on Monday to pick up some stuff. Neil and I put it all in the spare room. You should double-check you do not want anything. Everything else should be recycled or just put in the bin. You said you would hire a cleaner.'

'Yes, I will get one to come on Tuesday. It will make things easier.'

'What about the photographs?' Amanda looks right at me.

'We could split them?'

'You actually want some?'

'Why wouldn't I?'

'Because you hate him, you hate your childhood.'

'I am not going to take this, Amanda.'

'Take what?'

'Your constant abuse.'

Amanda laughs.

'I am not abusing you. You are the one who constantly says you had a terrible childhood.'

'Actually, I say I did not have a childhood. There is a difference.'

'Really?'

'Yes, because I was taking care of you and Paul. Cleaning up mess, being an adult. That does not mean I don't want any pictures of my mother or siblings.'

'But none of him.'

It is my turn to sigh.

'He is dead and yet you still cannot help yourself. Will you ever quit?'

Amanda does not say anything. She just stands there rubbing her bump and looking at me in a cold manner.

'I am going to get some bin bags from under the sink. We need to get started.' Maybe when I come back, she will have decided to let it go.

I get the bin bags and head back to the living room.

'Sorry, you are right. Let's stop fighting and get on with it.'

'That would be great.' She actually sounds genuine. I am taken aback by Amanda's change in mood, but I decide to go with it.

'Come and see this. You will never believe.'

Amanda beckons me to follow her so I do. I start to hesitate when I realise, we are heading to our father's bedroom. I do not want to go in there. It has nothing but bad memories.

Amanda notices me hesitating.

'Come on, it's okay. You will want to see this.'

I put one foot in and look around. It looks the same way it did when both of my parents slept here. Every cell in my body wants to move but I just stand there. Amanda opens a cupboard.

'Here. Come here. Look.'

I walk over and look in the cupboard.

'It is all of Mum's stuff. It is intact. He kept it all. It has been wrapped in plastic and boxed. It is a pretty big cupboard and it is all here.'

I look at the stuff. Great. Double the emotional trauma.

'Don't you think this is wonderful?' Amanda said, smiling at me. I am resisting the urge to slap her.

'No, I don't. I think it is even more work and even more crap.'

Amanda looks disappointed. Any other time I would have yielded to make her happy but not this time. I am sick of this shit and just want it to end. I want to start partaking in the future. I have had enough of the past.

'Do you want to start in here?' I ask Amanda.

'We may as well. You love Mum so you might want some of this stuff.'

I look at it. I touch a dress hanging on a rail, putting my hand underneath the plastic cover to feel the fabric. It feels soft.

'I will get Neil to box it and get it to you. The stuff on the bed is what I would like to keep. I turn and look at the bed. It has clothes, shoes, some jewellery and a trinket box. None of it is worth the fight. I already have some of our mother's stuff. When she first died, I had gone through all of this stuff. I was the one who boxed everything up and put the clothes in the plastic covers. I know everything that is in here. That would never occur to Amanda. I wonder what Sheila had thought about it. I hope it pissed her off every day.

'Why don't you have the rest of it? Mum had great taste in fashion. I think you were the same shoe size too,' I tell Amanda.

She looks delighted and hugs me.

'That is great, thank you, and I know you still have some of her designer clothes and jewellery. Well, this room is done now. Let's move to the next one!'

Ah, turns out she did not forget.

I hear the door. Finally, that must be Rob.

'That must be Paul.' Amanda practically runs down the stairs, freaking me out that she might stumble.

'Oh, it's you.'

I can hear the surprise in her voice. She has not even noticed my engagement ring. I walk down the stairs smiling. There he is at the bottom. He smiles back.

'I am sorry, Natalie, but for some reason Rob has turned up. Should I tell him to bugger off? I know you dumped him.'

'Hello, darling,' I say as I walk down the stairs and put my arms around his neck, giving him a passionate kiss.

It is at this point that Amanda finally notices the ring.

'Oh my God, what is that?'

We finish the kiss before we answer.

'It is my engagement ring.'

'Engagement ring? You guys were not even together and now you are engaged?'

'Rob rescued me from my car accident. I begged for his forgiveness and here we are. Back where we belong.'

Amanda just looks at us. She is not smiling, nor does she congratulate us. This is what I hate most about my sister. She is never happy for anyone else.

'Aren't you going to congratulate us?' Rob asks her.

She seems flustered and splutters out a 'congratulations'.

She rubs her bump again.

'Oh well. That is great, guys. Maybe you will have a baby soon too.'

Do not hit a pregnant woman, do not hit a pregnant woman. Rob looks at me and smiles as he squeezes my hand.

'Come on in,' I tell him, thankful he is back in my life. The only family that I have.

'Yes, of course! Sorry, Rob. Do come in. What can I get you? Tea, coffee? I think we also have some lemonade.'

Hmm. I was not offered any of this stuff.

'A coffee would be great, thank you, Amanda.'

I look at Amanda. Eventually she looks back.

'Natalie, would you like a coffee too?'

'That would be great.'

She smiles at him and then heads towards the kitchen.

'The break-up. It was because of things like that, right?'

'Right.'

Rob nods at me. I nod back. A part of me feels like crying but controlling my emotions while inside everything is a whirlwind is my special skill. I feel like my insides are a blender, almost permanently on.

'What needs doing?'

'Hopefully not much. The charity shop is coming to take stuff on Monday, I have a cleaner coming on Tuesday. Paul will pick his stuff up today. I don't want anything. I am sure Amanda has sorted what she wants and what she is going to do with it.'

'Neil and I have done most of the work. The spare room will be empty on Monday, our parents' bedroom will be cleared by Neil and I. If we just go room by room, making sure there will be no junk or clutter. Anything that can be recycled let's do so, otherwise things can go in the bin. Old food and stuff.' Amanda says as she comes back from the kitchen, two mugs in hand.

'Okay, sounds very organised of you and Neil. Well done. I will go into the kitchen and just chuck stuff out then.'

Rob takes the coffee Amanda is handing out and heads towards the kitchen.

'Oh, and Rob.'

'Yes.'

'Neil loves working for you.'

'That is great. We love having him. He is talented.'

'I know, he is so good at his job.'

Rob starts heading towards the kitchen and Amanda looks at me.

'Well done you. I was really worried about you. I would not want to start again at your age.'

'Thanks.' I do not even try to remove the sarcasm from my voice.

'There is a shoebox full of stuff for you in the living room. You might want to go through it. I have some other stuff too.'

'Okay.'

I go into the living room. There are so many things that happened in this room. Even some recently, but it had stopped being a family home. All of the conversations were always stilted, held back by years of bad memories and recrimination.

I look around for the shoebox. I spot it sitting on one of the chairs. It has my name on it. I open it. It is full of pictures and paper.

I look at the first picture. It is a picture of us all before the incident. My mother is pregnant with Paul, and Amanda looks so small. Everyone is smiling and happy. Amanda is sitting on our father's knee, cuddling into him as she always did. A daddy's girl from the first.

I expect to feel something, but these people seem like strangers to me now. I put my hand in the box and pull out a magazine clipping. It is an article I had written for a health magazine.

I had barely been talking to my father at this point, but I could not help but be touched that he found this article and kept it. It must mean that he genuinely cared. Even a little. But even as I was touched, I knew the facts: he always found it easier to care when you were far away.

I look further for more things from my childhood, or even my adulthood. There is a lot of yellowed paper, some newspaper clippings of various health ailments that I did not write. I feel disappointed. I thought maybe this box was about me and only me. It is a selfish thought, but would I have been asking too much?

I do not know why people hoard so much stuff. This room is full of crap. There are out-of-date magazines everywhere. Some of them are from ten years ago. There are even some broken ornaments and coins stuffed into the shoebox. What was the point of keeping so much stuff?

I hear a noise and look behind me. It is Amanda.

'It is okay to feel overwhelmed. It is a lot of stuff,' Amanda said. Defrosting for the first time this morning. I smiled at her, appreciating the comment.

'It's selfish in a way. To keep all of this stuff. Knowing that your relatives will have to get rid of it when you are gone,' Amanda said, looking around. 'But I guess people never really think they are going to die. I mean, they know, but they don't know.'

'That is true,' I say and smile at my sister.

Here it is. Another tentative truce. This one is much needed.

'I found this article that I wrote. Dad must have kept it all of these years.'

'Yeah, he kept all of your stuff. He followed your career obsessively. He was so proud.'

'I never thought he would do that. It is nice to know. I never thought he cared about my career. He never mentioned it to my face. Not in a positive way anyway.'

There is an awkward silence. Amanda just looks at me. I cannot tell what she is thinking.

'Maybe we should just get rid of all of this stuff. Do we really need do go through it?'

'I think we should. There might be something important somewhere,' Amanda countered. She looks serious.

'Okay.'

Was my relationship with my sister always like this? So full of tension. I always thought we had our ups and downs, but the ups were full of fun. Now we can barely talk to each other.

'We should crack on. Let me just check on Rob first. I will text Paul, he is taking so long.'

I go into the kitchen. Rob is clearing out the fridge.

'This is not a fun job. This stuff has been here for a while.' He makes a face like he is about to throw up. I laugh.

'I was just checking on you. Love you.'

'Love you too.'

I head back towards the living room and I notice Amanda is loitering in the doorway.

'Let's get this done.'

I grab a clear recycling sack and I put all of the magazines and newspapers in. Everything that is paper goes in. I work fast and make good ground. Initially Amanda just gapes, but then she starts to help out.

'There were only two things for me in the shoebox.'

'Oh, sorry. I had some other things. I will give them to you in a moment.'

'Thanks.'

'Do you ever wonder what went wrong?' I ask Amanda.

'With Mum and Dad?'

'No, with us.'

I look at Amanda.

'Everything seems like resentment and apprehension. We can barely talk to each other.'

'I think a lot of stuff has happened.'

'So you agree our relationship is not great?'

'Yes, of course.'

'Why do you think that is?'

I try to think what to say. How honest I should be. The truth is sometimes I feel like we are more like a married couple than sisters. The relationship had become exhausting because of the third person who was always hovering in the distance. Even in death. Amanda loved our father; I hated him. I always would.

'I think Dad came between us.'

'Only because you let him. Why did I have to choose?'

'You didn't, Amanda. Our relationship is terrible at the moment because you kept dragging me in. You bullied me. I never stopped you seeing him. It was none of my business, but my relationship with him was none of yours.'

Amanda sighs. Again. God, it really is irritating.

'You always think you are being bullied when people stand up to you.'

I take a deep breath. This is so exhausting. What price blood? All of my energy seems to leave me.

Amanda reaches into a box and pulls out a stack of letters and hands them to me.

'He wrote to you all of the time, but never posted them. He asked me to give some to you once. But I told him I didn't want to get involved. I feel guilty about that now. I am sorry. Maybe it would have made a difference.'

'Don't be. You did the right thing.'

I take all of the letters and then head into the hall to put them in my bag. I go back into the living room. I look around and feel despondent. We will not finish all of this today, but hopefully we have made a dent.

'You expected too much of him. He was only a human being,' Amanda said to me tentatively.

'I think expecting someone to not lie and cheat and leave their family is a minimum. He blew up our entire family, put himself before all of us. Separated siblings. He was a drunk for years. I mean, it is not like he was a good person that did the occasional bad things. He was just a bad person who did the occasional good thing. So, yeah, a human being. But a really shitty one.'

'You are acting like you haven't even lost your father.'

'You don't get it. I'm not mourning him. I have already mourned my entire life because I never had a father. This pain you are feeling? Already done it. Only I never lied to myself and pretended he was anything other than an asshole.'

We look at each other. It is a stand-off. Neither of us want to argue, but both of us have a lot to say. We just stand there. Wondering which one of us will go first.

'That was shitty, but he just fell in love with someone else.'

I inhale my rage. I did not want to do this today.

'No, he did not just fall in love with someone else. And you putting it like that is disloyal to our mother. It is a simplification of the annihilation of a family. Our family. It is making excuses for a man who not only walked out on his daughters, but also his newborn son. There are no excuses for what he did. It was selfish, it was awful and it shows his true character: that of a selfish monster who put his own happiness before everything and everyone else, including his responsibilities.'

'He tried to fix it,' Amanda yelled.

I look at her. Her love for her father blinded her. It was the worst kind of love. The kind that left you beholden to another person, unable to deflect any possibility that they were anything less than a god. It put one person on a pedestal and another one at their feet. It was unhealthy and I could not help think that maybe it was Stockholm syndrome.

Or just complete betrayal of our mother. I wanted Amanda to admit the truth. That what our father had done was wrong and that his actions had echoed throughout the rest of our lives. It drove me mad that Amanda was such a robot when it came to our father. Such a stupid, silly girl.

'Mum was not blameless. She would scream at him. And she was depressed all the time. Sheila…'

I did not let Amanda finish her sentence.

'She screamed because he was a lying, cheating bastard. She was depressed because of how he treated her and don't you fucking dare say that woman's name to me. You just want to blame the victim because that is what Dad taught you to do. If you had a backbone, you would have hated him just like me and Paul.'

'Paul doesn't hate…'

'Yes, he does! We all do. Everyone who met him knew he was a prick. A drunk, lying, screwing, womanising prick. Your biology screws you into loving him, but he is nothing but a monster. Admit that for once instead of your misogynistic bullshit. Christ, I cannot believe you are my sister. Look at you, a delusional bitch. Everyone has made excuses for you defending him all of these years but get your head out of your arse. You are such a disappointing and stupid, little girl.'

I can tell Amanda is in shock. I have never talked to her like this before.

'And you are always living in the past. This happened decades ago, but all you can do is hold a grudge and be a bitch. You have let one mistake ruin your life and everyone's around you. You looked like a deranged bitch running after Sheila at the funeral.

'I'm blind? You are blind to all of Mum's mistakes. You think she was a fucking saint. Maybe she cheated on Dad? She was always mean to him. Why can't you just forgive and move on. It wasn't Dad ruining our family. It was you and your decades-long grudge. Never letting anyone forget, not even for a moment. Always bringing up the wounds of the past. Always acting like a stroppy teenager. You ruined our family, not Dad.'

I look at my sister. I never thought she could hurt me like this.

'He was a crappy human being and an even worse father. That is not past nor conjecture. It is the truth. Something you have never had a very good relationship with. Good luck with the house. You are going to need it.'

I go into the hall.

'Rob, come on, we are leaving.'

Rob comes out of the kitchen. A *what the fuck* expression on his face. He had clearly heard.

'Natalie, don't forget the letters. They are for you,' Amanda called after me.

'Yeah, fuck you very much,' I mumble under my breath.

With that, I walk out of the family home and my sister's life. There is only so many times you can try and repair something that is broken.

Chapter Sixteen

Then
Jacqueline

The tears mix with my mascara and sting my eyes. I must look like a panda now. My worst fears have been confirmed. The nagging doubt was no longer. I could no longer choose blissful ignorance over reality. No matter how much the latter hurt. I put my hand to my swollen belly. It would be due any day now. Born into a family that was not a family any more.

Tim does not know that I know yet. But I found underwear in his pockets along with some notes. That bitch clearly wanted me to know. I could not believe that one woman could do that to another. Have sex with another woman's husband, especially when they had children together. Especially when the wife is pregnant. It was the lowest of the lowest.

It took so much effort to get out of bed every day. To take care of my children and pretend that everything is okay. Pretend to be happy. When Tim touched me, it made me feel sick. The worst thing was that I did not know what to do. Should I leave him? Become a single mother to three children? Or should I stay and try to work things out? I doubt my self-respect could take it.

Maybe my family would take me back, but that would be humiliating. I did not fit into my own family any more. My parents had downsized; there was no room for four more people.

I felt embarrassed and full of shame. How could my judgement have been off so badly? But then again, if I had not met Tim, I would not have my children, and they were worth the price. Despite everything.

'Are you okay, Mommy?'

I look up and see Amanda. Her curly blonde hair is messy and she is rubbing her beautiful blue eyes. She is perfection. She is still sleepy from her nap and looks happy she has found her mummy. I wipe my eyes and smile. I could not tell Amanda the truth. She worships her father. Her love for him was so pure and beautiful. I did not want to take that away. Or worse, make her grow up too fast. I would protect my daughters' childhood at all costs.

'I am okay, my love. I just had something in my eye. Let's go get a snack. You must be hungry after your nap.'

'Yes I am. I want bread, and cheese, and tomatoes and cucumber.' Amanda has run up to me and put her arms around me. Well, as much as she could considering the huge stomach between us.

'I would also like to have some biscuits. Please.'

Amanda looks up at me. Her cute little face and big eyes pleading with me. I cannot say no to that face.

'Oh, okay then. But only because you asked so nicely.'

'Yes. Thank you, Mummy. I love biscuits, but not as much as I love you.'

With that last comment, Amanda kissed me on the cheek and gave me a big squeeze hug.

'I am so happy. I really have the best mummy ever. And I also have the best daddy ever.'

The words break my heart all over again. How would Amanda feel if I left her father? Would it destroy her childhood? I pick her up and carry her to the kitchen. She puts her little head on my shoulder. I cuddle into her head. Her hair is so soft and she smells amazing. I hold my daughter and I know that this is the purest love in the world. She is everything. My daughters are all that matters.

Tim

I feel like I am suffocating. I made one little mistake with my secretary at a work party and now I am really paying for it. It had been a moment of weakness. In fact, I did not even kiss her back, but now she was pursuing me. Sending me the most obscene stuff. I am a man, for God's sake. When I see a naked woman, I react. That is only normal. Not that anything had actually happened at that party. It happened later. And I regretted it immediately.

Becoming domestic has not always suited me. Life is now monotonous, and I miss my bachelor days. It wasn't that I did not love my wife and kids, I just missed my wild days. I did not see why I should give them up. The worst thing was that I had hurt my wife.

I thought I could carry on the affair without her knowing. Have my cake and eat it too. Life was too short, that was what the problem was. My wife had her place; she was married and had her children. What more could she want? She wanted to study but how realistic was that? She did not even need the money. Her parents put up the deposit for the house. And I know they gave her money. It was ad hoc and probably not a lot but it was still just given to her. She did not have to work for it. I know she would never ask them for money.

I know that my wage does not keep her in the style in which she lived before she met me. She was a princess I had knocked off her pedestal. The thought made me feel guilty and resentful in equal measures. Our love had been pure when we first met. A lustful and wild love that had taken us everywhere. We had travelled and fucked our way around Europe. Then America and Thailand. She paid for most of it, and it was embarrassing. The heiress and the pauper. But I always kept that from my mind. We were living the good life and I did not care much about the means.

Then the baby arrived. Then another one and now she was pregnant with a third. Now we would have three children. Yet still I cheated on my wife. It had changed her. I could tell. She cried a lot. I wished she could pull herself together for the children. She thought they did not notice, and mostly they didn't. But she looked sad a lot. I was sick of the guilt. Sick of always being the bad guy. Nothing good that I did, counted. I had been faithful for years. Did everything I could to be a good husband. It almost killed me. The domestic life was so boring. I felt like I was trapped in a cage.

The children were enough for Jacqueline, but all I did was work and go home. Sure, I had a few nights out with the boys, but our life had changed so much. Sure, I had wanted to get married and have children, because that was what a man needed to do. Get a wife and have children, to carry on his line. A family. It was important. But did it really have to be the end of everything? I would die one day. I wanted to live as much as possible before that happened.

My eyes were hurting now. I hate computers. I hate working in construction. Sure, it brought in money. We had property and people always needed more houses, but I wished I had a more exciting job.

I looked at my phone. Jacqueline was due any day now. I was surprised that finding out about the affair did not bring the labour on. I wished she had not found out when she was heavily pregnant. It was not good for her or the baby.

In the moment she finally managed to get me to confess, after being so relentless I could not take it any more, I saw her faith in me go. In that moment, I knew my marriage was over. Even if she did not throw me out, we could never put the pieces back together again. The thought gnawed at me. I never wanted to be a weekend dad. But then again, maybe I would have my life back.

I hope the new baby is a boy. I have always wanted a boy. I did not want to spend my life surrounded by women. They were always the end of me. All of my mistakes involved women. Well, unless you included alcohol or an occasional pill. But those mistakes never changed your life. I stopped staring at the phone. The more I stared at it, the less likely it was to ring.

So I got back to my work. The work I hate which paid for a life that did not feel like it belonged to me any more. I was a member of the rat race now and with this new baby, it would only get worse. Another mouth to feed. Please let it be a boy. I am sick of all of the oestrogen flowing throughout the house. Women didn't understand, they never did. The phone starts to ring and it makes me jump. I panic as I pick it up.

'Hello?'

I hold my baby boy in my arms. Finally, I have a son. I could not be happier. This was it. I had to pull my life together. Give up Sheila. It was time to put my family first. I looked over at my exhausted wife. This labour had been a tough one.

It was beyond irritating when Jacqueline said it was because of the "stress she was under". She did not have to go out and work every day. What the hell did she know about stress?

Going out to work every day. That was real stress. It was as I thought of that I felt it. That bit of resentment I always had for my wife and her easy life and her constant moaning. But I had to bury it down. If only for my little boy. He was the start of everything. Life would only get better now my baby boy was here.

Jacqueline

The snow crunched underneath my feet. A new baby and a white Christmas. Maybe this was a good omen. That despite all of the humiliation and hurt, Tim would now be the person I thought he was on that day that we met. That we would be a family again. A happy one. Without any mistresses, secrets or lies. It would take a long time for us to heal but I hoped we would, if only for the sake of the children. The whiteness of the snow made me squint my eyes.

Paul had been a difficult birth which ended up requiring an emergency C-section. There were times when I thought I would never get out of that hospital. It felt like a prison. All I wanted to do was get back to my other children. I dreaded to think how tough it must be for them with only Tim to look after them. He could not cook, or never learned to, anyway. He never did any housework and he was not the most organised man I had ever met. But he did love the children. So that was something. Even if that something was not enough. I am angry at him, which I hoped meant he would try his best. And now here we were. About to go home to the faces of my two beautiful daughters so they could meet their little brother for the first time. Despite everything, the thought excites me. I may have a terrible husband, but I have three wonderful children, and that is an abundance of riches.

Chapter Seventeen

Now
Rob

I lay out the press clippings all over my desk. The campaign has been a staggering success. We have managed to turn around a vapid heiress with a reputation for partying and all of the vices that come with it. Now she is an activist who helps other people with their addictions and mental illness. She is the voice of a generation now. Filling up the pages of women's magazines and blogs with her story of triumph.

The phone rings and I answer it. It is my secretary.

'Your sister-in-law is on line one.'

I think for a moment. Why would Amanda call me? For a moment I panic.

'Put her through.'

'Rob?'

'Hi, Amanda. Is everything okay?'

'Yes. Everything is great. Thank you for asking. How are you?'

'I am good, thank you.'

An awkward pause follows. I am not sure how to fill it. I start to ask something about the weather when Amanda starts talking again.

'I wanted to talk to you about Natalie.'

Ah.

'Okay.'

'Well, our relationship hasn't been so good lately. I mean, it hasn't been very good for a while.'

She stops and I wait. Not wanting to fill in any gaps.

'I think maybe she has something going on, or something that is upsetting her. I thought maybe you could help her. I would like us to be sisters again.'

She says the last part quietly.

'I know you have had a few arguments recently. I am sure if you called her then you could talk it through.' I say gently.

Amanda sighs down the phone. I expected this. In all of the years I have known Amanda, I do not remember her taking responsibility even once.

'I think she has issues, Rob. I thought maybe it was just because the two of you broke up and she was worried she would not find anyone else. I would not want to be in my late thirties and single.'

I rub the bridge of my nose in-between my fingers. I can feel a headache coming on.

'Amanda, I think you have issues between you. Mostly your father. I also know that when we were not together, Natalie felt very bullied by you and Paul. You were allowed to love your father and have a relationship with him, Natalie was allowed to not want anything to do with him. She had it really rough with him and you do not even know the half of it.'

243

'Of course, you would take her side.'

She sounds like she is in a huff.

'It is the truth, Amanda. You need to see Natalie's point of view for once. You are unfair on her. So was Paul.'

I get another sigh for this.

'I think you need to take a step back, Amanda, and think things through.'

'She brings our father up all of the time. It is her way of pushing people away and being a bitch.'

'Amanda, that is not okay. You can be very difficult. I know you do not want to hear that, but it is the truth. Stop blaming Natalie for everything. You have as much a part to play in your terrible relationship.'

I hear a sniffle. Is she crying? I hope not.

'Did she say we had a terrible relationship?' Amanda said through sobs.

Crap.

'No. She did not say that. But I think things are not great between you.'

I hear more crying and worry I have been too harsh.

'I want a good relationship with my sister. She just does not love me. She never has.'

'That is not true, Amanda. Natalie does love you. She always has and she always will.'

'Really?'

'Yes, really.'

'I do not know how that is going to happen unless she lets go of the past. She just holds on to everything negative and blames Dad for everything. She has a serious issue. How can you not see it?' Amanda pleads with me.

'She does not always live in the past. You are the one that brings up your father all of the time. He was there all of the time with you. Years have gone by at times when she has not seen him or had to deal with him. It is not fair to blame her for that. You were the one trying to push him into her life. She never wanted that.'

'Family is family.' Amanda says sternly. A bossy tone to her voice.

'Family is earned. She believes that and so do I. Tim never earned that. He was always disgusting to her. I never liked him. He was a terrible person. I am sorry you cannot see that, but it is just the truth.'

Amanda starts crying again.

'How dare you say that. He is dead. He cannot even stick up for himself. Natalie has always taken it so personally that I chose our father that day. It does not even seem to matter to her that I was a child at the time. Even younger than Natalie in fact. She never let us be a family again. Our dad was always there, included but separate. It hurts that she cannot just let bygones be bygones. We could have all been a family again. Without the recriminations and resentment. I always thought that Paul would have got along better with our father if Natalie had just let him. She has been so uncompromising. Where was the fairness? Where was the compassion? She's incapable.'

'Being dead does not turn someone into a good person. You say Natalie has issues, but you clearly have your own.'

I can hear a sharp intake of breath on the other end. Amanda does not like hearing the truth. I do not think anyone other than Natalie has ever stood up to her. Neil certainly does not. He is besotted with her and treats her like a queen.

'She has been a monster to me since I got married. In fact, since I became pregnant, she has been a proper she-devil. She resents me all of the time for having a relationship with my own dad. In a baby shop we were buying stuff and she just blew up at me for no reason. I do not care what you say, she definitely has some issues.'

Now I do not know what to say. I was not there and I have not seen anything, but this could be true. It was the reason she left me on the side of the road after all. That was an extreme reaction. Maybe there was more. Amanda has clearly acknowledged my silence and she jumps on it.

'You know I am right. Is it because she is older and jealous? I mean, why is she being such a bitch? Hell, our mother was more forgiving than Natalie, and she was the one that was cheated on. How fucked up is that?'

I wish Amanda could hear how bitchy she sounds. I do not think she means it. She has just never had that filter that people generally have. Yet she thinks everyone else is the one with the problem.

'Well, didn't you say you went shopping? She hates shopping. It always puts her in a bad mood. That is how you unleash angry Natalie.'

I say this to try and brighten the mood. It does not work. I can just hear a silence on the other end. I can only guess at the look I am getting.

'I think it is best to take this seriously, Rob.'

'If you want to do that then actually care about her and take responsibility for your own actions, Amanda. See things from her perspective. You have bullied her.'

I see I have no choice but to be strong now. Even though she does not want to hear this. I understand because no one likes admitting when they are wrong. Taking responsibility is always a bitter pill to swallow. I wait, waiting for the eruption.

'Thank you, Rob. I will have a think about what you have said. I really want to fix things with my sister.'

With that she hangs up, leaving me stunned. Talk about personal growth.

I immediately ring Natalie. I do not expect to get her, but it is worth a shot. She is probably pulling a baby out of a woman right now. It rings out and I go to put the phone back down.

'Hello?'

I hear a tiny voice.

'Hi, it is me.'

'I know.'

I love the way she said that.

'Everything okay?'

She is worried. She always expects the worst.

''Everything is fine. I was just talking to your sister.'

'Oh.'

She sounds both surprised and worried.

'Should I apologise? She can be a bit temperamental.'

'You do not have to, actually. She was mature for once. Being married and pregnant is good for her.'

'Hmm.'

Natalie does not sound convinced. I am also aware that I am probably picking at a scab. The very scab that broke us up.

'She wants to fix things between you. She sounded genuine. I was honest with her and I told her that she has been bullying you. She said she would have a think.'

'Well, that would be nice, but I will not get my hopes up.'

'We don't we try properly for a baby?' I ask Natalie tentatively.

'You really want to?'

'Do you?'

'Yes. I really do.'

'Well then let's go all in. I know IVF would be hard on you, but we have the money. Let's just give it everything we have and then if it doesn't work, it doesn't work. Being child-free has its advantages. We would have no regrets and could have long weekends in Paris. Endless lie-ins, spare cash, good holidays. We would have complete freedom to do whatever we wanted when we wanted.'

'Okay, Rob, stop talking now if you do want children because that is a lifestyle that sounds amazing.'

I laugh. She has a point.

'Okay, let's do it. I know a really good doctor. We should start as soon as possible. I will try to get an appointment this weekend.'

I try to not get excited, but it is not working. The possibility of a baby is making my heart soar. Natalie is the only thing I want more in life than being a father. To have both would be my biggest dream.

'Yes.'

It is all I can get out.

'Try to not get too excited. It might not work.'

'Of course,' I tell her.

Too late.

There is a beautiful silence while we both allow ourselves to hope.

'I better go. Babies do not wait.'

'Okay. See you tonight. I miss you.'

'I miss you too.'

'Love you.'

'Love you more.'

She hangs up and I leave the phone there for a moment. Somehow it still feels connected to her. I give myself a moment to think about my dreams and what it would feel like if they came true. For the first time in a long time, it feels okay to allow myself to have those dreams. Just maybe they are within my reach.

Natalie

I tiptoe into our home so tired it feels like I have a hangover. August is not rush season in baby-making terms: that is September, but baby after baby arrived tonight. I think I did five C-sections in a row. I haven't had a drink for hours and I had to blast rock music to keep myself awake on the drive back. I should start taking taxis.

I go into the kitchen to get some water. My lips are cracked from dehydration and I have a headache. Rob must be in bed. The house is dark and tidy. Rob has almost OCD tendencies. He tidies and declutters relentlessly. I barely notice my surroundings unless I am stress cleaning. But then, I almost never sit still.

I drink my water and look around. I love this house. When we first moved in, it needed work and lacked soul. Now it was perfect. Our home.

The busy shift was a godsend. I had not thought of Amanda once. Now I am away from the hospital, she crept back into my head. For decades I have wanted my sister to become an adult so Rob's words should have made me happy. But they did not. I find it hard to think Amanda has just grown up overnight. I also find it hard to believe that she has had some kind of personality transplant. It takes more than marriage and getting knocked up to go from bitch to Bambi.

I know this is my own bitchiness talking and I hate myself for it. I know I should just move past my resentment and become a forgiving person. But the past never remains so in our family. The wounds never heal because the cuts keep on coming. How can you move past something that stabs you over and over again?

I see my handbag on the kitchen counter and then I remember: the letters. I open the bag and I take them out. There is a proper handful here. How many letters could a handful be? Twenty? Thirty?

My siblings clearly think I should have forgiven my father and become one big, happy family again.

How could that be? The father figure in our life was never there, or pissed when he was. He had more than one affair.

I loved my mother more than anything. I do not think she knew how much. I was extremely hard on her. I guess I am hard on everyone. I always thought that was okay because I am also hard on myself. Harder on myself in fact. Maybe I am wrong.

I try to think that maybe they are right and I am wrong. I was the one ruining our family. By not forgiving someone who made a mistake. I cannot believe I am in my late thirties and yet I still find it hard to comprehend all of these emotions I am feeling.

I did feel warmer to my father before he died. I wanted him to prove me wrong, but he never did. The jabs always came, the memories always lurked. Age softened him, weakened him even and keeping up the level of hate I had felt for him my entire life became too exhausting. My mother drilled it into me that you treated everyone like a human being. No matter if that person was a terrible human being or not. Sure, the adage that you treat people how they treat you is a good one, but it meant that if someone was terrible to you, should you be terrible back to them?

No, I never hide my feelings from my father, but as a grown-up, I had always been civil and polite the few times I did see him. That was a lot more than he deserved from me.

I lost my childhood to that man while he drank and screwed around. He took far more from me than he took from my siblings. A thank you would have been great. I take the first letter and I open it. I lay it on the kitchen counter. I pause for a moment before I read it. The letters could make everything worse. Snakes that played on my emotions. I finish my water and start to read.

Dear Natalie,

I am not always sure why I write to you. I am pretty sure you don't want me to, but I just like to think I am not the monster you think I am. I am flawed and I know that. I have been selfish in my life and hurt a lot of people, but I am your father and I always will be. Please always know that.

Love,

Dad.

I looked at it. "I am your father and I always will be". Yes, that had been the problem. He was my father. I was long past the point in my life where it mattered to me that someone had the same DNA as me. Love was about action. So was being a parent. So was responsibility. I was sick of all of this crap. I just wanted to get back to my life. My life which had been perfectly happy until my sister got pregnant and my father died.

I opened another.

Dear Natalie,

I hear now that you are a doctor. I am so very proud of you. It is a tremendous achievement. You were always so nurturing and caring so it makes sense to me that you would become a doctor and help sick people. On another note, I have always been scared of doctors, so it fits well there too. Ha ha.

Well done again. All my love,

Dad.

I hate how these letters made him sound like a normal human being. Like he had actually given a fuck about me in real life. As for telling me I was nurturing? I would not have had to be so nurturing and looked after everyone if he had decided to be a real parent. Rather than the sorry excuse for a dad that we ended up with. I read through the rest and they make me angry. That old familiar feeling. There was nothing here and I knew it. But then I realised what it was, helped by a line in the letter, "I was always sorry that I hurt your mother and I was very sorry when she died". It was my mother all over again. His death brought up the memory of her death.

Then there was the fact I was an orphan now. I wished my father dead many times in my youth and now that he had died it was still painful. The only comfort I had was the comfort that I would never have to see him again. Those sad, old eyes that masked that other man inside. The man who broke our family and always put himself first. Who destroyed my childhood and made me grow up too fast. He destroyed my mother and robbed me of a future with her. He was gone now but all of the things he had done had not gone with him. They lingered on, echoing into the future. Consequences that reached far and wide. At least he could not cause any more harm. I took comfort from that and as I stood there, it started to get just a little bit better. I decided to open one more letter.

Dear Natalie,

I am sorry for all of the hurt I have caused. I have heard from Amanda that you are still upset at me. She is getting married soon and I would like to try and make amends. I was a human being and I gave in to my weakness. Please find it in your heart to forgive me. We can become friends again and move on for Amanda. Please don't hate me forever. I know you have forgiveness in you. I will meet you anywhere and at any time. My number is 07924926494. Call me please. Let's put the past behind us.

Lots of love,

Dad.

In this one, I saw it and it helped even more. The manipulation, the dismissing. How he downplayed things. How he tried to make me sound unreasonable. Yes, that sounded a lot more like him. I took all of the letters and I put them in the shredder. As I watched them being ripped into tiny little shreds, a sense of happiness came over me. I was letting it go and it felt amazing.

'Hey, you.'

It is Rob. Looking gorgeous and sleepy in his pyjamas.

'Sorry, did the shredder wake you up?'

'No. The lack of your hot body in my bed woke me up.'

I laugh. He always makes me feel loved and adored. Like I am the only woman in the world. Life with Rob was like a Hallmark card. We were cheesy together. I remember once we were kissing in a line at the supermarket and the man in front of us got upset and asked us to stop slurping in his ear. A little old lady had defended us, 'Aw come on, they are so cute together.'

That was last year. We had been together for seven years and I still loved him as much as I did the day I first met him.

'Do you think I should forgive my father?'

'No.'

'Do you think I am too harsh on my father?'

'No.'

'But?'

'But I think we have to put this to rest. Let's talk it through. I want you to work it out in your head.'

'Okay.'

I stand there and hesitate. I do not have the energy.

'But not tonight. I can tell you are tired. You just had a long shift. You should always think things through. Get your head together. Then we will sort everything out. You and me against the world.'

I smile at him. My perfect man. He comes over and kisses me. Then he lifts me up, taking me into his arms.

'Let's get you to bed.'

'Time for a quickie.'

It is Rob's turn to smile.

'Absolutely.'

He practically runs up the stairs. It is a good job he is fit.

Chapter Eighteen
Natalie

I walk fast, needed to get to where I am going before my shift starts. The heat does not help. It is twenty-nine degrees. I know it is August, but this is too much. I finally reach my destination a sweaty mess. I do not think Brits are equipped to deal with this kind of weather. I wipe off my sweat moustache and head down the path surrounded by stones.

The walking is good for me. I put on a stone in break-up weight. I am not sure how I managed it. Comfort food, I guess. Too many doughnuts and too much wine whenever I had a chance. I can feel my stomach wiggle as I walk and my thighs are rubbing together. I need to get those chub rub things I saw advertised on Facebook. It is a ten-minute walk and then I am there.

The stone is beautiful. Marble, polished. A dark grey with Italic engraving.

Jacqueline Holmes.
Much missed wife and mother.
1952-1998.

'Hi Mum.'

I touch the headstone. Despite the heat it has a coolness to it. I close my eyes and breathe in. I am not always sure what I believe but I feel closer to my mother standing here. Amanda wanted to bury our parents together. I would never have allowed him to be here. An eternity next to him. He would have ruined our time together too.

The matter had thankfully been resolved when we found a make-shift unsigned will in a drawer and it turned out he wanted to be buried near his family in Streatham. It was a rare moment of my father making my life easier.

I think of my beautiful mother as I stand here. She died far too soon. I still miss her every single day. I did not miss my father. I just wished things could have been different.

My mother was a warm person. She had love and patience in droves. She was kind to people, even those who did not deserve it. She got a degree from the Open University while taking care of three children on her own.

I put the flowers down. White roses. They were her favourite. I stand and contemplate. Coming here just makes me feel better.

'Hello, you.'

I jump. It is Paul.

'Hey, I didn't know you came here.'

'I don't usually. The family has taken quite a knock recently and I just wanted. Well, I don't know what I wanted. I was just missing Mum. I wanted to get as close to her as I can.'

An awkward silence follows. We have not talked much. Not as much as we used to anyway. We were so close but so much has happened.

'Do you feel free now?'

I look at him. Searching his face for the old Paul I loved so much.

'What do you mean?'

'Now that he is dead.'

The comment stings. I am not a monster.

'I never wanted him dead, Paul. I just didn't want to hang out with him.'

Paul does not know what to say. Then he hugs me.

'He did love you, you know.'

I have an inward scream. What a way to ruin a hug. I pull away from the hug.

'I better go to work. I cannot be late.'

'Of course.'

I walk away as my eyes sting. I need to hold the tears in until I am far enough away. I thought coming here would help somehow, but now I just feel more broken. I have wanted a family my entire life. That nuclear family: two stable parents and a childhood spent in a loving environment. I am further away from that now more than ever. There is only one thing for it. I have to make my own family. Somehow, no matter what.

Here I am again. Stepping towards the pain. Because that is where hope is. On the flip side of devastation. The last time we did this it was brutal. The endless checking of the temperature and the cervical mucus. Having sex every other day. The agony of the two-week wait, followed by the devastating disappointment of a negative pregnancy test. The pressure had been too much. We decided to take a break from it to relieve the stress. But I asked for this. I said that we should have one more go before I hit my even later thirties. Forty seemed to loom over me. After that the odds would be tiny. A scary cut-off number. It would be much harder, if not impossible.

I was not taking any prisoners this time. I bought a mountain of ovulation tests and I was already booked in to see the top fertility specialist in London. There was hope now. I had got past what was haunting me. If it did not happen then we would be sad, but we could move on with no regrets.

I pee on the ovulation stick and wait.

Not today. Oh well. I pull up my pants and wash my hands. I can hear Rob in the kitchen.

'Not today, darling.'

'Really.' He says as he raises an eyebrow.

I can feel the heat he is putting in me. I take my top off and pull down the knickers. I am ready. For a moment he just stares with his mouth open.

'Wow.'

'Want to have some recreational fun?'

'Come over here right now.'

I walk over to Rob as he takes his clothes off. He lifts me up and puts me on top of the kitchen counter and fucks me hard. It feels amazing.

It is efficient sex: fun and quick. It hits the spot. When we finish, he breathes into my neck and kisses me. We stay in an embrace. He smells amazing. Finally, he pulls back.

'Let me get you some food. You deserve some after that.'

Rob starts cooking but does not put on any clothes. This makes me happy. I love his muscular body. He has long legs like a racehorse. He works out and it shows. His bottom is perfectly pert. How the hell could I have let this man go even for a second? I must be a complete idiot.

'You were right, you know.'

'What was I right about, darling?'

'The baby thing.'

'Well, I usually am right about everything,' Rob said, teasing, but also believing it because he was born with total confidence.

I reach forward a bit with my foot and give his bottom a gentle kick.

'Oi!'

I laugh.

'Hey, enough with the cockiness.'

'Really? I thought that was why you loved me?' He raises his eyebrows then winks at me.

'What I was trying to say was that you were right when you said there were other options. I mean, let's be honest. Being child-free sounds like fun. I mean, imagine the travel and the disposable income.

'There are other options too. Adopting would be great. We would be doing good while gaining a child. I would love that. Or fostering. There are so many options. We are both so privileged. We have a lot, and no one gets everything. So, if we don't have our own biological children then, it just is what it is.'

'Exactly. Well said, my Natalie.'

'So, whatever happens today happens.'

Rob comes up and hands me freshly made pancakes with a drizzle of honey and a cup of coffee.

I kiss him and say thank you.

We eat up and head to the fertility clinic, my heart banging in my chest.

We arrive too quickly. I am not ready. My legs feel like they might not work. Rob takes my hand and we head in. We are seen as soon as we arrive. That is usually the case with private doctors. We answer a huge number of questions, then the tests come next.

I lie down and the ultrasound probe goes into my vagina. Oh, the indignity of being a woman. This baby-making thing was not fun at all.

The doctor tested my blood earlier in the month. On day three and day twenty-one of my cycle for progesterone.

Then Rob had to go for a sperm test. All of that had come up fine. My follicle-stimulating hormone and Anti-Müllerian Hormone levels were normal. I was ovulating and had a good number of eggs left. There was nothing obviously wrong, but it was still frustrating. If we knew what was wrong, we could have fixed it. But so far so good, but also; not.

So now here I am. Getting an internal and external ultrasound. I have had my bits checked so many times already and I have a feeling this would just be the start of it. Next would be a Hysterosalpingogram test. Dye injected into my womb and then an X-ray so they could watch it going through, just to check that there was no blockage in my tubes. That sounded like fun, I thought sarcastically and then sighed.

'All okay?' the doctor asked.

'Yes, all okay. Sorry, it is just, well, this is not fun.' I laugh and so did the doctor and Rob.

'It won't be long now. I know it is not pleasant.'

I smiled at him and scanned his face, trying to see in his expression whether or not something was wrong. But he had his poker face on. So I lay back and hoped for the best.

'Right, you can get dressed now. Here is some tissue to wipe yourself.'

The doctor left and I got dressed.

I wonder what he had seen. During the entire process I tried to not get my hopes up and yet tried to remain hopeful. The entire thing was a roller coaster. When it came to wanting something this bad, hope was always the enemy. But I was going to give it all I had. I decided to stay positive. I stopped drinking, was taking prenatal vitamins, eating healthily and I was determined that I would lose the weight I had put on. I would give this everything I had and then if it was not to be, then it was not to be.

'I am ready now,' I said so the medical team would come back in.

Rob squeezes my hand.

The doctor pushed the curtain to the side and smiled at me.

'We will get the results to you in a week. I can tell you now that I did not see anything that would indicate any kind of problem, so that is good news.'

I breathe a sigh of relief. That is good news. Even if the problem remained infuriatingly unspecific.

'You can't see anything wrong at all?' I ask.

'No, there is nothing there that is worrying me. Obviously, I cannot give you a full result at the moment. I will have to check the scans more thoroughly later on.'

'Of course, thank you. That is great news.'

I gather my belongings and we head out of the door. Next up will be the IVF process. I cannot wait.

2004
Natalie

I stand at the threshold. I have been unable to move for five minutes. To walk further would be to step back into chaos. I already had too much of that in my life. It was his phone call that brought me here. Drunk sure, that was the usual, but there had been something else to his voice. A call for help that could not be ignored. And so I was here. Again.

It was time to be brave or leave, and I was always brave, so I walked in. The door was unlocked. Which was good. I did not have a key any more. My eyes had to adjust to the darkness. As I looked around, I wondered how anyone could live like this. The place was a mess, but it was more than that. The place was musky. It made me feel ill. Well, even more ill than I already felt. My nerves had been shot since last night.

'Natalie, you came. I knew you would.'

I jump. There he is. Dishevelled and not even dressed even though it is the afternoon. I just look at him. I cannot think of anything to say. I never could.

'Hi,' I said.

I was going to say hi Tim, but I reckoned, as he was obviously fragile, I should practise kindness. Calling him Dad on the other hand. That was never an option.

'You have been calling me non-stop,' I said, trying to keep the irritation out of my voice. I had to take sick leave from my studies to be here. I had never called in sick before and I resented it. I would have to work twice as hard to catch up now.

'I am sorry about that, love. It is just, I'm very sick. I have been very sick. Amanda and Paul are both away. Come on, help out your pa.'

I look at this pathetic excuse for a man and wish I was not related to him. It is embarrassing. I wish I was not as good a person as I am. I wish I could shut off my conscious. I wish I was more like him. When it came to ruthlessness anyway.

'What is it that you need, Tim?' This time I did not hold back. I was the parent again. He was making me the parent again. So he could deal with the consequences.

He flinched when he heard his name. He always flinched but you would think that he would get used to it. I look at him. He looks pathetic. He is in his boxer shorts and a vest. They were both probably white once but not now. Now they were yellowed. His hair is greasy and is plastered against his head. The smell coming off him is not just booze. No, it is clearly a mixture of delights. It is awful and made me wretch if I got too close. That is not going to happen anyway. The house is just as much of a mess as he is. If such a thing is possible. There are plates everywhere with half-eaten food, dirty clothes on every surface, newspapers and magazines piled up. It is hard to believe that this had been my childhood home. That there was actually about four good years that I had actually been happy here.

'Well, I just need someone to look after me. I need to eat, don't I? There is nothing in the house,' Tim said aggressively.

It was like it was my fault or something.

'Have you been taking drugs, Tim? You seem a little out of it.' I am scared to ask this question, but I have to. I am also confident I could get away if he lunged at me.

Tim's face darkens and he furrows his brow. The question did not make him happy.

'I just need to eat, Natalie. I am sick and I need help. I would prefer some gratitude, y'know. I did raise you after all. I looked after you and Paul and Amanda.'

I laughed at that. He could not even look after himself never mind his children. Tim gave me another glare. He clearly did not like being laughed at. I did not care.

'I will go and get you some food, Tim. Then I have to go back to uni. I am busy, I don't have time to deal with your hangovers or whatnot.'

I look straight at Tim as I say it. Daring him to argue with me. To say or do anything. He doesn't, because he knows I would leave then and he needs supplies.

'I will give you a list. Get me some pen and paper.'

I look around. 'Where from?'

'The drawer in the TV unit behind you.'

I pull out the drawer and find a pen and some paper. I hand it to Tim, holding my breath as I do. He is pungent.

It takes him five minutes to write his list. He thrusts it back in my direction. I take it, and he tries to pull it back as I do, so I let it go. He hands it back out again and lets me take it this time. I take a step back and then put my hand out. Tim looks at it blankly before it dawns on him.

'Oh, I don't have any money.'

I look at him with disgust. He should have plenty, but I guess he has either spent it all or is lying to me.

'Great. Guess I am paying for this then.'

Tim's face brightens and he smiles at me.

'Thank you so much, my sweet daughter. That would be so great of you.'

I try to not feel the level of hate and anger that is seeping upwards. I am a poor student who is doing crap minimum wage jobs to get by. With an occasional well-paid promotional job thrown in for good measure. The nerve of him. I hate him. I can actually feel it.

'You must have some money. Your student loan, and Amanda said you were working. That some of your jobs paid very well. You would not have some money, would you? It is just that I cannot afford the heating, or food, or a little drink once in a while. It's no way to live.' Tim smiles at me, a yellow smile that shows that half his teeth are missing.

I feel the anger rise in me. He knows I find it hard to say no. I always break in the end. I wish I could stand up to him. He has always been able to rely on me. Only I do not have any money. I am struggling myself. Some groceries, fine. But any more than that is not fair. I do not know what to say so I just look at him. This clearly angers him.

'Natalie, I have blown through the money. I have re-mortgaged this place. You are my daughter and it is your place to help me. I have a problem. It is not my fault. You must know that. Addiction is an illness. I am trying to get better, love.'

'I will see what I can do, Tim.'

My heart feels like it is falling to the floor. Tim smiles at me as I leave.

I purposely did not look at the list when he handed it to me. I figured there would be a few things on there that would piss me off. And yes, there they were. Alcohol. Cigarettes. Hell, I was surprised there was no drugs on here. I sigh and then put a pound in the trolly. I want to finish this as soon as possible. I go to the vegetables and fruit aisle first and load up on tomatoes, mushrooms, sweet potato, cucumber and peppers. Then I go to the other aisles, picking up pulses and grains. I add bread, butter and milk. Essentials and healthy foods that he is not going to like. Nope, he would not like this at all. But I did not care. He is his own worst enemy and I am sick of being dragged down with him.

I take it all to the till and it costs me a fortune. I will probably have to eat beans and toast for the foreseeable future. My rent is huge, my living expenses astronomical, never mind the cost of studying. A kernel of resentment is growing. I have to leave this man behind or he will keep dragging me down. He has the power to destroy me. I have to put myself first now. I have to escape. But could I do it? He is my father. My blood and DNA. He has an illness, clearly. I am studying to fix people after all.

I hope I will find the strength inside of me to get some space from him. I need a break from the toxic cycle of bingeing and recovery. I get into my car and head back to the family home. The family home which contains no family. When I get there, I grab all of the bags at once. They are very heavy and they pull on my arms, jarring the shoulder. Luckily the distance to the front door is not far, otherwise it feels like my arms would come out of their sockets.

I put all of the bags down on the mat outside the front door. I give myself a moment and then knock. Then I turn and quickly get back into my car and drive away. I have done enough. I do not have any more to give. I look in the rear-view mirror as I drive away and I watch him open the door and see the bags. He looks happy enough. But then, that was all he wanted. It was never about doing anything for anyone else.

My tutors were happy to see me back so soon and told me as much. I told them it had turned out to just be a twenty-four-hour bug. Returning to my own life was a tremendous relief. The amount of space between my father and I was a good start. I wish it was the distance to the moon, but oh well. He had been calling me all day, but I figured either he wanted something else, or he was not happy that I had only bought a few things from his list. I ignored the phone all day, choosing happiness over politeness, because I was done with all of that. The day of hardcore studying made me happy. Throwing myself into work was the only thing I had. The only thing that kept me sane and on track. I walked out of uni and into the street, pulling my phone out of my pocket as I did. I would listen to his messages now. I looked at my notifications. There were twenty-eight. Jeez. This was going to be fun. I guessed he had nothing better to do.

I put the phone to my ear and waited for the first message. It only took me a moment to regret it. He was in one of his abusive moods.

'Natalie, I thought you were actually smart. I gave you a list. A clearly written list and you just couldn't follow it. I don't know if you are just stupid or if you were being a bitch like your mother. I need the things I asked you for. If you come back immediately with them, I will forgive you. If not…'

He did not finish the sentence, maybe thinking better of it. A rare moment of self-restraint. I listened to the rest of the messages. Each one was more abusive than the last. I felt the tears roll down my cheeks. I tried to control myself, but it was no use. He had called me a bitch, a terrible person and a whore. He had even brought up my mother who had been nothing but a saint for putting up with him.

I tried to console myself with the fact it was probably the booze or the comedown from whatever else he had taken, but it did not excuse his behaviour. He had no right to treat me like that. I would not stand for it. This was the end of our relationship. I would never allow this to happen again. It was time to realise that blood was not enough, and that it never had been.

Rob

I sit at the edge of the bed and watch Natalie sleep. Last night was another late one, but we had managed to fit in a quickie. We were having sex every other day. Even when she was not ovulating. It was full on baby-making mode. One hoped anyway.

She looked so peaceful. It was one of her pass-out-from-exhaustion sleeps. I stroke her chestnut dark brown hair. It is incredibly soft. I cannot help myself. I kiss her on the forehead. I stand up and go to leave.

'Hey, you. Come back here and snuggle me.'

I smile and climb into the bed. I put my arm around Natalie and she nuzzles into my chest.

'I am so happy.'

'So am I.'

Natalie's phone buzzes. I take it from the nightstand and hand it to her.

'It is Amanda. She says they have a buyer for the house,' she says, sounding happy.

'That's great.'

'I guess so but I will believe it when I see it. These things tend to be drawn out.'

'No apology.'

'Nope.'

'You have to make sure you get your fair share of the money.'

'I will.'

I pause and think for a second. I have never been particularly close to my parents, but they were reasonable people. Their marriage was a happy one and it has lasted for forty years so far. I cannot even begin to understand what life has been like for Natalie.

'That was the last thing I had to do with him. Before Paul and Amanda decided he would be part of our family again.'

'Giving him the money?'

'Yes. He was really abusive to me that time I saw him, I think I told you about that. He was clearly on a comedown and he wanted money from me. I got him some shopping and he left all of these abusive messages on my phone.'

'He really was a creep.'

'Years later he turned up at a hospital I was working at and told me the house was about to be taken by the bank. He manipulated me by saying I should help Amanda and Paul. Anyway, I did in the end. I managed to fix something with the bank. Take out yet another mortgage, managed to pay it off, but I never had anything else to do with him. It took me ages to find my voice and stand up to him. When I did, I felt free. Life without him was always happy. I think that is why I was so angry when he was brought back into my life, and I was being bullied all over again. Not by one person, but by three.'

'You have every right to be angry. He treated you appallingly. He did not treat Paul or Amanda like that. Otherwise, it would be a different story. Hold on one moment.'

I get up and run downstairs, grab the box I am looking for and get back into bed.

'What is that?'

'It is a little box of mementoes. Stuff I have collected from your childhood. I have put it all in this one box. We are going to go through it and sort out all of this crap today. Then we are going to get closure.'

Natalie opens the box. It is full of family pictures, letters, diaries, birth and death certificates. Everything I could find went into this box.

I watch as Natalie goes through it. Her face a mixture of sadness and mental exhaustion. I can tell she wants this to end soon. It has to. We have to let go of the stress and put the past to bed for our future.

Then I see a calmness come over her.

'This stuff does not have the same effect on me any more. I can look through this stuff and feel detached. But also, normal. I am not broken. It is because of you. You make me happy. I feel like I have a home with you.'

'You do have a home with me. We are each other's family. We are all we need.'

'I don't think this is going to make me forgive my father. Or love him for that matter. If he did any of the things he did in isolation, then maybe I could have forgiven him. Alcoholism is a disease, infidelity, I could have forgiven him for that. For being weak. There was occasional drug use. That is not forgivable. But he was never a father. He never looked after us. If you add it all together then it's just.'

Natalie stops and thinks.

'It is just that this is not going to make me love my father.'

'Well, that's not the aim.'

'How can that not be the aim?'

'Closure's the aim.'

'Ah. That old gem. But is closure ever achievable? Can you ever file something away in your brain and it just stays there, not fucking you up?'

'That, my dear Natalie, is a very good question. So, let's do this. Did you have good times?'

'No.'

'Was he a father?'

'No.'

'Was there something in the relationship that was good that you no longer have?'

'No.'

'It's about you realising that you were right. You didn't miss anything. The closure is that all of these people are saying you should have fixed your relationship. There was nothing to fix. He was an asshole. I mean, really. The biggest asshole I ever met in my life. He had very rare moments where he was a human being. And it is sad for you that you didn't get a father. I am sure there is a hole in your life because of that, and that is shitty, but everyone has something in their life that they don't get. There is no such thing as a perfect family. You know I have had issues with my dad. That my mother is a fire-breathing dragon.'

Natalie laughs and takes my hand. My mother has always been horrible to her and she has always taken it well.

'But if your father was my father, I would have punched him every time I saw him. I wouldn't have been as nice as you. You raised your siblings. You have always been their rock. You held your family together. Paul knows that, I know that. Hell, I think even Neil knows that. Your sister has always been a spoilt child, but I reckon even she knows that. So, head up and screw them. Closure done.'

Natalie leans in and gives me a huge kiss. Then she stays there, nose to nose with me. I sigh a happy sigh.

'Now come on. There is someone we have to say this to.'

'What? Who?' Natalie asks as I start putting my clothes on. I beckon her to do the same.

'No, I do not want to get dressed. I want to stay in bed all day.'

'Tough, get up. We need to do this.'

The rain pours down, fat droplets land in sizeable puddles. It is almost September and I think maybe it is time to stop dressing for summer. We are in the middle of Streatham cemetery and now we are both damp.

'I cannot believe you dragged me out here. Do you not remember what happened last time? They probably have a picture of me up somewhere.'

I laugh.

'You did have a bit of a moment.'

'But you were so sweet.'

I smile at her. It was a moment of connection during a brutal time.

'It was a moment of hope. I always wished we would get back together. Even though you were such a mean girl.'

Natalie strokes me.

'I'm sorry, I was a mean girl.'

'You were also mean at the karaoke.'

She fixes me a look.

'I thought you were big on forgiveness at the moment.'

'Yes sorry, but feel free to make it up to me at some point.'

'Oh, I will,' she replies with a flirty look. I smile back at her.

'Come on. Get on with it.'

Natalie stands there tentatively.

'Go on. Tell him.'

Natalie nods and then she starts.

'I forgive you. I am not saying that what you did was okay, or that I will ever be okay with it. But I am going to let it go, just like I'm going to let you go. You were never the father I wanted you to be, but I forgive you for that. We don't always get what we want in life. Some holes remain empty, unfilled with promises that others couldn't be bothered to keep and that is okay, because I am happy with my life. I didn't get a father, but I have a family, and I love them. For who they are and who they are not. I lay you to rest, but more importantly, I lay our relationship to rest. All it was, was what it was. Nothing more and nothing less. And I forgive you for that.'

The last comment brings tears to her eyes. Which became fiercer and fiercer until she is weeping. I put my arms around her and hold her tight.

'Do you feel any better?'

'I do.'

I hope that is true. The ghosts need to be put to rest.

Chapter Nineteen

Natalie

The nurses are prepping my latest patient. I wait in the on-call room and send Rob a text.

All tests have come back negative. Good news.xx

It is good news, but I cannot help feeling sad. If we knew what was wrong, we could fix it. That is what I spend my life doing. I know I am a control freak, so the unknown is not my friend.

I need to go and do a laparoscopy. Some poor woman has had an ectopic pregnancy. They are one of the worst things about my job.

The surgery goes well and I head to the labour ward. I have been beeped. They need a consult on a possible C-section for a woman who has been labouring for a while. Now her baby is in distress.

The woman is a twenty-something called Sharon. She looks scared. The midwife fills me in as I smile her way, trying to put her at ease. When she finishes, I go and sit by her bed.

'Hello, Sharon. My name is Natalie and I am the consultant here. I understand you have been labouring for a while now and we think that baby is tired. We recommend that you have a Caesarean section now. What do you think about that?'

Sharon nods. I can tell she is relieved.

'Okay, I just need you to read this form and sign it.'

Sharon does not read it. She just signs as quickly as possible. George walks in.

'She has already had an epidural. She just needs topped up.' I tell him.

'Okay. I will do that now.'

I head off to prepare and get the theatre ready. These are the moments that I live for. The moments where I actually make a difference.

After the operation, I bump into George in the on-call room.

'You look exhausted.'

'Thanks.'

George pulls a face. 'It's not an insult.'

'Sorry. I probably am.'

'Too much shagging the boyfriend probably.'

I laugh.

'No one says "shagging" any more.'

'Don't they? I guess I must be old then.'

'Well, I didn't want to say.'

George pretends to be offended. I laugh some more. I am happy to have him as a friend.

'How are things?'

'Things are good. Rob and I are happy. I am back in my house. We worked through it.'

'Good.'

'How are the wife and kids?'

'They are all good.'

It is small talk, but it never feels that way with George.

'Rob and I are thinking of trying for a baby.'

George looks surprised.

'That is wonderful news. You would be an amazing mother.'

I feel happy. George's comment means the world to me.

'Thank you. It might not happen though. I am thirty-seven.'

'Wasn't Meghan Markle thirty-seven when she had her first?'

'Yeah.'

'It is fine. You should know, Natalie. You are a doctor for God's sake.'

'Yes, but that means I have seen the other side.'

'Try and then have IVF. You have good odds.'

'You're right.'

I pause. I do not want to talk about this as much as I do want to talk about it.

'We have been trying actually. For years. We had a miscarriage.'

George looks upset.

'Natalie, I had no idea. I'm so sorry.'

'It's okay.'

'No, it's not. You do not have to pretend to be okay. If you ever want to talk about it then let me know.'

George comes and takes my hand.

'Maybe we should go straight for IVF.'

'I think so. Do you have a doctor in mind?'

'Yes. I have a good recommendation. I had a fertility check-up recently and they didn't find anything wrong.'

'Perfect. I would go private. The NHS is a bit of a lottery and you might struggle to fit it in around work. You and Rob have money, right?'

'Yes, we are very lucky. Thanks, George. I think it is time to be brave and get on with it.'

'You are one of the bravest people I know. Onwards you go.'

I smile at George. I feel better.

Then
Jacqueline

I look at Natalie and I cannot believe how much she has grown. Her legs are so long. I had to take more of her clothes to the charity shop this week.

I watch as Tim picks her up and twirls her around. She can be such a daddy's girl. She loves him so much and follows him around everywhere, usually with Amanda toddling along behind. It is so sweet to watch.

But then he is twirling her too fast and I get an ache in my stomach. Tim always tells me I worry too much. Tim has never been one to think about consequences. He tends to just jump into the deep end. I think my life would be easier if I felt I could leave him alone with our daughters. He is just too unobservant. Everything feels like a risk.

It is not that he is a bad person, or that he would deliberately harm his children; he is just reckless. More of a child himself than a man. I don't even wish I knew that before I met him now, because then I would not have our beautiful children. And he was good with them. In his own way. He loved them and played with them. He fawned over the new baby who he said looked just like him. I wasn't sure about that, but, whatever. He is a gorgeous, little bundle. Though his cry could wake the dead. Not Tim though, he has never got up during the night. Not even once. Which I resent.

I understand he has to go to work, but I have to take care of three tiny human beings. A night off would not hurt him. The worst that would happen to him was that he would lose his job. I, on the other hand, am responsible for the lives of our children. The margin for error is much more severe. Now I have three. Yikes. I really am outnumbered.

We called the baby Paul. He is five days old now and since his birth, a truce seems to have started between us. Maybe it is because he finally got the son he wanted, or maybe he was feeling bad that he had been so awful during the birth. He was cooking a lot and he even brought back some flowers the last time he went to get groceries. Maybe my dreams of a proper family will pay off after all. Forgiving him was the right thing to do.

He has been playing with Natalie for a while now. It is rare for him to focus all of his attention on her for such a large block of time. Amanda is napping so maybe he just appreciates the one-on-one with her. It is sweet and it makes me smile. Yes, I am hoping that this is the start of a change.

Now
Natalie

I open the door for George and Bethany.

'Hello, thank you so much for coming.'

'Thank you for having us,' Bethany said.

'Yes, thank you, Natalie,' George said.

I kiss them both on the cheek and then move out of the way so they can get in. They take their shoes off and follow me through to the kitchen.

'This is Rob. I think you might have met him before, George.'

'I think I did, at something or another.'

They shake hands.

'Nice to see you again, Rob.'

'Nice to see you, George, lovely to meet you, Bethany.'

Rob kisses Bethany on the cheek.

'You have such a lovely home. This kitchen is amazing.'

'Thank you, we got it renovated a while ago. We have done the house up bit by bit. We bought it six years ago. I have no idea what it is worth now.'

George looks impressed.

'A fortune, I am sure. Property prices in London are insane. We bought ours a long time ago. Could never afford it now,' George said.

'What can I get you to drink? Wine? Coffee? Tea?'

'Some wine would be great,' George said.

'George is such a lush.' I tease him.

'Red or white?' Rob asks, ignoring my crack.

'Red, thanks.'

'Red for me too.'

Rob hands George and Bethany their glasses and then hands me a glass too. I take it and drink a sip but then I put it down.

'So, Rob, what do you do?'

As Rob gets into the details of his work life, I feel my phone vibrate. I look at the screen. It is Paul. Other than our awkward encounter in the graveyard I have not heard from my brother in a while. I wonder how he and Amanda got along with clearing out the house.

Amanda and I are sorry. We would love to speak to you.

I ignore it. I do not have time for this BS and drama tonight. I hear my phone ping again.

I would also like to apologise personally. I was mean to you in the graveyard. I should have respected your feelings on Dad. I should never have tried to force the relationship. I hope you can forgive me and we can be friends again. I miss you.

This one makes me smile. It takes a big person to admit their fault and apologise. It is all I have ever wanted. I text back.

Thank you. I appreciate that. Let's meet up soon. xx

'Ah, Nat.'

I look at Rob.

'We have guests, darling.'

'Sorry, I know it is rude to be on the phone. It is Paul and he has finally apologised.'

'That is amazing, Natalie. I am pleased for you. I hope your sister apologises too now. It is so crap, everything you have been through.'

'Thank you, George.' I am touched by his kindness.

'That is great news, my darling. I am so happy for you.'

'Siblings are such hard work, aren't they? I have not talked to my sister in years.'

I look at Bethany, surprised. I never knew she had a sister.

'Yes, they are. Well, they can be. Maybe there is a perfect family out there somewhere.'

'I doubt it. Every family has issues,' Rob said.

We all nod in agreement.

'Let's all sit down. The food will be ready soon.'

'I am glad you could come tonight. I feel so sorry for everything I put you through. That awful dinner with my family, and then my father dying while I was staying with you. You are both such good friends.'

'Natalie, stop apologising. None of that was your fault. We were happy to be there for you. You needed someone on your side,' George said.

'You definitely made our suburban life more interesting,' Bethany adds.

'God, yes, nothing was ever dull while you stayed with us.'

We all laugh but I can see a little sadness in Rob's eyes. This was the period when I left him. Apart from jokey comments we have never really talked much about what happened when we were apart. It has become too difficult for either of us to talk about unless it was in a jokey way. We just want to forget about it and move on. I take his hand and squeeze it. He squeezes it back and gives me a smile.

We all sit down and talk about everything from family to Brexit. I look at my friends and I look at my fiancé. Life seems close to perfect but I cannot help thinking about my sister. Our relationship broke years ago. We tried to repair the fractures sometimes, but the breaks always appeared again. Maybe I just had to do what Bethany did and cut her out, but I do not want to do that. It makes me feel sad that Bethany does not talk to her sister. Amanda is my sister and I love her. Despite everything, she is my family. I need her in my life. I need to do something to fix our relationship, but I do not know how.

Rob can see that I am feeling sad and he kisses my hand and keeps off the subject. The rest of the evening is fun and ends far too fast.

'Thank you so much for coming,' I tell them.

They thank us and leave. Just as they walk away, I see a shape near the gate. A pregnant shape. Amanda?

I walk down, and as I do, I hear George saying hello to her. As I get closer, she sees me and turns.

'Hi, Natalie.'

'Hi.'

'You really should go inside. It's cold,' George said.

'Yes, come inside, Amanda. It's freezing.'

She looks relieved and breaks out into a smile.

'Thanks, Natalie.'

'Bye, guys,' I say to George and Bethany and give them a wave. They wave back.

'Nice to see you again, Amanda,' George says and weaves a little as he walks. We put a good amount of wine into them.

'Get home safe.'

They nod and walk away.

I look at Amanda. She must be over three months now and her bump is really showing.

'You look great,' I tell her. I mean it.

'Thank you.'

I walk inside and she follows me.

'Hi, Amanda,' Rob says as she walks past. I can tell he is wary. He probably wanted the rest of the evening to be a quiet one. I am sure that isn't going to happen now.

When Amanda came back with our father, we had slowly and tentatively rebuilt our relationship. We had always tiptoed around each other when it came to Father, or Amanda leaving with him. That was when our relationship worked. When we avoided our differences and focused on the things that made us sisters. Not having my father in my life left no void. I simply did not care. But not having Amanda there always left a hole.

She walks through to the kitchen and we just look at each other. Neither giving anything away. Neither of us saying a word. I do not give. Then I see it. A tear falls down Amanda's cheek.

'He was a drunk. He showed no remorse at all. He was always on-guard and dismissive about all of the crappy stuff he did. What he did was awful and unforgivable. And Mum. Mum was doing her best in an impossible situation. He was all she had and so she had no one. I remember he said about the affair once,

"Sometimes you just have to hurt people", and he did that a lot. Because he was selfish and awful and heartless. But he was also my father and he was the only father that I had and I have a heart, and my heart could never manage to stop loving him. I am sorry for that. I am so sorry. He was always good to me, so I forgave him everything. I needed a father in my life and I made sure that happened at any cost. Mum forgave me for leaving with him. Her love was pure.'

Amanda is crying now. Hard and fast. Wracking sobs of past trauma coming up for the first time. She is almost hysterical. I go to her and pull her in. I cuddle her and kiss her on the cheek.

'It is okay. It's all going to be okay. We have each other, and we have Paul and Nathaniel. And we have Neil and Rob. It is all okay.' I say this over and over to her as I stroke her hair. We stay there for the longest time and things finally feel like they are going to be all right.

I can see Amanda looking longingly at the wine she cannot have as I help myself to some leftovers. I am so happy to have my sister in my life again. I love her so much. For every bad thing about her there are hundreds of good ones. Just like everyone else, I guess. I have been too hard on her, I know that. I was projecting and it caused harm.

'I am sorry too, Amanda. I have not been fair to you. I was projecting.'

'Don't be silly, Natalie. I was being mean. I know that. I was being a bully. You are completely right. I should have respected you and your feelings about Dad.'

I smile. I have wanted to hear these words for so long. There were times I have felt that maybe it was all in my head. That the problems were only mine.

'That means a lot. Thank you for saying it. I want you to know that I'm really sorry. I have not been honest with you and that isn't fair.'

Amanda looks at me. I have to somehow find the courage. I have never been good at laying myself bare.

'Rob and I have been trying for a baby.'

Amanda squeals and puts her hands to her face.

'That is amazing. I'm so happy for you!'

'But it has been years and nothing has happened.'

Amanda's face drops as she takes the words in.

'Oh, Natalie. I'm so sorry.'

'So, I have gone off the rails a bit this summer because of that, and Dad, and maybe even some other things. I have just found things very tough. I broke up with Rob because I thought I would never give him a child and then Dad died. Things just escalated and I am so happy you can see my point of view now. But I also want you to know that I could have been kinder.'

Now it is my turn to cry. Amanda comes and puts her arms around me. She kisses me on the top of my head.

'Then I am doubly sorry because I have been so insensitive. I hope you can forgive me and all of my mean comments.'

'Of course. Don't be silly.'

'You will have a baby. I just know it and when you do you will be an amazing mother.'

I smile.

'Thank you. I hope you are right. We are having IVF now. I have to inject myself every day and go to the clinic every other day. It is intense.'

'Jesus. You on hormones. I think I might hide in a bunker.'

I laugh.

'You are such a bitch.'

'I know, but I am a funny bitch.'

'Hmm. The jury is out.'

'Poor Rob too.'

'Yeah okay, you are not exactly an easy-going person yourself.'

'Well, that is true.'

We look at each other. Honesty melding us together again. Sisters at last.

'We need to talk to each other more.'

'I know, Amanda. I am sorry. I will be more open.'

We stand there and hug for a while.

'Let's let Paul know we have made up. We should tell him about the baby thing too.'

I feel awful.

'Paul already knows,' I say sheepishly.

Amanda sighs.

'You two always leave me out.'

I think about how untrue this was over the summer. I have been the one left out. On the narrowest of margins. I let it go.

'Well, we won't any more. I promise.'

'Good.'

Amanda FaceTimes Paul. He answers and looks elated when he sees my face.

'Well, this is exciting!'

'We made up,' Amanda said.

'And we are never going to fall out ever again,' I say.

'Really?' Amanda looks at me, not believing it.

'Yeah, we can argue but let's not fall out again. It's silly.'

'Yeah! I agree.'

'Does this mean I have also been forgiven?' Paul asks.

We both look at him with poker faces.

'I will think about it,' I tell him.

Paul gives me a puppy dog look.

'Oh, okay then.'

'Look at that. We are a family again,' Amanda said.

'Yes, we are,' I agree.

I feel so happy. Letting go never felt so good.

There is a crying on the other end.

'I have to go. That is Nathaniel. He keeps having nightmares.'

'Bye, give him our love,' I tell him.

'I will. See you both soon.'

Paul hangs up.

'I have some no-alcohol wine we should crack open.'

Amanda screws up her nose.

'You mean grape juice?'

'Yes, but fizzy grape juice.'

'Well, a bit of fizz always makes everything better.'

I go and get the bottle and open it. As I do I see Rob hovering in the door.

'It is safe to come in, darling.'

'Phew. I was thinking the worst.'

'Sorry for the intrusion into your evening, Rob.'

'Completely worth it if you two have made up, Amanda. Nice to have the family back together.'

'Thank you. It is, isn't it?'

I hand Amanda a glass and have one myself.

'Do you want some no-alcohol wine?' I ask Rob.

'God no. That sounds like an abomination.'

Amanda and I laugh.

'It is not that bad,' Amanda says after taking a sip.

'So, talk to me about the baby stuff. Are you having enough sex? You might just be missing your fertile days.'

I spit out my wine and Rob looks like he might faint.

'Amanda!'

'What?'

'I forgot that you have no filter.'

'You love the fact I have no filter.'

I think about this.

'You're right, I do.'

'So?'

'It is unexplained infertility. So, we are going to have IVF just in case. My age does not help.'

'I will cross my fingers. It would be so cool if we had children the same age.'

'I agree. Then they could terrorise each other like we did. It would build up their character.'

I laugh but Amanda does not find it as funny.

'Hmm.'

Suddenly the smile falls from her face and she looks like she is about to cry. She comes in to hug me.

'I missed you so much. I really did.'

I put my arms around her and hug her back. I stroke her back as she cries into my shoulder. I look over at Rob. He smiles at me and leaves the room, giving us space.

'It's okay, Amanda. We are friends again. We will work through everything. It's all going to be okay.'

Amanda pulls away and wipes her eyes.

'I hope so.'

Amanda looks embarrassed for a moment but then she looks around and notices that Rob has gone.

'I mean it, Natalie. I want us to fix our relationship. I am willing to go to therapy. I am willing to talk it out. I think that we got stuck into who we were as children.

You were always the adult and we relied on you too much. It wasn't fair.'

'I would like that, Amanda. I want to fix things. We need to move on. You're right.'

We both stand there, the ice thawing.

'Can I get you anything? Tea, coffee? I think we have some lemonade.'

'A tea would be great.'

'Okay. I have decaf.'

I fill up the kettle and switch it on. I go to the cupboard and I get the teabags, then I remember that Amanda takes sugar in her tea. Neither Rob nor I take sugar in our tea, but I try to always have some sachets in the house. After some searching, I find some sachets I pinched on a drunken jaunt to McDonald's.

I hand her the tea.

'How is the pregnancy going? Any morning sickness?'

'A little. The pregnancy hasn't been too bad. I'm glad I am past the twelve-week mark now.'

I can see Amanda looking around, thinking about things.

'This is such a beautiful house. You have done it up so well.'

'Thank you.'

We both stand there and a feeling of sadness comes over me. This is all small talk. I want to be able to talk about everything with my sister. I want us to be best friends again.

'I really hope the IVF works.'

Amanda's face breaks out into a smile.

'Me too. At least you have the money to do it privately. Is that why you got so upset when we were shopping for baby clothes?'

'Yes. It was. That was not about Dad. I just used him as an excuse. I'm sorry I did that.'

'Don't be sorry. I understand now. It all makes sense. You getting upset, you breaking up with Rob. I am sorry that I hurt you and caused you pain.'

'It wasn't your fault. A lot was going on. I should have handled it better.'

'Come on. Let's go into the living room. It will be more comfortable.'

We head into the living room with our tea and sit down. We sit on the sofa together and I turn on the TV. There is some comforting trashy reality television programme on. Amanda puts her head on my shoulder and we watch the show together. I look at her and feel happy. I finally have my sister back. We are a family again.

Rob

I leave Natalie and her sister to it. It is nice to see them becoming friends again. Maybe things are getting back to where they are supposed to be. I walk up to our bedroom and sit in the chair by the window. Some of the leaves have already fallen off the trees and turned that beautiful shade of autumn orange. Summer may be in full swing but autumn is nipping at its heels.

I can hear them in the kitchen and listen as they walk to the living room. It is best that they have some time together to bond. I pick up my book to read but my phone vibrating in my pocket stops me. It is Neil.

'Hi, mate. How are you?'

'I am good. How is it going?'

I laugh.

'You know she is here then?'

'Of course. I drove her. I'm in the car outside.'

I have a think.

'Okay, let's go to the pub. I think they are going to be a while.'

I change into some jeans then I walk down the stairs.

'I'm going out,' I shout.

'Okay, darling. See you later.'

I walk down the garden path and look around. I cannot see him. A beep diverts my attention. Ah, there he is. He is parked quite far away on the other side of the road. I walk towards him, enjoying the cool air on my face.

Neil opens the door as I approach. I get in.

'Hi.'

'Hi.'

Neil looks at me expectantly.

'They have made up.'

Neil fist punches the air.

'Yes. I was hoping that would happen.'

'I'm happy about it. It's sad the family's had such a tough time.'

'I agree.'

'Should we go to the pub, mate? It looks a bit weird, two men just sitting in a car.'

'Yeah, of course.'

Neil drives off.

'This one here is good.'

I point to the Golden Goose. It is a family pub that is close to us. It has great food and is not too expensive.

Neil spends ten minutes finding a parking space and then we head in.

'What do you want, Neil?'

'A beer would be great.'

'Okay.'

I go and order two beers as Neil finds us some seats. He is fiddling on his phone when I bring them over.

'I texted Amanda to let her know we are here.'

'Good, she will let Natalie know.'

We both take a sip and look around. There are few better places to be on a weekend than in a pub having a pint.

'How did she take it when she told her?'

'Told her what?'

'About the twins.'

I almost spit out my beer.

'You are having twins. Wow.'

'Oh. You didn't know, did you?'

'No. I did not.'

'Why hasn't she told Natalie? That is what she went to do.'

I take this in. Shit. I thought she went there to apologise. Not inadvertently rub salt into the wound.

'You okay? You look worried.'

'No. It is fine. She apologised.'

Neil just looks at me.

'Amanda apologised to Natalie. I thought that is what she came to do.'

Neil is still just looking at me.

'Oh. That is good, I guess. Amanda apologised and they made up.'

'It is good.'

'I hope Natalie apologised too.'

'Well, she did. Not that she had to as much as Amanda. It has been awful how badly Amanda and Paul have been treating Natalie.'

Neil just stays quiet. There is always that boss/employee dynamic in the background.

'It was so weird how they fell out. Amanda thinks it was because people kept asking Natalie when she was going to get married and settle down, you know, have kids and such, and she just freaked out. Then she took it out on Amanda. Amanda thinks you two probably had fertility problems. It was so weird you never had kids. Then the stuff with their father too. Not a good mix. Of course, she broke up with you in that crazy way. It is so good of you to take her back. None of it was your fault,

Rob. Some people just can't do commitment. Some people are not family orientated.'

I feel a flash of anger. So much for my assumption on boss/employee deference.

'Neil, Natalie practically raised two children. She was like another mother to Amanda. She did everything, so do not say she is not family orientated. There is no one who cares about family more than Natalie.'

I try to hide just how pissed off I am about the comment, but it clearly doesn't work. Neil looks at me sheepishly.

'Sorry. I did not mean to offend you. I guess it is all perspective, isn't it? We both just love our women.'

'It's fine. Just please do not mention the break-up again. We are over that and we sorted it all out.'

'Okay.'

'A relationship only happens between two people. No one else knows what really happens.'

'That is true, mate.'

We sit in the awkwardness for a moment.

'God, are you really having twins?'

That will break it.

'Yes. Amanda is happy because now she knows why she is carrying so big.'

I suppress a laugh. I wonder if Neil has told Amanda she is "carrying big" to her face. Neil notices that I am trying to not laugh but thankfully finds the humour in it.

'Yeah, I know, mate. You have to say "carrying big". If you value your life anyway. Not that she is fat or anything. But I did think that was one big baby.'

We both laugh but then the sad thoughts come back again.

'You all right? What is wrong?'

'Yeah, sorry. I was just worrying how Natalie would take the news.'

I think it is best to be honest. Amanda will tell him everything Natalie said anyway.

'Yeah, so is Amanda. She told Natalie she was pregnant straight away and she didn't seem to take it well. I mean, she thought she was happy, but something else was there.'

'When did she tell her?'

'Oh, I can't remember,' Neil said, although it was clear that he did.

I look at him.

'Okay, fine. It was the day before she broke up with you.'

'That makes sense. We have been trying to have a baby for a while. That is why she took it badly.'

Neil looks surprised and then sad.

'I'm sorry. I had no idea.'

'It's okay. It is what it is.'

'Do you want to talk about it?'

'Not really. We are having IVF at the moment. Hopefully that will work. If not, maybe we will adopt.'

I can see guilt pass over Neil's face.

'I'm sorry I was going on about having twins. I feel awful now.'

'Don't be silly. It really is okay. I am happy for you. Natalie is happy for Amanda too.'

'Phew, good.' Neil says in a jokey way to try and lighten the mood.

'We should talk about sport now or something. Let's get back into the safe zone.'

Neil laughs.

'Yes, let's do that, mate.'

Chapter Twenty

Natalie

The walls could do with another lick of paint I think as I lie down, satisfied and happy. Feeling the weight of Rob lying on me. I missed this. The weight of him. The smell of him. How big and strong his hands are. I love this man with every fibre of my being. He is everything to me. So much so that I had purposefully hurt him. Yet here he is again. There had always been this chemistry between us. We could never be apart. Something very real bonded us together. It is love, I know that. In its purest form.

I nuzzle into him and stroke his back.

'I'm sorry,' I said, meaning it, and wishing it would erase all that I had done. 'I was such a bitch.'

Rob lifted himself off me and to the side. Bringing me in as he did so my head was on his shoulder.

'You have already apologised. Stop being silly. It is in the past now. It belongs in the past. It should stay there.'

I laugh. His forgiveness means the world to me, but I am not sure that I will be able to forgive myself. I had gone off the deep end in the summer and now I am glad that things are getting better. I have to make up properly with Paul now. I know that. The constant talking and fixing things is exhausting. Why is family never easy? I look at the time. Shit. I have to get to work. I jump up and run to the shower. Rob whistles at me as I am naked.

'Wow. What a body,' he shouts after me.

I laugh but also, I feel happy that he still finds me attractive.

I arrive at work and walk through the hospital corridors. The hustle and bustle of a hospital. I love it. A lot of people think I am weird for thinking so but there is so much life here. True, there is also a lot of death. Illness is not a nice thing. Maybe that is why I choose to be in obstetrics and gynaecology. There is life in this field, joy and birth. It is even a surgical field. It has everything.

I have my gynaecology patients this morning and then I have an elective Caesarean section to do in the afternoon. I need to get my head into that space. I see George and I wave to him.

'See you at one this afternoon for Mrs Fortescue's C-section.'

He nods and I keep walking. I walk to my locker and I get changed. I close my eyes and I breathe in and out. This is how I prepare. I have to get into my calm, happy place, but getting into my headspace has to be quick because there is no time. So just breathe in, breathe out, breathe in, breathe out. I do this three times. Then I am good to go.

I do my rounds on the ward. The first patient of the day I see is someone who has had a sexual misadventure and got something stuck up there. Joy of joys, I have to retrieve it. I do my best to not judge my patients. We all have our things and our weirdness. The next woman I see has endometriosis and is now finally pregnant. It took her seven years. The thought makes me happy.

The afternoon comes and we are in theatre by the time we know it. A scalpel and then here it is: the baby. Crying, beautiful. This moment always gets me. A new life coming into the world.

Baby goes to the midwife and is checked over and weighed. Then mum has a cuddle. After that the father takes the baby and I stitch mum back up. I have done so many of these I could probably do them with my eyes closed.

It is done quickly and then I go and write up my notes.

This is just the first C-section today. There will be more. But there are also mothers who want water births, natural births, births with epidurals and, in some cases, all of the drugs. There is no right way to do this. It is hard and painful and gory. Yet it is a miracle.

But there it is, that moment when a stab of darkness comes in. Recently I have thought that maybe it is time to do something else. Being surrounded by babies has always been okay because even though I did not have any of my own, it still meant so much to me that I was helping life come into this world. I close my eyes and push the thought away. Today has confirmed this. I need this in my life. I need to make a difference somehow.

The rest of the day goes by in a blur of babies born through the tunnel and the sunroof and gynae patients. I am always on my feet and something is always happening. I love it.

After a long shift I arrive home. I put my stuff down near the door and give a happy sigh. The fresh air on the way back from the hospital was refreshing and kept me awake but the bus was crowded and full of drunks. Football fans sang and jumped up and down for the entire journey. I wanted to punch them. Twenty babies came into the world.

I took the bus because I need to stop using Rob's car. I know he does not mind but I need to get my own. It only takes forty-five minutes. I walk through the door and he is sitting by the window. He is wearing his dark blue suit with a white shirt. The two top buttons of the shirt are undone. This is my favourite suit that he owns. He looks so hot in it. He smiles when he sees me. I go to him and he stands up as I do. He pulls me to him and kisses me. A gentleman to the end.

'Hello, my love, how was your day?'

'Twenty new babies entered the world today.'

'Wow.'

'I did not deliver them all obviously.'

'I know.'

'But it is pretty cool. How was your day?'

'It was good. I got a lot done. The new campaign is going very well. We are trying to improve the image of that soft drink company.'

'Ah. I remember that one.'

'How did things go with Amanda? We didn't really get a chance to cover it.'

'It went well. I guess. That was the first time she has ever admitted that Tim was anything other than a saint. I have been projecting on to her as well so, I guess we were both at fault.'

'What about the babies?'

'Babies? Plural?'

I take a moment. Rob now has an "oh shit" look on his face.

'Oh, for fuck's sake. She is having twins, isn't she?'

'Neil told me that is why they came round. To tell you.'

'Well, she did not.'

I let out a long breath. Of course, she is having twins. The golden child that all is bestowed upon. Why does everything in her life have to be so easy?

'I'm happy for her. It is great she is having twins.'

'I am so sorry. I was worried she didn't tell you. She should have; it is not fair on you.'

'No, I'm okay. I'm happy for her, but I don't know why life always has to be so fucking unfair.'

'I know. It's not fair.'

Rob takes his hand and puts it on mine. He strokes my hand. I feel a lot better. There is a niggle now. These things always happen with Amanda. She does not consider other people. The only way to have a relationship with her is to either ignore it or pull back. Even though I am glad we have made up, I cannot help but think I need to pull back. I try to bury the negativity deep down. Internalising used to be my speciality, but something seems to have broken in me.

I start to cry. A little at first and then it feels like a tsunami. Grief of things and people lost. Grief of things that I do not know if I will ever have in my life. Grief of mistakes and broken promises. Love and lost chances. Rob holds me in his arms and he soothes me and loves me. He tells me it will be okay and I know it is true, because as long as he is there, it will be.

Rob goes to make tea after my tears subside. I feel much better now. I needed the emotional release. Sometimes you just have to cry and let it all out. Rob comes back in with the tea and I noticed he has put biscuits on the side. A little touch that makes me love him even more. He is so detail orientated and caring. He always does the little things. It is all a fiancée can ask for. He put the tray with the pot and cups on the dining table and sat back down on the chair.

'I'm happy you got that out. It has been too much. You need to cry more and allow yourself to be human, Natalie. I'm not trying to make you feel bad, but we have seen what happens when you keep things in. The past year has been tough on you, and trying for a baby is a huge strain on anyone. Maybe we should take a break. Would you like that? I am hoping you can take some time off.'

'You are right. I will stop holding it in. It is not helpful. Thank you for being so understanding. You are the greatest man I have ever known.'

'Do you know what day tomorrow is?'

'How could I forget? We find out if the embryos implanted.'

Rob rolls his eyes at the scientist.

'We find out if we are going to have a baby. If it doesn't happen, it doesn't happen, but if it does, it will be wonderful.'

I smile at him.

'Let me cook tonight. I want to make you something amazing.'

'Why don't we get a takeaway? You had a long shift and I had a lot of crap to deal with at work.'

'Deal.'

Rob scrolls through the app and finds our favourite restaurant.

'Do you want your usual?'

'Yes. Just reorder from last time.'

I look at his hands. I love those hands. So strong and sure.

'Why don't we leave?'

Rob looks up at me.

'Leave? Now? We just ordered food.'

'I mean leave London. Even leave the UK. Just leave everything and everyone behind. A fresh new start.'

Rob looks surprised and I am surprised myself.

'That came from nowhere.'

Rob is right. This did come from nowhere, yet I feel it has been building up for a long time. That need to escape. I keep going around in a circle with my issues with my sister and now with my brother. I just want to live my own life without the constant feeling of suffocation my family bring. Relationships should not be this much work.

'We could move to Paris. Or somewhere like that. The world is a big place.'

Rob has moved from surprise to something else, but I cannot place it. Then he jumps up and puts his hands on my waist. He lifts me up and kisses me.

'Yes, let's do it. We will do the IVF and we will find somewhere to go on a big adventure. We're still young. We have been stagnant for too long.'

He twirls me around and I laugh. When he stops and puts me back down, I look at him and smile. I breathe in and out. It feels like the first time my breath has reached my lungs in months.

Chapter Twenty-One

Then
Tim

It is Christmas Day. Christmas Day. I keep saying that to myself while I look around this crap hotel room. But mostly it hits me when I look at my tiny little daughter on the bed watching cartoons and eating crisps. Jacqueline and I have pretty much been arguing since Paul was born. For the first few days we had managed to hold a truce together. But we had fought solidly for a week and now I could not take any more.

It was the guilt mostly, but it was also her. She had not done anything wrong to me. Ever. There was nothing comparable about our behaviour. She was too good for me. It had been utter madness to go out and see Sheila just after the baby was born. And then again. And again. She had known. Deep down, straight away. But then. Then it seemed to suck everything out of her and I saw her give up. That had been the worst.

With everything I had done, with the drinking and the occasional pot, with a minor indiscretion and with Sheila. But even with all of that. I never thought I would lose my wife. She was the only solid thing in my life. The consequences of my actions hit me. I could lose my entire family over this. In this moment, I hate myself, because I had never even thought about that before.

The mistakes of the past would stay with me forever now. I could never come back from this. I have blown up my entire family and for what? Some silly woman who would not leave me alone. She had been a heat-seeking missile. I stood no chance against her constant advances. She gave me everything and she listened. More importantly, we had no baggage.

Sure, Jacqueline and I had memories. Many happy ones, but lately the memories became like a weight around my neck. So much has happened between us, it seems impossible to ever start again. The past has become a heavy thing that would not allow us to move forward, but merely weighed on us, growing heavier each day. The suffocation of a lifetime of slights and grudges.

Which is how I came to this hotel room, on Christmas Day. With my family torn apart, burdened by every mistake I had ever made. I did not know how to make this right. I knew that I was the grown-up, that I was supposed to have all of the answers. But this was beyond me. One thing after another had escalated into oblivion. It felt impossible to get back. I had taken my family for granted, under the idiotic assumption that we were unbreakable.

I look at my daughter. The only thing now was to make her Christmas amazing. I sit down next to her. She is still in her pyjamas. Another flash of guilt hit me. My children have been let down by both of their parents. All we had done for weeks was argue.

'Right, we are going to order lots of room service and watch a marathon of Christmas movies. Does that sound like fun?'

'Yes, Daddy, yes! I have never had room service before. Can I order anything I want?'

Amanda was ecstatic. It never took much to make her happy. She was such an easy child.

'Of course you can. It is Christmas and Christmas is all about gluttony. We can have crisps and cakes and steaks and lots of soda.'

'Yes! I love it here. I want to stay here with you forever, Daddy. You are so much fun and so perfect. You are the perfect daddy. I love you.'

Amanda jumps off the bed and launches herself at me, wrapping her tiny arms around me and burrowing her head into my legs. This display of affection melts my heart. Amanda has always been such an adorable little girl.

Natalie had always been my favourite as she was my firstborn, but I felt her pulling away from me. Now there was a boy, of course. A baby that would finally carry on the family name. When I argued with Jacqueline, Natalie would always go to Jacqueline and hug her or hold her hand. It irked me. Or the looks Natalie would give me, so different from the looks she gave her mother. It was clear who was her favourite. It hurt as it had once been me. My daughter may still be a child, but she has chosen a side. Maybe that was why I stopped for Amanda. I just did not have it in me to lose another child. To not be the favourite. For once I needed someone on my side. And more than that, I needed someone on my side who knew that deep down I was a good guy.

Christmas Day had been a surprising success for us. It turned out that it did not take much to make a small child happy. You just had to loosen the rules and let them eat whatever they wanted while they watched whatever they wanted.

We finished Christmas Day off by jumping up and down on the beds. I wish I had known that parenting could be this much fun. I am surprised by how much joy my daughter has. There is none of the cynicism or moodiness that Natalie already has despite her youth. Truth was, Natalie has always been mature, but that was not always a good thing. Especially not when it made her too perceptive for her age. Her eyes were like lasers that saw into my soul. Opening out every single thing I have done wrong in my life.

I look at Amanda now, eating her cereal and drinking orange juice. From the moment she stepped into the car, her adoration for me never wavered. I needed that.

'Right, you, let's go shopping for clothes and presents,' I say in my most excitable voice. I want her to remember this Christmas forever, and I want that memory to be a good one.

Amanda's face brightens up.

'Yeah! Shopping. I love shopping. Can I get a pretty dress, Daddy?'

'You can have the prettiest dress in the entire world. You will look like a princess.'

Amanda screams in delight.

'Yes! Thank you so much, Daddy. I'm so excited. This is the best Christmas ever.'

I almost tell Amanda to get her coat and then I realise that she does not have one. Nor shoes. Just her pyjamas and socks. She does not even have a toothbrush. She ran out with just a teddy bear in her hand.

I go to my suitcase and open it. Hoping that somehow there will be something that Amanda can wear that will not make her look like a kidnap victim.

As I think about this it scares me. Jacqueline could call the police. What I have done is probably illegal. I am pretty certain it is.

Not that it's fair. I am Amanda's father, but nobody will care. I am always the bad guy. As I sift through my suitcase, I see a waterproof jacket that I packed, a jumper and some scarves. Thank God I packed in a hurry. I really had just put anything that touched my hands into the case. Then I got lucky: one of Jacqueline's cardigans. It will do. I put that on Amanda, along with a scarf. I will have to carry her to the car, and to the shop, but it will be fine. Even better, it is the Boxing Day sales. I could really spoil my daughter today. I look at Amanda in her mishmash of clothes and smile. It may be unorthodox, but it would do.

The Boxing Day crowds are something to behold. Masses of people all out for a bargain. Weird, I thought, as they must have done lots of shopping in December. When I walk in with Amanda, I get a lot of funny looks. I understand why, but it doesn't make it easier. A man walking around in the snow with a child with no shoes and no coat and who was clearly wearing an adult's cardigan and scarf. That would seem weird even to me.

I try to play it off by giving everyone I see a huge smile while loudly talking to Amanda about what present she wants from her daddy. We certainly have loaded up. After the scram to buy shoes and a coat we go for the non-essentials: Barbies, toys, dresses, more shoes, chocolate. I am exhausted from the shopping and hoping the end is in sight when we spot a tiara. I see Amanda's eyes light up.

'Do you want it?' I ask her.

She turns to me with her eyes wide.

'Daddy, am I really allowed to have that?'

It was a question of disbelief, not a request.

'Yes. You can have that because you are my princess and you deserve a tiara.'

Amanda looks so happy she might cry. I take it down off the shelf and we go to pay. From the moment it is paid for it's on her head and never leaves. Not even when she goes for a bath.

Now
Natalie

A new sense of lightness has come over me. I pull up my sleeves to let my forearms get some sun. Most of the summer has been in the high twenties or low thirties and sometimes there was no cool breeze to offset the humidity. Not today. Today was a perfect twenty-four degrees with the lightest breeze. Perfect weather for today.

I sit on the blanket for some much-needed rest. I have been blowing bubbles for my nephew for fifteen minutes. The bubbles keep going over to other picnickers. Some even landed in one guy's face. I give a meek wave and a mumbled sorry. When kids want their bubbles, it is hard to say no.

I look at Paul. He looks sad.

'A penny for your thoughts.'

Paul looks at me.

'Do people still say that?'

I laugh.

'I do.'

'Yeah, that is because you are old.'

He gives me a wink.

'How very dare you. I am not old, I am older.'

We smile at each other as we try to get back to a place where we effortlessly made fun of each other. There was never any small talk. Everything with Paul used to be easy. Nothing felt easy any more.

We look across Wimbledon Park and watch Nathaniel as he feeds the ducks seeds. The lake looks perfect today: the most tranquil blue I have ever seen.

My nephew looks tall. He has grown inches as he tends to do every summer holiday.

'I have got back together with Stacey. I know you have not always liked her, but we still have feelings for each other. I want to give things a shot.'

Relief follows his words. I have been full of guilt since we decided on our big adventure. Leaving my single-father brother alone to raise his child with no family help made me feel awful. But he would have Amanda and now, Stacey.

'I am happy for you both. I do not dislike Stacey. I just always take your side on everything.'

'She's had a lot of help for her postnatal depression. She is building an amazing relationship with Nathaniel. I'm proud of her.'

'So am I. She has done so well.'

'Well, thank you for your recommendations. The therapist was amazing.'

'Annabel is amazing. She always impresses me.'

'We will sort the house stuff out when Amanda gets here.'

'Good.'

We sit and watch Nathaniel some more. I do not know how to break this to him.

'We are leaving.'

Paul looks at me, confusion on his face.

'What do you mean?'

'Rob and I, we have decided we need a change. Everything's been too much, so we are moving to Paris.'

'Paris.'

Paul looks shocked. I can tell he is trying to comprehend this.

'I'm sorry. We need a change of scenery. This summer has been so intense. We are still young, so we want to be more...' I try and think of a word without sounding like an idiot. 'Daring.'

I can tell Paul is thinking. He is still unsure what to say.

I unwrap my baguette and take a bite. Salmon, egg mayonnaise, gherkins and salad. It is weird and yet somehow it works. I open a can of Orangina. I love the feeling and the sound of opening the can. The satisfying pop.

'I'm pleased for you.'

Paul has finally found his voice.

'It is not because of me, is it?' he asks, his voice pained.

'Of course not, we just need a change of scenery.'

The lie comes out of my mouth so easily. It is not all him. I can see the other reason walking towards us now. She is glowing. Or do my pangs of jealousy just project that onto her? Is it possible for a woman who is trying for a baby to be totally happy for a woman who is pregnant? There must be some saint somewhere, but not here. Yet I am happy for her. That makes me happy. I am not a total monster.

'Amanda is here.'

Paul follows my gaze.

'Does she know?'

'No.'

'This should be fun.'

I sigh. He is right. I doubt she will take this well. I am dreading it.

I put a smile on my face as she gets closer. Paul stands up to greet her so I do too.

Amanda is wearing a long yellow dress. You would think it would clash with her hair, but it just accentuates her light-golden blondness. Her curls are swept up into a top knot and some escape and frame her face. She is wearing gold sandals and a delicate gold necklace with a heart pendant. She looks angelic.

In the foreground I can see Neil struggling with a picnic basket. He is wearing a pale blue polo shirt and jeans.

'Hi, Amanda.'

'Hey.'

She comes over and gives me a hug. Then she kisses me on the cheek. Her bump is prominent and brushes against me.

I hear huffing and puffing behind Amanda. Neil has caught up.

'Hi, Neil.'

'Hi, Natalie,' Neil said as he put the hamper down. It looks heavy.

Amanda and Paul greet each other warmly. This summer has really brought them together.

'Where is Rob?' Neil asks.

'He is just getting some drinks. Non-alcoholic ones, and snacks.'

'Ah, okay.'

It is a bit of a hike for Rob, but he should be back soon. I hope so anyway. I feel outnumbered.

'I got the exciting email about expanding the business. I cannot wait to talk to him about it.'

'Yes, it is all exciting.'

I do not give any more information even though I know Neil wants it.

'He has not been in the office as much.'

Neil says this in an accusing way. I cannot help but smile. Rob and I have been obsessed with our careers, but now we think there might be better things in life than just working all of the time.

'Where is Nathaniel?'

'He is near the lake feeding the ducks.'

Jeez, just use your eyes, Neil. I never realised how annoying he is before.

'Look at this, the band is back together.'

Thank God, it is Rob. He greets the others and then sits down beside me and kisses me.

'Should we go straight into the house sale?'

Amanda gives me a look.

'Get straight to the point then, Natalie.'

'I like to get to the point. Why not?'

Amanda rolls her eyes. I see she is back to feeling comfortable.

'The house sale is going through. It will probably take another month or so to complete, but we got a good price and we are all going to get a good amount.'

I can see Amanda look at me. I know what she is thinking.

'We will, of course, pay off the debt to you, Natalie. That is only fair.'

'Thank you, Paul.'

'Not that you need the money,' Amanda says.

She could not help herself.

'Neither do you. I am not sure why you are always pleading poverty.'

Amanda's mouth gapes open. I can tell she is surprised I have stood up for myself. Bullies always are.

I see Neil catch Rob's eyes, but he gives him nothing. There is an uncomfortable silence.

'Anyway, Rob and I have some news.'

'Oh, my God! You are pregnant!'

'No, Amanda, I am not pregnant.'

'Oh. Oh well.'

I ignore this and barrel on.

'Rob and I are leaving.'

'What do you mean?'

I laugh because those are the same words Paul used.

'We are leaving, Amanda.'

She just stares at me. Clearly, she has no idea what to say. I look at Neil. He looks queasy.

'Where are you going?' Neil asks.

He knows this is real.

'France,' Rob answers.

'What about the business?'

'I thought you could run the London wing. If I get bored, we can always expand to France.'

Neil does not look queasy any more. He looks elated.

'What do you mean you are moving to France?'

Amanda still does not understand how I can do something that does not revolve around her.

'It means we are moving to France. It's not hard to understand.'

'What about your job?'

'I'm going to take a sabbatical, but babies are born everywhere.'

'What about trying for a baby?'

'You can do that anywhere, Amanda.'

She looks stung. The hurt is evident on her face, but I have spent my life caring for other people. At some point you need to do something for yourself.

'Retiring to France is what old people do. You are both in your thirties.'

'We are not retiring. We are shaking things up.'

'What about me?'

'What about you?'

'I am having a fucking baby, Natalie! No, actually, two fucking babies! All hands, on deck!'

I sigh. This makes her angry.

'Why are you being so selfish? What is wrong with you?'

'It is not my baby, Amanda! You are married, you have Neil's parents. You will have money. It is not my job to make your life easier.'

'Is that what this is about?'

'What?'

'You're jealous.'

Now I am the one who is fuming. How dare she? I exhale, wanting to take a moment before I say something I regret. Rob takes my hand and squeezes it.

'Amanda, that is inappropriate and, to be brutal, not very nice at all. Natalie has spent most of her life looking after you and making your life easier. Now we are going to go and live our life. It is time we went after our own happiness,' Rob tells her sternly.

Amanda takes this in and then nods. She looks deflated. It takes everything I have to not go over to her and yield. I have been conditioned to be her substitute mother. Rob squeezes my hand harder. I look at him. The loving look he gives me is the strength I need.

'Okay,' Amanda finally replies.

She sounds like a little girl. There is another uncomfortable silence. These silences seem to be the punctuation of our lives together. I need to lighten the mood.

'Besides, it is only Paris. It is probably easier to get to Paris on the EuroStar than it is to get to some parts of London.'

'You are moving to Paris.'

This does not seem to make Amanda happy.

'Yes.'

'When you said France, I thought you meant somewhere in the country.'

'You can always come and visit.'

She just looks at me. I know she loves Paris.

'Maybe.'

I can tell she is in a huff.

'You, Neil and the twins.'

She is startled by the comment. She realises that when she blurted out the comment about two babies, that was the first time she told me about the twins.

'I really could do with another pair of hands,' she says with a little laugh.

'I am not a nanny, Amanda, and I have to live my own life. Not just be your helper.'

'You don't think that's selfish?'

'No. It's not selfish. You chose to have your children. They are your responsibility. Frankly, I think it would be good for you to have some.'

This comment makes Amanda narrow her eyes.

'Right, now we have the news and business out of the way, let's move on to having fun,' Paul jumps in, trying to save things.

I feel sorry for her. Amanda cannot drink and cannot eat a lot of things. Saving things will be hard. Paul reaches into his bag and pulls out a chocolate cake. Okay, maybe he knows how to fix things after all. Amanda's eyes light up. I could do with some cake myself.

Paul dishes out the cake and Rob hands everyone a can of Coke. Nathaniel, seeing what is on offer, comes and joins us.

'Well done, Nate. The ducks are well fed now,' Rob said to Nathaniel and smiled at him, finishing it off with a hair ruffle. Rob has always loved Nathaniel. He's good with children.

'I was also skimming stones. I'm very good at it.'

'Well maybe after we eat lunch, we can do that some more.'

Nathaniel nods at Rob, happy with the suggestion.

'I would like that, Uncle Rob.'

We eat cake and overload our bodies with sugar in the summer heat. We are surrounded by families, children playing various sports, parents blowing bubbles. There are even some barbecues and to our right, someone is playing songs on the radio while their children dance with abandon.

I love days like this. Surrounded by the lush green of the trees and the azure blue of the lake, life is all around us and despite our differences as human beings, it is beautiful indeed.

We all walk to the playground after lunch to let Nathaniel burn off some of his energy. I walk in time with Paul.

'I am sorry Stacey couldn't come. We should meet up soon for lunch.'

'That would be great, she is working today. They do the occasional weekend at her work.'

'Finance seems like insane hours.'

'That coming from a doctor.'

We laugh. It feels good to be comfortable in each other's company.

'Are you sure you are doing the right thing?'

'Yes. Why wouldn't it be the right thing?'

'I don't want to think that you're running away.'

'That is a negative way of looking at it.'

'It is breaking the family apart. We have always lived near each other.'

'Well, I think that was always the problem. I have trouble setting boundaries and I have been left exhausted. I want to focus on my life and my relationship for a while.'

'But you have such an amazing job.'

'I guess I do, but I need to do this or I will burn out.'

I pause there and consider whether I should tell Paul the rest of the story. I decide to go for it.

'Also, the fertility treatment is really full on. It is daily injections, going to the clinic every other day. Lots of tests. I cannot do that and do my job. I also need to remove myself from stress. A part of me thinks that's always been the problem.'

'I understand.'

Paul links his arm through mine.

'And be Amanda's nanny apparently.'

Paul laughs.

'Yeah, she does tend to try and get as much as she can.'

I feel happy as we walk along. It is nice being with my brother.

'I hope the fertility treatment works.'

'So do I.'

'I also hope you can forgive me. I know we are raking over old ground, but I want us to have the relationship we used to have.'

'I forgive you. It doesn't matter. You said sorry and everything is sorted.'

Paul squeezes me tight to him and nods.

'Good.'

'It's just Paris. We are still close.'

Paul nods, not convinced.

He smiles and I smile back at him, but I do not have it in me to tell him that things will never be the same again.

Chapter Twenty-Two

Rob

The suit feels a bit tight on me. First there was the break-up comfort food, and then the we-are-so-in-love food. Damn, I wish I tried this suit on before today. Oh well. I will just have to suck in my stomach for the pictures.

I shave and brush my teeth. I look presentable. Phew.

I walk into the hall and I loiter tentatively outside our bedroom where Natalie is getting ready. I know I can go in, but it does not feel right.

The door opens and there she is: my bride. She looks gorgeous in her white, knee-length strappy dress. It looks like silk and on any other woman it would look like a simple dress. But not on Natalie. She is elegance and beauty personified. Her glossy dark brown hair is up in a messy chignon and her make-up is understated. I put my hand out and she takes it. She kisses me on the lips and we walk downstairs.

We walk all the way to Wandsworth Town Hall hand in hand. I feel like the luckiest man in the world. When we get to the entrance, I reach into my inside pocket and pull out a necklace I have bought her. It is pearls with a diamond clip. It is beautiful and elegant, just like her. She gasps when she sees it. I let her take a good look and then I put it around her neck and fix the clasp.

'Perfect,' I tell her.

'It is, thank you so much. You are perfect.'

We walk to the room where we will be married. Neil and Amanda are there. So are Paul, Stacey and Nathaniel. George is here with Bethany and their children. My parents are here; it is the first time I have seen them in years. There are a few other friends here, but we kept it small. The older you are, the smaller things seem to get. I always thought it was better that way.

I walk to the front and Neil stands beside me. I made him my best man. I may not be that keen on his wife, but I think he is a great guy. He is going to run the London operation and do an excellent job. I have no doubt.

Amanda stands next to Natalie. A maid of honour in name only. Natalie is still keeping her distance. I cannot blame her.

Everyone was surprised by our last-minute wedding. It was not last-minute, of course. We had done our banns seven weeks ago. We got lucky with our slot. There was a cancellation.

'Do you take Natalie…?'

Yes, I do. Yes, a million times and then a million more. From now until eternity.

'Do you take Rob?'

Phew. Yes, she does. Not long now. Any moment and we will be bonded together forever.

'I now pronounce you man and wife.'

We kiss and it is done. In this moment, I have no idea why it took us so long. We have known each other since our early twenties. We were both with other people at the wrong time. Eventually all of the wrong was swept away and then there was this: everything slotting into place.

Everybody cheers and the song starts. A classical song which I recognise and cannot place. Natalie chose it. It is perfect.

We walk out into a rain of eco-friendly recyclable confetti. iPhones point towards us and the wedding photographer snaps away.

There is a car outside. A Rolls-Royce with white ribbons on all the right places. It may not have been a big wedding, but we included our little touches.

We are not heading anywhere exotic just yet. We are heading to Amanda's and Neil's. They said they would do our reception for us. I would rather have gone to a restaurant, but I wanted them to feel included.

The driver hands me the keys. He is just delivering the car. I will take my wife where we need to go. My wife. I love those words.

We head to Amanda's house. I put the radio on. I look at Natalie. She is beaming. She has never looked more beautiful.

'Hello, wife.'

'Hello, husband.'

Neil asked me to take a longer route so everyone could get there. I told him to text me. We drive around until I feel a buzz in my pocket.

'Can you get my phone?'

Natalie reaches into my pocket and gets the phone.

'It says "we have all arrived".'

'Perfect.'

We are not far behind on our detour and we arrive quickly. I find somewhere to park and we get out.

When we open the door, everyone jumps up. There is a "just married" banner and poppers going off. Everyone has a glass of champagne in their hand. I doubt the poppers are environmentally friendly, but I think Natalie might let this one go.

Natalie and I look at each other and smile. This moment is perfect.

We walk in and Amanda hands us both a glass of champagne. The entire place looks amazing. They have moved all of the furniture and there are tables with white tablecloths, chairs with white covers, pink roses on the tables. There is even fabric draped from the ceiling. It looks incredible.

'Wow,' Natalie said.

'Wow,' I say in agreement.

Amanda proudly smiles.

'I am glad you like it. We wanted to welcome you to married life with a bang.'

'You should both feel proud. You have done an amazing job.'

'I agree,' Natalie said.

'Well, we are lucky. We have an open-plan living room and kitchen, so we had a lot of room. Go into the garden! It is so exciting.'

We head into the kitchen. There are white lights everywhere and flowers. Presents are piled up on a table with a white linen tablecloth over it. As we walk into the garden, we can hear music. There is a band. A full-on band with violins and percussion. They are under a white marquee. Canapés do the rounds, handed out by waiters in traditional black and white outfits. They must have spent a fortune.

This is perfect. Even if I worry about how much money they have spent. The band were just warming up when we arrived but as soon as they see us, they break into a version of the Ramones' "Baby I love you". One of our favourite songs. Natalie and I both look at each other and then smile at Neil and Amanda.

'Thank you so much, guys. We will remember this forever.'

They both say thank you and Amanda looks like she might cry. I mean every word. We mingle with people, drink our champagne and have some canapés.

We cut the wedding cake together. One hand over the other as everybody snaps away.

Then it is the wedding breakfast. We all sit down and eat. Somehow Neil and Amanda made all of this food themselves. Scallops with pea puree and bacon to start, followed by asparagus and salmon with a poached egg. We have the wedding cake for dessert.

Then it is time for the speeches. Neil goes first.

'I have known Rob for more years than I care to admit to. He is my boss which means I should probably err on the side of caution during my speech. That would be the smart thing to do. However.' Neil stops for effect and people laugh.

'Rob loves Natalie more than I have ever seen anyone love anyone else. Well, apart from me and my wife of course.'

People laugh. 'When she dumped him on the side of the road and they broke up we were all shocked.'

I could kill Neil right now. What the fuck. I look at Natalie. She has her face in her hands, but I can see a smile on her face. She is taking it in good humour.

'But we all knew deep down that this was not the end of the greatest love story. These two have a bond that could never be broken and they found their way back together. Now here we are. These two lovebirds are married and are going to start a new journey together. We all gather here today to celebrate their love and, most importantly, to celebrate with them. Let's raise a toast to Mr and Mrs Adams. Cheers to them!'

Everybody raises their glass and cheers. The band still play, but quietly. It is Amanda's turn now. As she stands up, I detect the smallest evil glare to Neil. I guess Neil said something to bother her.

'It is my honour to be my sister's maid of honour. She was the maid of honour at my wedding and she did an amazing job. I am so happy to return the favour.'

I try to not roll my eyes over this speech. It is all so me, me, me. I notice that as Amanda continues, she is cradling her bump.

'Rob and Natalie are a wonderful couple. I wish them a full and happy life together. Let's all raise our glasses again to the happy couple.'

We all raise our glasses again for the other toast. I put my glass down. The wedding breakfast is finished. Soon I will whisk my wife away on our honeymoon. I lean over and give her a kiss. Certain that this is one of the best days of our life.

Natalie

'Come with me.' Amanda tells me.

I follow Amanda up the stairs and into her bedroom. She goes into the nightstand near her bed. She pulls a small box from the drawer and hands it to me.

'I wanted to give you something before you left.'

I open the box. It is a silver charm bracelet. It is beautiful. I notice it has a "sisters" pendant on it and a heart one.

'Thank you, Amanda. This is beautiful.'

I hug her.

'Rob asked us to drop all of your other wedding presents off at your home while you were away.'

'That would be great. We are going straight to a hotel near the airport after this, then we are flying to Hawaii in the early hours.'

'That is what Rob said.'

'Well, thank you. For everything. For the wedding breakfast, for being a great maid of honour and for the present. Oh, and for keeping an eye on our house while we are on holiday.'

'No worries at all. I am always happy to help.'

Amanda's drawer is still open and I am surprised to see a tiara in it. That fucking tiara. For a moment, seeing it feels like a wound reopening, but I am not going back there ever again. There is no point arguing about the past any more. It is just a little momentary sting. Family is not easy. In fact, family is a constant negotiation, but mostly you are stuck with your family, for richer or poorer. The past is painful, which is why it is never a good idea to stay there. It is time to move on or let the bitterness kill me. Family is all about compromise.

Amanda follows my gaze and looks horrified when she sees what I am looking at.

She goes to the drawer and takes the tiara out. She holds it up with both of her hands, turning it around slowly as she does. Then she stops and looks at me.

'I'm sorry I left you. I really mean it,' Amanda said.

Her statement has a tone of sorriness that I have never heard before. It surprises me and I try to hide the shock I feel.

'It's okay.'

I tell her and after everything, I am happy to realise that, actually, it is. It does not matter any more.

'No, it's not. I hurt you and I hurt Mum. You have been angry ever since and I don't blame you. It wasn't nice. And I never apologised. I just saw you at school and I acted like nothing had happened and then when I came home, I had all of this stuff. We were best friends. We really were. I ruined that. You always looked out for me. All Dad did was throw money at me. I was so superficial, I confused it with actual love. It was a bitch move.'

I walk over to Amanda and put my arms around her.

'Anger is a strong word, but resentment is a good one.'

Amanda laughs and then I do too.

'Seriously, it is okay. You were a kid. I was even a kid. Everyone is a bitch sometimes. It is time we both let it go. All of it. We are a family and we love each other. But even more importantly, we cannot transfer our baggage to the next generation. We need to forgive and forget for them. They are going to learn from us. So it is okay. It really is.'

Amanda nods, but I can see she is crying. I hug her tighter.

'Frankly, if I was offered that fucking tiara, I would have chosen it over you too.'

The tears turn to laughter. It is a nice moment. I am glad I had this with my sister.

'I should throw it away. It is silly to keep it.'

'Don't be silly. Maybe one of the babies will be a girl. Hell, even if they are both boys, why can't one of them wear it?'

'Or it will be two girls and they will fight over it.'

I laugh.

'That would be karma.'

'Yes, it would.'

'We should go back downstairs. Rob is probably wondering where I am.'

'Yes, we should. We don't want to be rude.'

We both head downstairs. I give Amanda's shoulder a rub and then we go in opposite directions. She turns to me and I give her a kiss on the cheek.

'Thank you.'

She smiles back and I go and mingle.

We have been trying to leave for a while, but everyone seems to want to talk to us. It is understandable, I guess. I have been talking to George for about five minutes now. He is upset I am leaving the hospital, but he is happy for me. Being happy for other people: that is always what I loved about George. It is such a rare trait. It is certainly a better conversation than the one I just had with Rob's mother, with all her comments about us "maybe having babies now". I guess I should not blame her. Rob is her only son and she obviously wants to have grandchildren. It is her worst fear: a barren daughter-in-law.

'You will keep in touch, won't you?'

'Of course, I will. You and Bethany are two of my best friends. You should come and visit us too. It is very close on the EuroStar. I am telling everyone that so they know not to forsake us.'

I laugh and so does George, but the truth is the only person I have said it to and meant it is George. Everyone else can go to hell. I feel a hand on my shoulder. It is Rob.

'Let's go.'

George takes the hint. He kisses me on the cheek and then shakes Rob's hand.

'Congratulations again, you two. We are so happy for you.'

We try and sneak off. Making our way out as everyone says goodbye. We are almost at the door. I must be socially awkward. I never know how to leave things like this.

'The bride and groom are leaving. Everybody outside to wave them off.'

Great. Amanda has noticed and is making a big deal of it. We stop and look at each other. Oh well. Everybody piles out and we wait. Somehow, they make two lines and we walk through as they clap and cheer. We get into the car and they all wave us off. I am glad that it is all done. It worked well but it was stressful. Now we can just be happy and married. The two of us together against the world.

Then
Jacqueline

It is the depth of winter and I can feel it in my bones. The snow is falling outside so heavy that it is blinding. I have always loved winter. I was never sure why and other people think it is strange, but being inside when it is snowing and cold outside is such a cosy feeling. I have always loved walking in the snow too. Not this snow; this looks more like a blizzard.

The pain in my body is a lot now, but I have done my share of raging against the injustices of the world. Life can deal you the blows, I know that more than anyone, but as I lay here, knowing that my life would not be a very long one, I still feel blessed.

The pain that I will not see my children grow up, not know if they will get married or have children, not know what they will end up doing with their lives, that is one that will never go away. But despite everything, I have lived. And I have loved. They are everything to me. My three musketeers.

My faith helps me. I do not just believe that there is something else there, I know it in my bones. I believe in faith and love and everything that is good in the world. I have come to terms with dying. The only thing is my children. It will be hard on Natalie, and I only hope that when her younger siblings grow up, she will finally take the time to live her own life. I do not expect Tim to be much of a father. I merely hope he will keep a roof over their heads. Natalie will be the one who holds the family together.

It saddens me even though I am grateful for it. This little girl who I love so much is already an adult. Since I was diagnosed, I tried to spend every moment with my children. To drink them up and feel their love, all the while hoping they could feel my love for them and carry it with them all their lives. Because that is all I want now. For my children to remember how much their mother loved them. To know that they were really the only thing in my life worth a damn.

I would have given up everything for them a million times over. All I wish for is their happiness and as I close my eyes the thought of them fills me with a warm glow and brings a smile to my face. I can feel peace come over me. I can feel pure love.

Chapter Twenty-Three
Epilogue

Now
Natalie

Three months of summer had turned into autumn and then became winter. The snow lay on the ground now. I love the crunch of it underneath my feet. Winter in Paris is beautiful. I feel happy and privileged to be here.

Everything has gone so well. The family house sold and then our house sold in only twelve weeks. All for a number our estate agent said was "good". As soon as we put the plan into action it felt like everything fell into place.

Hawaii seems like a lifetime ago now winter has brought its coldness. I button up my coat and pull my scarf tighter around my neck. I love to walk along the Seine. I feel like I have lived my entire life on fast forward and now I feel like I am actually living and experiencing life, day by day.

Winter makes me feel closer to my mother. She died on a day like this. When I found her, she had the most beautiful smile on her face. Like she had died in a halo of warmth. I take my glove off and I touch the snow. My finger leaves its mark. I smile and look up at the sky.

'I love you, Mum. I miss you.'

I put my glove back on and I keep walking. I am meeting Rob at our favourite restaurant. Our sabbatical has been glorious. I never thought two workaholics could step off the treadmill of life and be happy.

I can see him now at the door of the restaurant. My tall, handsome husband. My face involuntary smiles every time I see him. I would run but I do not want to slip. He gives me a wave and matches my smile.

'How are you, my beautiful wife?'

'I am well.'

Rob kneels down and puts his head to my tummy.

'And how are you, little seed? Are you having a fun time in Mummy's tummy?'

He leaves a pause.

'Oh, you are. Well, I do not blame you. It is a fun place to be. You have all you need in there, little one.'

I love it when he talks to the bump. Or "little seed" as he calls the baby. We did not need more fertility treatment in the end. The one cycle we had failed but then I got pregnant naturally on my next cycle.

I could not believe it. That was probably fifty thousand pounds saved. We conceived the baby on our honeymoon in Hawaii. All we needed was Hawaii, it seemed. George said he thought that might happen. The moment stress is removed from the equation, a lot of couples conceive naturally. I think the baby just did not want to be born so close to its full-on aunt and uncle.

We have not told anyone else other than George and Bethany yet. They had come to visit and I spent most of the day throwing up. I like having a secret. Especially in this day and age. Sometimes it feels like privacy does not exist any more.

Amanda would be huge now. She is due in February. We would go and see the babies after they were born. She had mentioned coming over for Christmas, but I doubt it will happen. I have not seen any of the family since we moved. I feel clearer and happier than I can ever remember feeling. I FaceTime Paul, Stacey and Nathaniel and Rob FaceTimes with his parents.

We have bought a house in the fifth arrondissement of Paris on the Left Bank. It is near the Sorbonne, the Latin Quarter and the Pantheon. I had a lot of fun decorating it and buying things. I want it to look just so. At some point I will do the occasional consultancy work, so will Rob. Life, at the moment, is perfect.

We are lucky that we have enough money to not worry about anything and live like this. We will go back to work at some point, I guess. But not right now. This time is for living.

Finding out we were having a baby was the best moment of our lives. I had taken the pregnancy test, not thinking for one second it would be positive. We both looked at it in disbelief. Then we bought another one.

We conceived the baby in September and it is due in June. Even now, I can barely believe it. I am going to be a mother.

Rob stops his little conversation with the seed and we go into the restaurant and sit down. It is hard being pregnant in France. They love rare meat and smelly cheese. Neither of which I can have.

I order a Coke and Rob joins me in solidarity. It makes me love the bones of him. I order sea bass and chips. A posh take on fish and chips.

'I was thinking. If it is a girl, we should call her Jacqueline.' Rob says.

I look at Rob and smile.

'I would love that. She would have loved that.'

'Good. Then it is a deal.'

'Deal.'

June 2019
Natalie

I have been in labour for fourteen hours now. The pain was manageable before. The break in-between contractions felt like heaven. But now my body feels like it is going to split apart. I think about all of the women I helped give birth. I did not give them the proper respect. I always thought I had, but this pain is unbelievable. I am in the second stage of labour and this is real. I hope it ends soon. Otherwise, I will hit a wall.

'Maybe I should have an epidural,' I say to the midwife.

'It is too late now, Natalie. You are ten centimetres and I need you to push into your bottom.'

Fuck. Why did I not just go for the drugs? I start to push. It is exhausting.

'We are almost there, Natalie. Just a few more pushes.'

Rob is holding my hand. I am trying to not grip him too hard. If I let myself go, I feel like I would break his fingers.

'Come on, Natalie. You are nearly there. You can do it.'

I gather all of my energy and I put all of the screams I want to do into the energy of pushing the baby out.

It works.

'The head is out. One more push, Natalie.'

'Come on, darling, you can do it.'

I push for all of my might. Then I hear it. The cry.

'She is out. Well done, Natalie.'

The midwife hands her to me. I put her to my breast and she attaches herself, just like that. I look at her and I cannot believe she is real. I look at Rob. I can tell he cannot believe it either. We have waited for her for years and now she is in our arms. She is covered in blood and a bit wrinkly, but she is the most beautiful thing I have ever seen in my life.

I wonder if this moment will ever stop being surreal. If after a certain number of sleepless nights and poopy nappies I will stop being grateful. I find the thought impossible. I think this will always feel surreal to me. Like she is somehow not real.

'She is real,' I tell Rob. As if he does not know.

'Yes, she is. Our little Jacqueline. Look how perfect she is, and so clever. She knew immediately how to feed.'

Little Jacqueline stops her feed and falls asleep in my arms. I just stare.

'I just have to weigh her and check her over.' The midwife takes her for what feels like an eternity. Turns out our little Jacqueline is seven pounds and eleven ounces of gorgeousness. Her Apgar score is ten all round.

I breathe a sigh of relief.

She hands my daughter back.

'Can I get you anything? Tea, toast, some cereal maybe?'

'I would love some tea. Thank you. Some toast would be great too.'

The midwife looks at Rob.

'I would love a cup of tea, thank you.'

The midwife leaves to get the food and drinks.

'I told Paul and Amanda, we would FaceTime them.'

I sigh. Family obligations. I am over them. I know that makes me sound like a bitch, but I do not care. Sometimes you need to embrace your inner bitch and just run with her.

'Okay, let's get it over and done with.'

Rob gets out his iPhone and we FaceTime. Rob sent them texts updating them throughout the birth. They all gathered together at Amanda's house.

They pick up on the second ring. Rob points the phone towards our daughter. Amanda screams.

'Oh, my God! That is one beautiful baby.'

'Is it a boy or a girl?' Paul asks.

We decided to not find out. That way we would have a surprise.

'It's a girl.'

Paul whoops.

'We could do with another girl in this family. Amanda and I all had boys. We needed to balance it out.'

I watch Amanda's face as she hears the news. She smiles but I can see a flicker of jealousy. But she has her beautiful boys. They really are beautiful. I also notice that Amanda looks tired. She has bags under her eyes and dark circles. I doubt she is getting much sleep.

Neil's face comes into view, along with Stacey and Nathaniel. They are all staring in awe at our beautiful bundle of joy. I feel proud.

'Wow. She is beautiful. Congrats, mate. And Natalie.'

'She really is, guys, well done!' says Stacey.

Nathaniel just stares and screws up his nose.

'What is that on her?'

'Blood,' I tell him.

'Ew.'

'Nathaniel,' Paul scolds.

'It is okay, Paul.'

'She is pretty though. Despite the blood,' Nathaniel says. High praise indeed.

'What is her name?' asks Stacey.

'It's Jacqueline.'

I can see them all smiling on the other end.

'That is beautiful, Natalie,' Amanda said.

'It really is, Natalie. Well done. It is a fitting tribute,' Paul adds.

'Thank you. We are really happy.'

'We better let you go, you will be exhausted,' Amanda said.

'Thank you, Amanda. I appreciate that.'

We say goodbye and Rob hangs up.

Rob and I look at each other and then look at our daughter.

'I still cannot believe she is here.'

'Me neither. We are both so lucky.'

Jacqueline wiggles around and then falls asleep. I am a mother. I say it over and over again in my head. I still cannot believe it, even as the evidence sleeps on me.

For a moment, the happiness is ripped through with the sadness of a missing mother. Jacqueline would have been a wonderful grandmother. It brings a tear to my eye to think that my mother will never meet her namesake. The pain of the birth is nothing compared to this. That pain was the price I paid for the child I always longed for.

Rob leans over and kisses me. He can always feel my sadness. Then he kisses his tiny daughter.

'I love you, Mrs Natalie. Well done. You made a beautiful little girl.'

'And thank you, Mr Rob, for giving me the beautiful little girl and for not giving up on me.'

'I would never give up on you. Not for a moment. You are my world. Well, tied with Jacqueline. There are three of us now.'

'Yes, there is. Our little family. Our fresh start.'

This time it would be done right. There would be no broken family and no broken children. We would all be a team. No matter what it took.

It is never too late to start again. Family is what you make it.

'I am the luckiest man in the world.'

I look at Rob and I feel the same. I never thought I would be allowed to be this happy but now I have everything I have always wanted, and all it took was a leap of faith towards happiness. And for someone to catch me at the other end.

Fin